THE
BOOK
OF
NAMES

THE
BOOK
OF
NAMES

JILL GREGORY
AND KAREN TINTORI

ST. MARTIN'S PRESS ✼ NEW YORK

This is a work of fiction. All of the characters, organizations, and events portrayed in this novel are either products of the authors' imaginations or are used fictitiously.

www.stmartins.com

Book design by Chris Zucker

Illustrations of Tower Card and Ouroboros copyright © 2007 by Steven Katz

Library of Congress Cataloging-in-Publication Data

Gregory, Jill.
    The book of names / Jill Gregory and Karen Tintori.—1st ed.
        p. cm.
    ISBN-13: 978-0-312-36632-2
    ISBN-10: 0-312-36632-9
    1. College teachers—Fiction. 2. Sacred books—Fiction. 3. Mysticism—Judaism—Fiction. I. Tintori, Karen. II. Title.

PS3557.R4343B66 2007
811'.54—dc22

                                    2006050600

First Edition: January 2007

10 9 8 7 6 5 4 3 2 1

To my precious family—my wonderful husband, Larry, and my incredible daughter, Rachel

And to the memory of my beloved parents

With love always
    — JG

*

To my gemstones—my brilliant husband, Lawrence, my rock-solid sons, Steven and Mitchel, and the glowing daughter Mitch brought us, Leslie
    — KT

ACKNOWLEDGMENTS

The inspiration for *The Book of Names* goes back fifteen years. It was sparked by Geri Levit, who first shared with us the legend of the Lamed Vovniks.

Many others have inspired and taught us during the writing of this book. We acknowledge them with appreciation and gratitude: Rosemary Ahern, Rabbi Jonathan Berkun, Rabbi Lauren Berkun, Jean Donnelly, Myrna Dosie, Ruthe Goldstein, Larry Greenberg, Rachel Greenberg, Charlotte Hughes, Lawrence Katz, Mitchel Katz, Leslie Katz, Steven Katz, Irving Koppel, Dr. Patti Nakfoor, Claudia Scroggins, Rae Ann Sharfman, Haim Sidor, the Safed Foundation, Rabbi Elimelech Silberberg, Rabbi Dr. Shlomo Sowilowsky, Jennifer Weiss, Rebecca Weiss, and Marianne Willman.

We are deeply grateful for the support and enthusiasm of three special women—our phenomenal editor, Nichole Argyres, and our dedicated agents, Ellen Levine and Sally Wofford-Girand.

The world must contain not less than thirty-six righteous people who are blessed by the *Shekhinah* (God's presence).

— RABBI ABBAYE, *TALMUD*

THE
BOOK
OF
NAMES

PROLOGUE

Two men shoveled the sand under cover of darkness. Their only light in the cave was a lantern set beside their packs. This series of caves and tombs, fifteen miles from Cairo, was a treasure trove of artifacts and antiquities. For three thousand years, Saqqara, the City of the Dead, had been the burial place of kings and commoners—archaeologists might spend several lifetimes and never discover all of its secrets. And neither would the tomb robbers.

Sir Rodney Davis, knighted for discovering the temple of Akhenaton and its dazzling treasures, felt the familiar tug of excitement. They were close. He knew it. He could almost feel the crisp papyri in his hands.

The Book of Names. Part of it. All of it. He didn't know. He only knew that it was here. It had to be here.

The same tingle of exhilaration had coursed through him on the hill of Ketef Hinnom in Israel the night he unearthed the gold scepter of King Solomon. Topped by a thumb-sized pomegranate carved of ivory and inscribed in tiny Hebrew script, it was the first artifact found intact to link the biblical king of the tenth century B.C. to the fortifications recently discovered there. But unearthing the Book of Names would dwarf that and every other discovery. It would ensure his place in history.

He trusted his instincts. They were like a divining rod pulling him toward matchless treasure. And tonight, in the sands where ancient kings had walked, Sir Rodney dug on, fueled by the lust of discovery, the thrill of uncovering what no one had seen since the days of angels and chariots.

Beside him, Raoul threw aside his shovel and reached for his water canteen. He drank deeply.

"Take a break, Raoul. You started an hour before me."

"You're the one who should rest, sir. They've been here all these millennia, they'll wait for us another three or four hours."

Sir Rodney paused and glanced over at the man who had been his loyal assistant for nearly a dozen years. How old had Raoul LaDouceur been when he'd started? Sixteen, seventeen? He was the most tireless worker Sir Rodney had ever seen. A reserved, dignified young man distinguished by his olive Mediterranean coloring and deep-set eyes—one the color of sapphires, the other the deep mahogany of Turkish coffee beans.

"I've been waiting half my life for this discovery, my friend. What is an additional hour's work at this point?" He shoveled another load of sand from the cave floor. Raoul watched in silence for a moment, then recapped his canteen and took up his own shovel.

They worked for more than an hour, the stillness broken only by the sound of their own labored breathing and the soft thud of shovel against sand. Suddenly, a chinking sound froze Sir Rodney's hand. He dropped to his knees, his weariness forgotten, and began to brush the sand aside with his long, calloused fingers. Raoul knelt beside him, shared excitement racing through his veins.

"The lantern, Raoul," Sir Rodney said softly as his hands rounded the curved sides of the clay vessel embedded in the sand. With small, careful rocking motions, he freed it.

Behind him Raoul lowered the lantern, the light revealing a roll of parchment tucked within the vessel's mouth.

"Good God, this could be it." Sir Rodney's hand actually trembled as he drew the papyri from their hiding place.

Raoul rushed to unroll the tarp and stood back while his mentor unrolled the yellowed sheaves across it. Both of them recognized the early Hebrew script and knew what they had found.

Sir Rodney bent closer, peering at the minute letters, his heart racing. The greatest find of his career was here beneath his fingertips.

"By God, Raoul, this could change the world."

"Indeed, sir. It certainly could."

Raoul set the lantern down at the edge of the canvas. He stepped back, one hand slipping into his pocket. Silently, he withdrew the coiled length of wire. His hands were steady as he snared Sir Rodney's neck in the garrote. The archaeologist couldn't even squeak.

It was over in a flash. With one movement, Raoul yanked him away from the precious parchments and snapped his neck.

The old man was right as usual, he mused as he gathered up the papyri. This find would change the world.

Raoul was too elated by his victory to notice the amber gemstone nestled at the bottom of the vessel left behind. Carved upon it were three Hebrew letters.

ליו

JANUARY, 7, 1986
HARTFORD HOSPITAL, CONNECTICUT

Dr. Harriet Gardner was slumped on the lumpy armless couch in the hospital lounge contemplating her first bite of food in twelve hours when her beeper summoned her right back to the ER.

Chomping at the apple, she raced down the hallway. This has to be a bad one, she thought, or Ramirez would be handling it on his own. She tossed the half-eaten apple in the wastebasket as she pounded past it, wondering if this was a car crash or a fire. She burst through the white metal doors to find three trauma teams working at warp speed. There were three kids on gurneys, one of them screaming. Five minutes ago the only sounds in this wing had been the quiet murmur of monitors, the periodic whoosh of blood pressure cuffs, and the occasional whimper of the five-year-old in bay six waiting for X-ray to confirm a broken leg.

Now paramedics and police swarmed the ER, and the surgical resident, Ramirez, was shoving an endo tube down a teenage girl's throat.

"Get that kid up to CT stat," he yelled to Ozzie, as the male nurse jockeyed a boy on a blood-soaked gurney toward the elevator. The teenager lay unmoving, his leg twisted at an impossible angle. There was a gash over his right eye and blood dripped from both ears.

"What do we have?" Harriet flew to the boy in the #18 Celtics jersey, and Teresa, the intern on rotation, stepped aside. The boy's jersey had been cut apart up the center, revealing a bloody chest.

"They fell off a roof," a paramedic answered. "A three-story drop with a gable in the way."

Kids. "Get some blood gasses over here," Harriet bit out. "And a stat portable chest X-ray." Even after three years in the ER her stomach still dropped when she had to work on kids.

Get over it, she told herself, as she peered at the monitor. His pulse was 130, blood pressure 80/60.

This kid was in trouble.

"This one is Senator Shepherd's son." Doshi wheeled the oxygen tank to the head of the gurney. "And the kid Ozzie took to CT is the son of the Swiss ambassador."

"What's this boy's name?"

Doshi peered at the chart. "David. David Shepherd."

Harriet frowned at David Shepherd's battered upper body. "Looks like flail chest, broken clavicle, dropped lung."

Deftly, Doshi inserted a plastic oxygen tube into his trachea. "The others have been drifting in and out, but he hasn't regained consciousness."

The cuff whooshed again. Harriet's gaze swung to the monitor. The kid's blood pressure was dropping like a rock.

Shit.

UNITED NATIONS, NEW YORK CITY

Thunderous applause rang through the room as Secretary-General Alberto Ortega concluded his remarks to the assembled nations. Smiling, Ortega made his way through the diplomats, shaking hands and accepting congratulations on the adoption of the Amendment of the Slavery Convention first signed in Geneva in 1926. His long-lidded gaze roamed the room and at last fell upon the familiar figure of his attaché.

Ortega's expression didn't change, not even when Ricardo slid through the throng and slipped a folded scrap of paper into his palm.

Once inside his own office, away from the noise and the press of bodies, he locked the carved oak door and unfolded the yellow square of paper. His eyes narrowed as he scanned the message.

LaDouceur bagged a prime specimen. The hunt goes on.

HARTFORD HOSPITAL, CONNECTICUT

Nothing hurts anymore. David gazed down at his body on the hospital gurney and was startled to see so much blood on his chest. *Five . . . six . . . seven . . . there were so many people leaning over him . . . so much commotion . . . why didn't they just leave him alone . . . let him sleep?*

Now Crispin was walking toward him. Strange, there was no floor under his feet either.

As he reached David's side they both looked down and noticed that the activity in the ER had reached a fever pitch.

David heard someone call his name, but at the same time Crispin pointed upward toward a brilliant light.

"Isn't that incredible?"

Yeah, David thought. *It is. Even more fantastic than the Northern Lights I saw last summer.*

Crispin started toward the light and he followed. Suddenly the dazzling brightness enveloped them. They were inside it, drifting down a long tunnel. A still more brilliant light glowed ahead and they quickened their pace.

David felt so peaceful now, so exhilarated. So safe.

Suddenly he saw movement within the lustrous aura ahead and a strange murmur began pulsing through the luminous silence. Crispin dropped back, hovering where he stopped, but David was pulled closer, as if a giant magnet was tugging him.

And then his mouth dropped open.

The murmur became a roar, filling his head. Before him he saw faces. Blurry, begging faces. Hundreds of them. Thousands.

Oh, God. Who are they?

He heard a long scream. It seemed a millennium before he recognized it was his own voice.

————

"We're losing him. Code blue!" Harriet yelled.

Doshi positioned the paddles over David's chest. "All clear!" she warned. And then she zapped him.

"Again!" Harriet ordered. Bending over the dark-haired kid, Harriet felt perspiration bead along her upper lip. "David, come back here. David! Listen to me now. Come back!"

Doshi stood by with the paddles ready as Harriet frowned at the monitor. Still in V-Fib. A heartbeat away from flatlining. Damn it.

"Doshi—again!"

Three hours later Dr. Harriet Gardner finished her paperwork. Some day. It started with a thirty-five-year-old female with a heart attack and a toddler with the tines of a fork embedded in his forehead. It ended with three kids who'd risked their lives on an icy winter afternoon climbing a fucking roof.

One got off with only a bruised larynx and a broken arm.

One had shattered his right femur and was locked deep in a coma.

And one she had barely snatched back from the jaws of death. She wondered if he'd seen the light.

Sighing, Dr. Harriet Gardner shoved the files across the nurses' counter and went home to feed her dog.

CHAPTER ONE

Athens, Greece
Nineteen years later

Raoul LaDouceur hummed as he opened the trunk of his rented Jaguar. As he slid the rifle from beneath a plaid wool ski blanket, he became aware that his stomach was grumbling. Well, not for long. He'd spotted an open air taverna some ten miles back and had a sudden irresistible yen for a platter of braised lamb shanks and a glass of ouzo.

He checked his watch. There should be time. He'd already dispatched the two security guards and rolled their bodies down the hillside. He was ahead of schedule and still had five hours before he had to return the rental car and fly back to London to await his next assignment. Time enough even for two glasses of ouzo.

He walked purposefully through the olive grove, feeling vaguely uncomfortable. Despite his sunglasses, he was aware of the waning, still-hot Mediterranean sun. He preferred to do his work in darkness.

But as he'd learned to tolerate the sun on so many scorching digs during his younger years, so, too, he would tolerate it today. Ignoring the perspiration running from his armpits, he selected his position, the one that best afforded him a view of the entire rear of the house. Then he took a puff from his inhaler and settled in to wait.

The fragrance of these olive trees made his throat burn. It brought back memories of his grandfather's farm in Tunisia, where he'd labored as a grafter from the age of six. Slicing off branches and rooting them into new olive trees, he'd spent ten hours a day at monotonous work beneath an unforgiving sun, his throat dry and raw as pipe ash.

And what did he get when he was done—a crust of bread, a scrap of cheese? And more often than not, a beating with a switch made from one of the very branches he had cut.

His grandfather was the first man he'd killed. He'd beaten him to death on the day he'd turned fifteen.

Today, too, must be someone's birthday, he thought, his gaze flitting over the balloons tied in bunches to the lounge chairs, then to the table piled high with gaily wrapped gifts.

The party was about to begin.

Beverly Panagoupolos had been baking all afternoon. It wasn't that her brother's chef was incapable of making a birthday cake, it was just that for *her* grandchildren, she liked to do it herself.

Her littlest granddaughter, Alerissa, was nine today. In an hour the birthday girl and her big brothers, Estevao, Nilo, and Takis, would all be gathered around the pool deck with their parents, their cousins, aunts, and uncles. Alerissa was so timid she would be shy throughout the party, then would talk of nothing else for days to come.

Beverly licked the cinnamon frosting from her thumb and strode outside to check that the pink and silver balloons and bright array of gifts were arranged as she intended.

She paused for a moment, gazing with pleasure at the silvery blue water of the pool, where soon all the children would be splashing before dinner.

She didn't hear a thing until the gunshots cracked through the palm trees.

She didn't feel a thing until the bullets razored across her back.

She didn't see the silvery blue water turn crimson with her blood.

She died with cinnamon frosting at the corners of her lips.

The car snaked out from the secluded hilltop and roared down the road. Flipping the radio dial in search of a classical station, Raoul caught the tail end of a news broadcast. Terrorists had blown up the Melbourne Airport's international terminal and thousands were feared dead inside the collapsed building.

He smiled to himself. He was good. The best. The proof was written across the ever-increasing chaos in the world. Soon he'd be hailed as one of the principal heroes of the new order.

The thirty-six Hidden Ones were dwindling. Beverly Panagoupolos was the fourteenth to die by his hand. No one else had ever killed so many. Now, only three of the thirty-six remained. Once they were eliminated, Raoul thought with pride, God's foul world would be finished.

Already it was deteriorating. War, earthquake, famine, fire, disease—one by one, every type of natural and man-made catastrophe was proliferating across the globe like never before. It was merely a matter of days now.

When the final three were gone—the light of the Hidden Ones extinguished—the time of the Gnoseos would dawn and the world would be no more.

BROOKLYN, NEW YORK

Time was running out.

Nearly five thousand miles away, in his small office on Avenue Z, Rabbi Eliezer ben Moshe closed his rheumy eyes and prayed.

Throughout his eighty-nine years, those eyes had seen much tragedy and evil, *simcha* and goodness in the world. But of late, the evil seemed to be multiplying. He knew it wasn't a coincidence.

Desperate fear filled his heart. He'd spent his entire life in the study of Kabbalah, meditating upon God's mystical secrets, calling upon His many names. He'd murmured them, praying for protection—not for himself—for the world.

For the world was in peril, a peril greater than the Flood. The dark souls of an ancient cult had found the Book of Names. He was convinced of it.

And all of the *Lamed Vovniks* listed in the ancient parchment were being killed, one by one. How many were left? Only God and the Gnoseos knew.

Sighing, he turned to the talismans arrayed on his desk. Some he understood. Some he did not. He picked them up, one by one, and stuffed them back inside the cracked leather satchel sitting open on his desk. His fingers ached from arthritis as he pulled the ancient volumes of the *Zohar* and the *Tanach* away from the bookshelf and spun the dial of the safe hidden behind them. Only when the lock clicked and the satchel was again secured within the fireproof metal did he pick up his worn Book of Psalms and shuffle toward the door.

His long silver beard quivered as his lips moved in prayer.

Dear God, give us the strength and the knowledge to stop the evil ones.

Beneath his desk, the tiny microphone carried his prayer.

But not to God.

CHAPTER TWO

GEORGETOWN UNIVERSITY
WASHINGTON, D.C.

When David Shepherd walked into Houligan's Bar after teaching his morning classes, the only things on his mind were a pounding headache and the desperate need for nourishment. He'd been too wired to sleep last night after having hosted Tony Blair's two-day visit to the campus. Blair's address had brought the students to their feet and the afterglow at Dean Myer's had lasted until nearly one.

Blair's visit had been considered a coup on his part, but really it was only luck. David had met the British statesman seven months ago when he'd been invited to present a seminar at Oxford. Following the seminar he'd been fêted at a dinner at Boisdale of Belgravia, and Blair, seated across from him, had complimented him on his latest book, *Empowering the Nations: The Struggle for Peace in an Era of Nuclear Proliferation.*

They'd exchanged e-mails, and to his surprise, the statesman had accepted his invitation to speak at Georgetown.

The visit had been a huge success but this morning had been pure hell. He'd floundered, sleepless, until four in the morning, snored through the alarm, and then rushed in late to deliver his 8 A.M. lecture. There hadn't even been time to gulp some Tylenol, much less grab a power drink from the fridge. He hadn't even shaved, he'd only taken time to jump in the shower and to slick back his thick dark hair.

"Dave, what gives?" He recognized Tom McIntyre's nasal voice above the din. Tom waved him over from two tables away.

"For Myer's golden boy, you sure look down in the mouth. Did your pal Tony have you contemplating the state of the world a little too deeply last night?"

The balding assistant professor with whom David shared an office in the poli-sci department signaled to the waitress across the room. Also single and in his mid-thirties, Tom was a brilliant sparring partner and one of the most popular professors on campus. Each semester Tom kept a running check on which of them filled up their classes first. David sensed more than friendly competition in the way Tom tried to needle him, but as the son of a U.S. senator, David had grown up surrounded by politics and was immune to it.

He usually shrugged off Tom's need to be top dog—except when the two of them took their annual rock-climbing trip out west. Tom was a good guy and a hell of a climber and excelled in the one area where David enjoyed competition—pitting himself against man and nature, testing himself against the cliffs.

With a groan, David folded his long muscular body into a hard-backed chair opposite Tom.

His office mate hoisted a beer. "One of these might cure what ails you."

"And a sledgehammer might knock this headache loose." David forced a smile. "You happen to have one of those handy?"

Tom's attention had already shifted away, his gaze fastened on the TV screen above the bar. "Chicken Little was right, my friend. The end is near."

"No argument from me." David ordered a hamburger, chili with onions, and a Heineken. He slouched back in his seat, rubbing his temples. His gaze automatically followed Tom's to CNN. *Another terrorist attack in Melbourne.* He grimaced. Disasters were erupting all over the world with the regularity of Old Faithful.

He'd been teaching political science for nearly ten years now, the last four here at Georgetown, but nothing in his career had been as challenging as this past semester. The words of Plato, Thoreau, Churchill, and other great political thinkers didn't come close to explaining the current turmoil storming through the world. Hurricanes, tsunamis, war, assassinations, terror—an amalgam of nature's caprice and man's violence against man. His students had more questions than he—or even Tony Blair—had answers.

By the time the waitress slid his beer in front of him, David was almost relieved to look away from the screen. Tom leaned forward and dropped his voice.

"Okay, my friend, this is your lucky day. Kate Wallace just parked her beautiful blond self two tables away. Get over there and invite her to the dean's Labor Day barbecue."

David resisted the urge to turn around. Kate Wallace was a thirty-one-year-old English professor who was writing a racy novel about Ferdinand and Isabella's court. And she was the first woman he'd seriously lusted after since Meredith filed for divorce. They'd had coffee in the staff lounge a couple of times, and so far he hadn't scared her off.

Hell, why not?

He quirked an eyebrow at Tom and wheeled out of his chair. Two minutes later he was scribbling down Kate's phone number and the directions to her town house.

When he got back to the table, Tom chuckled. "I'm impressed. It only took you a semester and a half to make your move."

"I hear timing is everything." David took a bite out of his hamburger and stared down at the scrap of paper.

He stopped chewing. *What the hell?*

Instead of "Kate Wallace," he'd written down something else.

Beverly Panagoupolos.

Oh, no, not again, he thought. The headache, which had receded slightly as he'd eaten, now suddenly pounded with renewed vigor. Another random name. There were so many. Where did they come from?

"Hey, Dave, you all right? Seriously—all of a sudden you look like the walking dead."

David tensed. Tom had no idea how close it was to the truth. But he never talked about the fall that had almost killed him when he was a kid. He'd never even shared it with Meredith.

"It's just this damned headache." He forced down another bite of his burger but he was no longer thinking about his food, or Tom, or Kate. He was thinking about Beverly Panagoupolos.

And he didn't want to.

An hour later, David drove past Eastern Market, doing a little over the speed limit for Capitol Hill. By the time he swung into the alley to park his Mazda6 at the rear of his town house, David could barely wait to see if Beverly Panagoupolos' name was in his journal. He was about to turn off his ignition when the CBS hourly news update began.

We have breaking news out of Athens: Police have surrounded the residence of Greek Prime Minister Nicholas Agnastou after his sister, Beverly Panagoupolos, was discovered brutally murdered there just hours ago. . . .

David's hand froze on the ignition key. Sweat beaded on his forehead, but he felt icy cold inside. *Why is her name in my head today—on the day she died? This has never happened before.* He yanked the scrap of paper from his pocket and stared at it, his mind racing. *Or had it?*

He ran up the front steps and jammed his key into the lock. He shot across the short hallway to his office as the door slammed shut behind him. His desk was in controlled chaos, strewn with the pieces of his life: partially graded papers, binders and books, a box of Sharpie fine-point pens, a framed photo of himself and Stacy on their last ski trip to Vail, and the milky gray-blue gemstone he kept perched in the hand of the red ceramic monkey that Judd Wanamaker, his father's best friend, had brought him from Thailand when he was eight.

Yanking open the center drawer of his rolltop desk, he fumbled under bank statements and bills until his fingers closed around the thick red notebook. Heart pounding, he scanned the pages where all the names were written.

One hundred forty-five pages, filled with names. Thousands and thousands of names.

And then he saw it. Right there in the middle of page forty-two. *Beverly Panagoupolos.*

He'd written it on October seventh, 1994. He always marked down the dates when the names found him. Beverly's had found him when he was twenty-two.

All those years ago, he'd written her name. And today he'd written it again. On the day she died.

He looked at the names. A United Nations of names. Encompassing, he was certain, every nationality on earth.

Throughout his teens, he'd thumbed through phone books in every city his family vacationed, trying to find the names he was writing.

He never had, and after a while he'd given up.

But today he knew for certain one of the names belonged to a murdered woman. A chill came over him as he wondered if there were more.

VILLA CASA DELLA FALCONARA, SICILY

Irina was in darkness. Cold. Afraid. Naked.

Holy Virgin, how long will they keep me here, waiting? For what?

The silk blindfold was soft against her eyelids, but she had no idea how long it had been on. Even when they brought her food and unbound her hands so she could eat and use the toilet, she was never permitted to remove the blindfold.

She wanted to go home, to sit by the front window and embroider her wedding pillowcases. She had five more to finish before she married Mario.

Would she marry Mario? Was he looking for her? Weeping for her? Would she ever see his face again?

Warm tears soaked the silk that bound her eyes. She shivered and sent up a silent prayer. The same one she said every day, over and over.

Where are you, God?

On moonlit nights in August, the Italian prime minister liked to sit in the garden of his hilltop villa and smoke the Cuban cigars his father had first let him smoke there on his eighth birthday. Casa della Falconara, which overlooked the age-old amphitheater at Segesta, had belonged to his family for over four generations. His parents had chosen its grand terrace with its spectacular views for their sunset wedding reception seventy years ago, but the garden was his own favorite sanctuary, where no one dared disturb him.

There, on hot August nights, he could close his eyes and savor the fragrance of the lemon groves wafting up from the valley while he listened to the ancient Greek and Latin plays reenacted in the amphitheater below.

Tonight the amphitheater was quiet and the garden deserted, but within the weathered walls of his villa, Eduardo DiStefano presided over a select group of guests, twenty men conversing in muted and dignified tones.

The prime minister's butler moved silently around the long table where they sat, refilling their goblets with thirty-five-year-old port. No one spoke of anything beyond the broiling weather, or the six-course meal they'd just enjoyed, until Silvio had slipped from the room and they heard the intricately-carved mahogany door click closed behind him. Then Eduardo DiStefano stood, locked the door, and began to speak with the charm and elegance for which he was known.

"Tonight, my faithful friends, we have reached a turning point. Thirty-three obstacles have been eliminated." DiStefano paused, appreciation shimmering in his penetrating eyes as vigorous applause broke out. He was a man of striking good looks, with an intelligent high forehead, a strong jaw, and a smile that could melt gold. Though he was nearing sixty, his dark hair was only slightly flecked with silver, which added a degree of elan as commanding as his Armani tuxedo. As his guests applauded, he twisted the gold ring of intertwined snakes on his middle finger and waited for silence.

"And, even more importantly," DiStefano continued, "our own Serpent is on the verge of a final breakthrough."

He turned with a smile toward the distinguished golden-haired banker, the man whose family had been entrusted with safeguarding their vast holdings since the sixteenth century. It was his son who had proved so invaluable in identifying the targets for the Dark Angels, his son whose brilliance made their long-sought triumph imminent.

Applause broke out and the banker bowed his head in acknowledgement.

"I'm told," DiStefano continued, "that again, your son hasn't left his computer in three days. Gentlemen, at this very moment, he could be seconds from unlocking the ultimate knowledge—the final three names."

The men at the table started, looking from one to the other with a combination of excitement and awe. For more than a hundred generations, they and their predecessors had struggled to attain this knowledge, to achieve this goal. The notion of imminent success, of total spiritual enlightenment, was nearly overwhelming, it was erotic—an enticing flame to scorch the flesh and free the soul.

"*Salut,* my friends." DiStefano raised his goblet, his gaze meeting that of his second-in-command, Alberto Ortega. The former secretary general of the United Nations smiled widely and raised his glass in response as DiStefano offered a toast.

"Let us prepare ourselves for the rest of the journey." He drank a sip of the dark rich port, savoring it, as did all the men assembled. The familiarity of this ritual soothed and exhilarated him.

He remembered the first time he'd been allowed to participate. He hadn't slept for a moment the night before, nor had he eaten anything throughout the day.

His father had never given him a hint of what went on in this room during the special meetings he hosted twice every year. All he knew as a child was that it took the staff days to prepare the banquet and that even his mother was not allowed to attend.

Sometimes, he would awaken at five in the morning to the sound of tires crunching the gravel driveway leading down the hillside as the dignitaries slipped away like stars blinking out before the dawn.

What were they doing all those hours, far into the night? He'd known his father was an important man—and all the men who attended twice a year were important men as well, many of them famous leaders and heads of state.

It was as if the UN was meeting in Sicily, in his home.

From the time he first saw the paneled double doors close, shutting him out in the marble tiled foyer, he'd longed to be a part of it, to sit by his father's side and listen, to soak up the power that was in that room.

But not until he was eighteen did he receive his own talisman— the gold ring he never took off—and his own invitation to the ceremonies.

He'd been revolted by what he'd seen.

Odd how he'd come to relish this ritual that crowned the evening. Fortunately, his father had been an intuitive and patient man, who had explained the necessity of what they did, and its grander purpose. The women they initiated would play a key role once the world was theirs. Hand-selected, isolated—the unwilling vessels would be needed. And used.

Now when he couldn't sleep the night before the ritual, it had nothing to do with anxiety.

He reached out a well-tanned hand, and with the press of a button the paneled wall behind him slid away.

She was waiting there in the shadows, raven-haired, blindfolded, naked.

Some of the men began to shift in their seats, thinking of the divine ecstasy to follow. Others remained perfectly still, their gazes hawk-like on the girl.

They were all intelligent men, dedicated and powerful. Like those who'd come before them, each had been handpicked at an early age for this honor, for this challenge, for this most bold and dangerous quest.

And no one outside the Circle was the wiser, he thought with satisfaction. Not a one of those fools mired in the physical earth knew a single thing about the Gnoseos.

The girl was brought forward.

Alberto Ortega went to the cabinet where the two ancient gemstones gleamed, like dark stars, in a lighted glass case. The amethyst and emerald dated back thousands of years. They were two of the twelve ageless gems upon which the birthstones of the zodiac were later modeled. Ortega was careful not to jostle their case as he reached to retrieve the ritual goblet and the small silver vial. Carefully, he shook the blue powder into the goblet until the granules covered the etching of a serpent biting its own tail at the vessel's bottom. As the blindfolded girl whimpered, DiStefano stepped forward to pour wine from a cut crystal decanter. He watched the ruby liquid rise to meet the embrace of a second serpent etched halfway up the bowl, then stirred it with his finger.

Eyes gleaming, he signaled for the blindfold to be removed. Ignoring the girl's terrified expression, he lifted the goblet and tipped it to the girl's trembling lips.

"No, please," she begged, frantically trying to twist her head aside.

"Stop whimpering," DiStefano murmured, fingering the curl that fell across her cheek before grabbing the hair at her nape, tilting her head back. "You should be thankful. You have been chosen for greatness."

As he dribbled nearly all of the bitter liquid down her throat, her eyes locked on his—seconds before she began to quiver. He passed off the goblet, first to Ortega, who tasted a droplet and then passed the ceremonial cup to Odiambo Mofulatsi, third in command. Quickly, it made its way around the table as each member of the Circle took a small symbolic sip.

And then the girl's shoulders began to shudder uncontrollably.

The world spun as wild colors leaped behind Irina's eyes. Her heart began to race, hurting inside her chest. She felt serpents, slithering, twining, around her shoulders, and then smelled the musk of men.

Her screams surfaced and swam through the room as the colors and the men and the terror pulled her under.

MARYLEBONE, LONDON

His eyes were so dry they ached. The lines of the graph on the twenty-four-inch flat-screen monitor blurred one onto the next. Three days in this chair, he thought wearily, three days of superimposing one graph upon another. Three days of searching the overlapping transcriptions, trying to identify the final three names. With a groan he flicked off the computer. *Enough.*

He'd be no good to anyone if he persisted at this point. He knew his limits and he'd already crossed them. There weren't enough Optrex Refreshing Drops in London to keep him going another hour.

Spinning his chair around, he blinked at the magnificently erotic Gustav Klimt canvas that filled one entire wall of his second-floor office. While he was working he was totally unaware of the luxury of his surroundings, of the polished ebony floors hewn from African woods that were echoed in the crown moldings, of the exquisite zebra-skin rugs, the Aubusson tapestries and the sculptures purchased from Christie's auction house. In his Oxford years, many of his acquaintances had thought him decadent—how right they were. He, like his father and a majority of the Circle, made hedonism an art.

Since the body was evil, why attempt to tame it? Why struggle against nature's impulses? The evil in the body was inherent—only the soul, like the Source with which it yearned to reunite, was pure. So when he worked, it was all work, intense, focused, and driven. When he played, he gave it everything he had—he denied himself nothing.

And now it was time to play.

He squinted at his watch, a Vacheron Constantin, and realized that the ancient ceremony in Sicily had begun.

He'd have a ceremony of his own tonight. It would rejuvenate him.

He reached for his cane and pushed himself to his feet. As he limped through the marble-floored corridors of his three-story home on Blandford Street, he realized he hadn't eaten solid food in over twenty-four hours. That would soon be remedied. He wanted to wrap his tongue around something spicy and hot.

He buzzed Gilbert from his bedroom. Indian cuisine would be perfect.

"Get me a reservation at Tamarind for tonight—the usual time, the usual table. I want a redhead. A Cate Blanchett type. Make sure she's there one half hour before I arrive."

He shuffled through his cavernous closet, the cane thumping with each step. He paused to finger the sleeve of his newest Ermenegildo

Zegna tuxedo. He'd set it off with the sapphire cufflinks he'd picked up in Florence last month.

Tossing his clothes across the bed, he removed the gold medallion that hung around his neck—a double ouroboros—two serpents, coiled into a figure eight, biting each other's tails. Their diamond eyes flashed against the lustrous gold.

His ouroboros talisman was grander than his father's, he thought with satisfaction. *As was befitting the Serpent.*

Icy water attacked his body from the multiple jets studding the granite walls of his shower. As always, the freezing water pleased and revived him. He lathered his shoulder-length dirty-blond hair and scrubbed at the tired muscles in his powerful sloped shoulders.

The end of the world must wait a few more days, he decided as he lathered his buttocks, where tattooed black snakes intertwined.

A burst of food, sex, pleasure would sharpen his brain for the finale. Soon enough, this mockery of an earth with its pathetic skyscrapers, droning factories, laughable churches, and deluded governments would dissipate into the ether. All of it was evil, only the soul and the Source was pure.

And for tonight he would put aside the quest for the ultimate purity—the truth of existence. He'd put out of his head the search for the last of those bloody names, and indulge the flesh.

His flesh.

All for the good of his soul.

CHAPTER THREE

Shen Jianchao
Glenda McPharon
Hassan Habari
Lubomir Zalewski
Donald Walston
Rufus Johnson
Noelania Trias
Henrik Kolenko
Sandra Hudson
Mzobanzi Nxele

Furiously, David flipped through his journal, typing names from random pages, Googling them one after another.

By midnight, he'd done a search of more than fifty of the names. A number of them came up "not found." Others landed numerous hits, but scant information.

Then he typed in Marika Dubrovska. A series of links to news headlines from Krakow popped up on the screen. A Marika Dubrovska had been shot in her sleep at the Wysotsky Hotel two years ago. Though David searched for updated material there was none, and it appeared that her murder was unsolved.

One Simon Rosenblatt turned out to be a Holocaust victim, gassed at Treblinka in 1942. Another was an American sailor killed in the bombing of Pearl Harbor. There were three other Simon Rosenblatts—all of whom died between 1940 and 1945.

LaToya Lincoln, a Detroit social worker, washed ashore on the Canadian side of the Detroit River in 1999.

David's fingers flew across the keys. He typed in another name, and another.

Donald Walston. A blizzard of hits filled the computer screen. He sorted through information on four Donald Walstons—an electrician in New Brunswick; a great-grandfather on a genealogical tree in South Africa; an author in Birmingham, England; and a dentist in Santa Barbara.

His hands began to tremble. All four were dead. Different times, different countries. With the exception of the great-grandfather in South Africa, who died of typhoid in 1918, the others had all died within months of each other—and all within the last year.

The electrician had been a murder victim, the author died in a hit and run, the dentist was killed in a fire.

By 7 A.M. he had gone through one hundred eighty of the names in his journal. He found hits on sixty—of those, forty-eight were dead. Like the three Donald Walstons, twenty-seven had been murdered, the other twenty-one died in accidents. Not one of them had died of natural causes.

Dazed, David read over the names. Their hometowns spanned the globe. Their dates of death spanned several centuries. They came from every walk of life, every ethnicity, every religion.

They came from his journal.

They came from his head.

CHAPTER FOUR

"There you have it, Dillon. Am I nuts?"

Father Dillon McGrath studied David through searing blue eyes that had seen and pondered much in forty-five years. "Hearing Beverly Panagoupolos's name in your head the same day she died and then finding it in your journal doesn't make you nuts. Psychic, perhaps, but not nuts."

"If I had one psychic bone in my body, I'd have won the lottery by now."

Dillon's face crinkled into the crooked smile that had made countless women curse his Roman collar. David had always thought that with his black curly hair and ruddy complexion, Dillon McGrath looked more like a pirate than a priest, but in the eight years they'd been friends, the only vices the burly chair of the Theology Department had ever displayed were a penchant for Glenmorangie and contraband Cuban cigars.

They'd both started on the tenure track at Georgetown University in the same autumn. They'd had practically nothing in common, but their friendship had formed at faculty functions and spilled over to their weekly Saturday morning search for the best lox and bagels breakfast in D.C.

Glancing at the wall of Dillon's office, with its bookshelves packed with volumes on philosophy, comparative religion, supernaturalism, and metaphysics, David had few illusions that any of them held the answer to what was happening to him.

"How long have you been writing down these names?" Dillon asked, taking a sip of coffee from the Orioles mug on his desk. "Can you recall?"

"Since my sophomore year in high school."

"So what happened that year that might have triggered it?"

"Nothing." David got to his feet and began to pace around the room. He wasn't sure he was ready to actually give voice to what had happened to him, even though that was why he'd come here.

"Spit it out, David. I know you too well. Whenever you start pacing, I know there's a thousand thoughts going on in that brilliant brain of yours. Don't make me drag them out one by one."

"Now you sound just like the psychiatrist my parents dragged me to right after the accident."

Dillon leaned forward. "Accident?"

With a sigh, David turned back and threw himself down in the chair. "I nearly killed myself and a couple of friends when I was thirteen. Two years before the names started. We fell off a roof. I smashed in my rib cage, and for a few minutes, they lost me."

He looked straight into Dillon's probing eyes. "And, yes," he said, preempting the question, "I went down the tunnel and saw the proverbial light."

Dillon stared at him in amazement. "And you never told me?" He gestured toward the bookshelves. "You know I wrote two books about metaphysics and the afterlife and you've never let me pick your brain?"

"Forgive me, Father, for I have sinned." David grinned, holding up both hands, palms up.

Dillon shook his head. "That near death experience must be connected to the names." His voice held an edge of excitement. "Two years is merely a blink to the subconscious."

"If you say so. . . ." David took a long breath. "I'm short on answers right now. That's why I'm here."

Dillon leaned back in his chair. "Why don't you start at the beginning," he suggested. "Don't hold back or edit your thoughts. Just tell me everything you remember about that experience."

So David told him. Told him about his father's important guests that snowy afternoon at their home in Connecticut. The Swiss ambassador, Erik Mueller; his wife and their son, Crispin, two years older than David, and as full of himself as anyone David had ever met. It had been David's job to entertain him.

Crispin was broad-shouldered, blond, and athletic, a skier who boasted that he'd scaled a section of the Matterhorn when he was seven. Crispin was restless that afternoon, and clearly showing off for David's best friend, Abby Lewis, who'd stared at the older boy like he was David Bowie.

David's stomach churned as he recounted the details: Crispin daring him to climb the roof of the neighbor's three-story gabled home, his own voice rising in false bravado as he accepted the challenge. Then there was Abby clambering up behind them, snow melting on her eyelashes. His feet slipping as he followed Crispin's tracks across the roof, trying to act as if he wasn't scared, as if the dizzying distance to the ground didn't matter.

Then Abby's feet flew out from under her, and her laughter turned to screams. David tried to grab her, his arms flailing, knocking Crispin off balance. They all fell together, in what seemed like slow-motion as the ice-packed ground rose up to slam them into silent blackness.

"And then . . ."

David's voice trailed off. Dillon cocked an eyebrow.

"And then . . . what?"

David felt sick and shaky. He hated talking about this, he hated the guilt it dredged up. He heard his father's voice again, thin and biting.

How could you do something so asinine? Crispin dared you, so you had to do it? Do you realize you nearly killed yourself? That boy could be in a coma for the rest of his life. Why the hell didn't you think, David? You're supposed to be so smart, why didn't you think?

His head pounded, remembering how his mother had shushed his father, drawn him away from the hospital bed, but it was too late. Those words had hung between them like the dingy gray curtains the nurses pulled around his bed to keep out the press.

"And then the next thing I knew I was in the hospital, hurting like hell and hooked up to wires and tubes—and the doctors were telling me they'd brought me back."

Dillon nodded. "And where did you go?"

"I'm not sure." David raked a hand through his hair, his eyes narrowed in concentration. "I only remember a tunnel, a bright light. The same thing everybody who experiences this remembers. Nothing more. I've read every book Elisabeth Kübler-Ross has written on the subject. And as far as I can tell, there was nothing unique about what happened to me."

Dillon spoke quietly. "It's less than what most people who've gone to the light have reported experiencing, David. There is definitely more to your experience. There has to be. You're blocking it." Dillon's voice was matter-of-fact.

"I'm betting that whatever you experienced in that tunnel has some bearing on these names. You've been writing them in your journal obsessively year after year for nearly a quarter of a century. Something like that doesn't just happen randomly. Not to someone who's as sane, functional, and practical as you are."

"But I'm *not* functioning so well, that's just it. I feel like I'm losing my mind. Lately, the names are with me more and more. How do I stop it?"

"You've got to get to the source." Dillon's eyebrows knitted in concern. "If you're that blocked, you need to see a hypnotherapist."

Alarm surged through David. He couldn't have been more startled if his best friend had just suggested electroshock therapy.

"Take it easy. This isn't hocus-pocus," Dillon assured him. "Alex Dorset works with crime victims and the D.C. police. He's a highly regarded hypnotherapist—and a friend."

He flipped through his Rolodex. "Here you go." Grabbing a pen, he scribbled on a sheet of lined paper. "I can't put you in better hands."

David stared at the paper the priest held out, but he didn't take it. "I'm not comfortable with touchy-feely stuff, Dillon—"

"Are you comfortable with the names taking over your life? I thought you were looking for answers."

David didn't reply. He rubbed his temples. He'd written a new name in his journal last night. He'd been trying not to think about it.

Dillon pressed the paper into his hand. "This is as good a place as any to start. Call Alex."

David folded the paper and shoved it into his wallet. "I'll let you know what happens."

"By the way," Dillon said, as David started toward the door. "You never mentioned what happened to your friends."

"Abby was okay." David's mouth twisted. "She only had a broken arm. But Crispin . . ."

His voice trailed off. Dillon waited, saying nothing.

"Crispin ended up in a coma. They said he'd probably never wake up. My father checked on him for a year or so, after they flew him back to Switzerland, but he hadn't improved." David shook his head. "Actually, I still have something that belonged to him. Though I never figured out why he'd have a rock with Hebrew lettering on it."

"What do you mean?" Dillon tilted his head.

David shrugged. "He had this blue stone—very smooth. An agate about the size of a grape. When he was daring Abby and me to go up on the roof, he waved it in the air and bragged that it had magical powers and would keep us from falling. Some magic, huh?" he said grimly.

"And you still have it?"

"I went back to where we fell after the snow melted, just poking around, and I spotted it in the grass. I'd forgotten all about it. I picked it up and kept it—a little reminder about the price of impulsivity."

Dillon was regarding him with interest. "Do you know what's written on the stone?"

David snorted. "Probably the words of the sages. Something like, 'Gravity sucks.'"

The priest's eyes grew thoughtful as David closed the door behind him. He went to the bookshelf and reached for the volume on Jewish magic. Pursing his lips, he checked the index and flipped to the page.

Half an hour later, he snapped the book closed and reached for the phone.

CHAPTER FIVE

On Friday morning David pulled onto D Street and headed toward Pennsylvania Avenue. He circled around the Capitol until he picked up Pennsylvania again, deliberately driving in silence through the brilliant August day—no radio, no CD. He wanted to clear his head before the session.

When he found a parking spot, he turned off the ignition and eyed the tall brick office building with a combination of anticipation and dread. The place didn't look the least bit threatening, so why did he have a knot in his chest?

Come on, man, you've scaled mountains, for God's sake. You can handle an hour of hypnosis. What are you afraid of?

And then it dawned on him. He was afraid this wasn't going to work, that hypnosis wasn't going to reveal a thing. That the names were never going to go away and would always remain a mystery.

Fear was something David had lived with intimately those first few years after the fall. Initially it had paralyzed him, making him terrified of escalators, open staircases, amusement park rides—any kind of height.

His parents had dragged him to one therapist after another, but in the end, it was David himself who found a way to conquer his fears. At sixteen, he got tired of always being afraid, disgusted with himself and with the panic kicking through his gut.

The previous year there had been a series of death threats against a number of senators, including his father. Robert Shepherd immediately hired a security detail for himself and his family. Karl Hutchinson, the bodyguard assigned to protect David, was a former Navy Seal, smart, agile, and unshakable. The two quickly struck up a friendship, and instead of resenting the man shadowing him, David found himself looking forward to his time with Hutch.

Hutch taught him how to lift weights and box, and as David's adolescent body took on a muscled definition, an inner confidence took shape as well. When the threats against the group of senators ceased, Hutch and the other guards were reassigned, but he and David continued to keep in touch. And when David finally decided to conquer his fear of heights, it was Hutch he asked to help him.

His parents agreed to send him to Hutch's family cabin in Arizona for two weeks. And there, David had faced his terror.

He'd asked Hutch to take him into the mountains. At first they'd merely hiked up rocky trails thick with brush and tumbleweed. Then David had decided to push his own limits and insisted Hutch drive him to Prescott to tackle the six-thousand-foot craggy face of Granite Mountain.

Hutch, to his credit, hadn't laughed at him. And though David only managed to climb a thousand feet on his first try, it was enough. He was hooked.

By the end of the most grueling, exhilarating two weeks of David's life, he returned to Connecticut wind-burned and covered with scratches and scrapes, but determined to keep climbing until he could conquer Granite Mountain. And that was the beginning.

He'd mastered his fear of heights, and now he knew he had to master his fear of the names.

He was just stepping out of his car when his cell phone rang. "Over the Rainbow," pealed out—Stacy's special ring. The two of them had watched *The Wizard of Oz* so many times together, he could still recite all the dialogue.

"Hey there, Munchkin." He smiled, glancing at his watch. It was just before eleven in Santa Monica. "Aren't you supposed to be in school?"

"Lunch break," his stepdaughter answered, and David felt a pang. Her voice was no longer the little-girl voice he remembered. At thirteen, she sounded like a typical teenager.

"I need to tell you something but I don't want to talk when Mom's around."

"Sounds serious." He turned his back on the building and leaned against the car. "What's wrong?"

"Everything."

He heard Stacy take a deep, trembling breath. He couldn't imagine what was coming next.

"Mom got married again this weekend. I have a new stepdad." She spit the last word out as if it was a piece of sour candy. "He's nothing like you."

"Hey, Munchkin, who is?" He kept his voice light, but he was shocked. He and Meredith had talked only a few weeks ago and she hadn't even mentioned dating anyone. "Don't you like him? Maybe you just need to give him a chance."

"Len's fine, I guess. He did get Mom to quit smoking again. But he tries too hard. I barely know him, but Mom already let him adopt me, and it's so wrong. They didn't even tell me ahead of time—I didn't know until the wedding."

Adopt? David was flabbergasted.

Stacy's voice thickened with tears. "If any one of Mom's husbands had to adopt me, I'd want it to be you." Her voice grew smaller. "And if it can't be you, I just want to keep my birth father's name and stay who I am."

David cursed Meredith for her impulsiveness. She never stopped to think how her actions impacted anyone else, most of all her daughter. He had to bite back his anger.

"Oh, Stace, this is tough. I wish I could change it."

"Oh, it gets worse. She and Len said they're taking me on a 'family' honeymoon. How gross is that? Len even bought me one of those world global cell phones like yours so I could call you from Italy."

David checked his watch. 2:02 P.M. His appointment had started without him.

"I feel for you, honey, but I know your mom only wants what's best for you. How about I call and talk to her later? Maybe I can convince her to let you come visit me instead of going on the honeymoon."

"Fat chance. She and Len are really into this family thing. But you're my family, David. I don't know why you and Mom got divorced anyway."

David grimaced. It was probably mostly his fault that things hadn't worked out with Meredith. She said he hadn't let her in, that she was tired of his moods, his introspection, even the headaches he'd never seen a doctor about. Though she'd never verbalized it, he knew she craved the easy affection he'd so effortlessly shared with her daughter. With Meredith—gorgeous, flighty Meredith—the connection, the communication, had been mainly sexual. Outside of the bedroom, he hadn't been able to give her what she wanted: attention, adoration, heart to heart talks about their innermost private feelings. The marriage had been a mistake, his mistake. And Stacy was the one suffering most for it. "Sometimes grownups don't have all the answers, Stace. But I can tell you this. Your mom and I might be divorced, but you and I aren't. You got that?"

"Then will you talk to my mom, and tell her I don't want to be Stacy Lachman?"

Stacy Lachman. David froze. For a moment he couldn't breathe, much less speak.

Stacy Lachman.

"David? You still there?"

"Yeah . . ." It was no more than a croak. He cleared his throat. "I'm here, sweetie. I'll give it my best shot, ok? Stace, I gotta go. Now do me a favor—go eat some lunch."

David shoved the phone in his pocket and hurried across the street. Cold dread filled every part of him. Stacy Lachman was a name he knew all too well. It was a name he'd been compelled to write in his journal over and over again.

His heart was pumping as he ran for the elevator. Stacy was the only good thing to have come out of his seven years with Meredith. Incredibly, the two of them had bonded the very first night they met, when Meredith had dragged him to Stacy's nursery school play. The three-year-old pixie had barely reached his knees. He'd laughed when Meredith told him that for weeks her daughter had been standing in front of the hall mirror, hour after hour, reciting her two simple lines.

David was all set to clap loudly for her, but then, just before her big moment, Stacy's little friend Emily had forgotten her lines, burst into wails and fled the stage.

Stacy had hesitated only a moment before dashing after her. At intermission, he and Meredith had found her backstage holding Emily's hand, both girls singing "Twinkle, twinkle little star," along with Emily's mother.

"Stacy, you messed up the play!" Meredith had chided an hour later at Ben & Jerry's. "Why didn't you wait and say your lines?"

"Emily was crying," she said between licks of her ice cream cone.

"But her mommy was there."

"I was closer," Stacy had insisted in a small firm voice.

Meredith had looked exasperated, but David had understood. There'd been something so pure in that three-year-old's eyes as she spoke those words. Something he couldn't quite name. He'd knelt down and gravely shaken her hand. "Emily's lucky to have a friend like you, Stacy. Maybe you and I can be friends, too."

Alex Dorset's receptionist knocked lightly on the hypnotherapist's door and pushed it open. David brushed quickly past her into a sunlit, paneled office.

Alex Dorset sat scribbling at his desk. He was an overweight balding black man with a walrus mustache and large sunken brown eyes. His office was cluttered and smelled of lemon polish. David counted four candy dishes overflowing with Good & Plenty and Reese's Pieces, all set within arm's reach of every chair in the room.

"Please." With a pudgy hand Dorset motioned David to a padded black recliner facing his desk. "Have a seat, Professor Shepherd, and try to relax. You look a bit rattled."

"I want you to hypnotize me." David placed his palms on Dorset's desk. His jaw was rigid. "Right now."

"I need some background first. What you told me on the phone was very sketchy. Why don't you start by telling me about those headaches you mentioned?"

"I don't give a damn about the headaches right now." He slammed his hand on the desk in frustration as tension throbbed in his neck. "I need to find out about the names."

Dorset's brows lifted. "You need to calm down before I can hypnotize you. Please, sit down and tell me about this obsession."

David forced himself to sit and to bite out a Cliffs Notes version of what he'd told Dillon. *What did Stacy have to do with this? Why was her new name in his journal?* He had to find out.

"From what you said on the phone, I knew this would be complicated." The hypnotherapist tapped a pencil on the desk.

"Damn straight it's complicated. Can we start now?"

"We can try."

David took a ragged breath and forced his eyes to close as Dorset lumbered around the desk to take the chair beside him. He settled back into the recliner and heard the click of a tape recorder. Dorset told him he would wake up refreshed, that he would remember everything he recalled under hypnosis. He directed David to focus on his voice.

The hypnotherapist's tone was soothing, his words low-timbered and rich, like a radio announcer's.

"Counting downward . . . five . . . now four . . ."

David soon found himself engulfed in liquid darkness. He was drifting . . . drifting past the tension throbbing in his shoulders . . . drifting past anxiety . . . past thought.

He followed the voice, that reassuring, even voice, followed it back to the winter of his thirteenth year, to the snow-packed roof of the tall handsome house where Crispin Mueller ran easily ahead of him.

"Abby! Grab my hand—Abby!"

"Abby's fine, David," Dorset said. "You're in the hospital now. The doctors are there. Can you see them?"

"I see myself. My chest—it's bloody. The doctors are bent over me."

"Do you feel any pain?"

"No, no pain, I'm just floating. Now Crispin's here—the doctors are gone. What's that light?"

"Find out. Go toward it, David. You're perfectly safe. Tell me what you see."

Light, beautiful silken light. He saw people within the light, shapes, faces. So many faces. They shouted to him, arms outstretched from within the shimmering rainbow. He was mesmerized by their faces— transparent, tortured, pleading faces.

Their shouts nearly drowned out the light, pounding at his head, roaring like thunder. Their names. They were shrieking their names. He heard hundreds of names, thousands, over and over. Then, in one voice, the tortured faces chanted a single word.

Zakhor.

Suddenly, the light went out.

When David opened his eyes, the dim light in Dorset's office seemed to burn his skull.

His head was splitting, his breath coming quick and shallow.

"Are you all right, David?"

"You tell me, Doctor." Shakily, he sat up.

Dorset handed him a glass of water. "So, do you remember everything you just told me?"

"Every word." David's face was pale. He was having a hard time digesting what he'd just revisited. Now, instead of answers, he had a lot more questions.

"I always remembered being pulled toward a brilliant light, but I had no memory of seeing all those faces. Of hearing their shouts." David's brow furrowed. "Who's Zakhor?" he said, almost to himself. "They all said it. *Zakhor*."

The other man regarded him intently. "Perhaps you should check your journal. And perhaps we should make another appointment for next week. You traveled a remarkable distance on your first try. Next time we may be able to probe on to another level."

"Can't you take me back down again now? I need to find out what these names mean."

"I can't do that. It would be counterproductive. Reliving such experiences drains the psyche. Give your subconscious some time to assimilate what you saw. Believe me, this is best."

David left the office, his chest tight with worry. He punched in Dillon McGrath's number as he crossed the street to his car.

"Dillon. Stacy's name is written in my journal. And I have no idea why. Some of these people have died, Dillon." The words tumbled out in a rush. "And what's Zakhor? They told me Zakhor."

"Who told you 'Zakhor'?"

"The people. The people at the end of the tunnel." David took a deep breath. "There were thousands of them. Shouting at me. Shouting their names. And then they all said 'Zakhor.'"

There was silence at the other end of the line.

"I may know someone who can help you figure this out," Dillon said finally. "I think you must consult a rabbi, David. I know you have no affinity for religion," he said quickly, before David could interrupt. "And that you haven't seen the inside of a synagogue since your bar mitzvah. But those voices spoke to you in Hebrew."

"Hebrew?" David stopped in his tracks, two feet from his car. "Zakhor is Hebrew?"

"It means 'remember.' Those people you saw in the light, in the tunnel. They want you to remember."

"Remember *what?*" David scraped a hand through his hair and squinted up at the sky.

Dillon's voice came low and patient. "It's obvious, David. They want you to remember their names. And so you have."

CHAPTER SIX

"You're the metaphysics genius," David said into his cell phone. He swung the car onto 18th Street. "*You* tell me what this means."

"That I can't do," Dillon said promptly. "The fact that they spoke to you in Hebrew suggests to me that a rabbi is your best guide. The reason they want you to remember must be inside of you, David, just like their names. I have a colleague I believe can help you. Rabbi Eliezer ben Moshe is a revered Kabbalist, a teacher of the Jewish mystical tradition. You've had a mystical experience, David. Now if you needed an exorcism," he said, "that might be more in my league."

Kabbalah? All David knew about Kabbalah was that some movie stars had made it a cause célèbre, tying red strings to their wrists and adopting Hebrew names.

As if reading his thoughts, Dillon said, "No, it's not the Madonna version of Kabbalah. And yes, I've already called him. He's very interested not only in your journal, but in that gemstone you've saved since your accident. Bring both of them with you when you go to

Brooklyn. In the meantime, he asked that you fax him several pages of the journal so he can study them before you arrive."

David's brow creased as he made a sharp right. His mind was spinning as Dillon continued.

"Ben Moshe comes from a long line of learned rabbis who have made the study of Kabbalah, and the unraveling of universal mysteries, their lifelong purpose."

Learned rabbis. The words triggered vague memories from his childhood—his mother telling him stories about her ancestor, Reb Zalman of Kiev, a famous mystic. Supposedly he could teach students in two different cities, three hundred miles apart, on the same evening. He'd always thought she'd made the stories up.

"You're kidding me, right?"

"David, there are things in life you can't measure with science and empirical data. Try to be open-minded."

David drew a deep breath. "I'm not convinced. . . ."

"You have a better idea?" Dillon countered.

David rubbed his forehead. "Whereabout in Brooklyn?" He wondered what Dean Myer would say when he informed him he had an out-of-town emergency.

CHAPTER SEVEN

A hard drizzle was slapping the pavement when David stepped out of the cab on Avenue Z in Brooklyn. He hoisted his duffel bag onto his shoulder and ran up the steps of the nondescript brownstone on the corner. After pushing the buzzer, he studied the ornate silver *mezzuzah* affixed to the doorframe of the B'nai Yisroel Center.

A thin youngish man starkly dressed in a white shirt, black slacks, and a knitted black yarmulke ushered him through what David guessed had once been the front room of a private home. The brownstone had been converted into a comfortable maze of offices.

"I'm Rabbi Tzvi Goldstein, Rabbi ben Moshe's assistant," he said, leading David down a hallway and into a classroom where a wide green blackboard sat perpendicular to the two long walls lined with shelves of books. David scanned their spines, noting they were all in Hebrew. The room smelled pleasantly of chalk and old leather and floor wax.

"We've been studying the journal pages you faxed to Rabbi ben

Moshe." Rabbi Goldstein was smiling and seemed barely able to contain his excitement. "He is very anxious to see you."

Good. Maybe now I'll get some answers, David thought.

Lately, every time he picked up his journal, he found himself gravitating toward the page with Stacy's new name.

And it was making him increasingly uneasy.

"Can I get you some tea while I let the rabbi know you're here?"

"No, thanks." David shoved his hands in his pockets as the young rabbi left. He moved toward the room's single window, where rain trickled in rivulets, blurring the view of the street below. His thoughts drifted to the images of the Iranian tanker explosion he'd seen on the airport TV while waiting for his boarding call. It seemed like the only news broadcast lately was bad news.

He jumped as a quiet voice spoke behind him, interrupting his thoughts.

"Shalom, David. Please, come this way. We can talk upstairs in my office."

David felt a twinge of surprise. He'd expected a Yiddish or Russian accent, but the elderly rabbi standing before him spoke with a faint New England intonation. His voice was creaky, somehow matching his gaunt frame. Rabbi Eliezer ben Moshe was a slight man who looked every bit as ancient and well-worn as the books on his shelves. He had a full head of faded gray hair and a silver beard that wisped in cloudlike curls to the middle of his chest. As David followed him up the carpeted stairs, he noticed how frail the rabbi appeared. His plain black suit coat hung from his bony shoulders, looking two sizes too big, as if its owner had shrunk since the time it was purchased.

But his walnut brown eyes, as he watched David take a seat in his cramped office, were sharp with worry, curiosity, hope.

"Did you bring your journal—and the stone?"

So much for preliminaries. David reached into his duffel and pulled out his journal. The rabbi's eyes lit when he set the red leather book down on the desk. As he pulled the rock from his pocket, David spotted the pages he'd faxed sitting alongside the rabbi's computer. There were notations on them, but he couldn't read what they said.

The rabbi stretched out a gnarled hand for the stone, and hesitating only a moment, David placed it in the man's palm.

Rabbi ben Moshe stared at the smooth variegated agate, unblinking and silent. He drew in a breath and his frail chest quivered.

"There are no facets," he whispered.

David watched in silence as he quickly opened a desk drawer to withdraw a magnifying glass. He turned the stone from side to side and, peering through the glass, examined it from every angle.

Out of all that had happened, the notion that this rock—something he'd kept on his desk since he was thirteen—held any significance, was the thing that baffled him the most. But the rabbi was brushing his finger across the Hebrew lettering with such reverence, such awe, that David curbed his impatience to rush into a discussion of the names.

"This is an ancient holy stone." Rabbi ben Moshe glanced up and met his eyes. "See how it's cut—rounded and shiny? The agate is polished, yet it doesn't glimmer or reflect the light. That's because it was cut in a convex style known as cabochon. Until the middle ages all stones were cut this way."

David glanced once more at the milky blue stone he'd so casually kept in the hand of the ceramic monkey.

"You're telling me it dates back to the Middle Ages?"

"Oh, no. It is much older than that. It dates back thousands of years—to biblical times."

Biblical times. David was stunned. And skeptical. *How would Crispin Mueller have gotten his hands on a biblical stone?*

"I was told it had magic powers." David half-expected the rabbi to laugh.

But ben Moshe nodded, holding his gaze. "And so it is written."

Then the rabbi closed his palm around the stone and murmured a prayer in Hebrew.

"You are Jewish. Do you understand the *Shehehiyanu* prayer?

I have just thanked God for allowing me to live long enough for this moment."

David's spine tingled. *What was he talking about? What was so special about this moment? And what did Crispin's rock have to do with Stacy's name being written in his journal?*

He leaned forward as the rabbi set the stone carefully down beside the journal.

"You say it's magical. In what way?"

"It belongs to a very special set of twelve. You told me on the phone that you're not religious, David, but I assume you know who Moses was."

David nodded. "That much I know."

"And his brother, Aaron—the high priest?"

"Now you've lost me." David was wondering whether he'd made a mistake in coming here. He felt he was moving further away from answers about the names, getting sidetracked with gemology and Bible study. As he struggled to contain his impatience, his gaze returned to the stone. Suddenly he remembered the reason he'd kept it in the first place—as a reminder to pause and think. He forced himself to bite back his questions about the journal and to concentrate on the rabbi's words.

"In the book of Exodus," ben Moshe continued, "we read that Aaron was the first high priest, the most glorious Jewish position, and that God told Moses to make his brother three holy garments—a breastplate, an *ephod*, and a robe."

"You've lost me again, rabbi." David shrugged. "Ephod?"

"It's another word for the linen apron Aaron wore during the holy rites. But the breastplate is what we're concerned with." The rabbi continued. "It was made according to instructions God gave to Moses. It was a woven square fashioned by an artist from threads of gold and blue, purple and scarlet."

Ben Moshe met David's eyes and explained. "According to the Book of Exodus, whenever Aaron entered the holiest part of the Temple to pray to God, he was instructed to wear upon his heart this 'Breastplate of Judgment,' which contained the names of the Children of Israel—the names of the Twelve Tribes."

David went still. *Names?*

"The names were engraved on twelve gemstones which were set in gold and sewn onto the breastplate with gold thread."

Suddenly David realized where this was headed. "And you're telling me that this rock is one of those stones?" he asked, incredulous.

The rabbi picked up the agate and came around the desk. "Look at what it says."

"I don't remember much of my Hebrew."

Ben Moshe ignored the admission. He held the agate before David and pointed one by one to the five tiny letters, tracing them from right to left. "*Nun pey tav lamed yud,*" he read. "They spell out *Naphtali*—one of the Twelve Tribes of Israel."

David's mind raced. "So there was a stone for each of them?"

"Exactly. And each stone was different. Naphtali's was an agate— the stone of protection, the one that prevents a man from stumbling and falling—"

David gave a bark of laughter. "In that case, it didn't work," he told the rabbi. "That's how I got this stone. The person who had it before me told me it was magic and would keep us from falling off a snow-covered roof. It didn't."

The rabbi didn't appear the least bit flummoxed. He merely looked at David with those faded brown eyes and said in a quiet tone, "Later, I must hear more about this person who had the stone. But for now, I can tell you that he didn't understand the nature of it. This stone—as well as each of the other eleven—has a larger purpose. This stone was never meant to protect one person. It is meant to protect the Children of Israel—and the entire world. The twelve stones represent God's mercy on His children."

The rabbi drew a long breath. "There's a reason you're here in my office today, David. It's no accident. Just as it's no accident that you're in possession of the names you've written in your journal and also of this sacred stone." An urgency burned in the rabbi's eyes. "May I see the book?"

A sense of unreality washed over David as the rabbi picked up his journal and opened it to the first page.

This all had to be some wild coincidence. After all, the stone had only come to him by accident. . . .

Accident.

The same accident, he realized, leaning back dazedly, that brought him to the names.

The stone and the names.

Could they really be connected?

"I believe these names belong to those people you told me you saw in your near death experience." Ben Moshe stroked his curling beard, his voice more somber than it had been before. David felt a chill tingle up his back.

"But who are they and why are their names always in my head?"

"You may scoff, David, but a nonreligious person can have a mystical experience. And you have. So—there's a mystical answer to your question. You are not the first to write these names in a book. And these are not just random names—they are special. Very special."

David braced himself for whatever was coming next.

From the third floor walk-up apartment above the Java Juice coffee shop in another part of Brooklyn, a man in an Eminem t-shirt and a backward Yankees cap lowered the volume on his headphones. He'd heard enough.

Picking up the safe phone, he hit redial while the video screens and monitors of the state-of-the-art communications center flickered all around him. This job was geek heaven. From the center of his horseshoe-shaped console, he could eavesdrop on conversations across three continents and watch history in the making, while two floors below, the caffeine addicts were lining up like lemmings to swallow flavored cups of mud.

"What gives?" The blond hulk in the back of the bakery van parked on Avenue Z snapped the words into the phone. James Gillis was antsy, and his ass burned from sitting here waiting. This was his first opportunity as lead Dark Angel, and he was impatient to prove himself.

"Damn it, Sanjay, how much longer do you expect us to just sit here? Shepherd's been in there for forty minutes already."

"Hold on to your balls, big guy. Here's the drill. Shepherd's got the gemstone and the journal with him. Get them both. And after you've eliminated everyone, find the damned safe. We need to get whatever that old Jew has in there."

"No problemo." Gillis glanced at Enrique, the Puerto Rican locksmith with his toolbelt and Glock strapped beneath his Armani blazer. Enrique sat in the captain's chair beside him, staring at the rain splattering the van's windows. He was always cool—as patient and expressionless as a Mafia hitman.

In the communications center, Sanjay checked that the bank of digital recorders on his left were still blinking.

"In that case," he said, raising the volume and returning to the conversation in the brownstone. "Dark Angels—go. You are cleared to fly."

CHAPTER EIGHT

"These names you've written . . ." The rabbi touched a hand to the pages beside his computer, the ones David had faxed him. "They match names that have been recorded in ancient papyri discovered in the Middle East."

David felt like the floor was sliding away beneath his chair.

"That's impossible."

"Confirmation came in only this morning. Hear me out before you close your mind," ben Moshe chided. "These names, and all those in your journal, were first written thousands of years ago — they were written down by Adam."

He held up a hand as David started to argue. "According to the Kabbalah, Adam copied down God's *Book of Names* — the names of birds, beasts, and every living creature — for himself and for his sons. They, in turn, passed copies on to their sons, and so on, until eventually the Book reached Moses."

David leaped from his chair, unable to contain his incredulity a moment longer.

"Rabbi, with all due respect, I find it impossible to believe that Adam knew my stepdaughter's name back in the Garden of Eden." He pulled the journal toward him and began reading random names aloud. "Or Shen Jianchao's. Or Noelania Trias's. Or Beverly Panagoupolos's." David tossed the book down. "Come on, now."

Ben Moshe remained unfazed. "I don't expect you to understand this all at once. The study of Kabbalah is a lifelong journey. It requires a mature mind and many years to uncover the mystical layers of the Torah. In past centuries, its secrets were restricted, passed down only from the rabbis to their most devoted students. But, David, I have dedicated my life to this study for over sixty years and I know as well as I know my own name what I am about to tell you."

David suddenly flashed on his mother's tales of her great-grandfather, the mystic, Reb Zalman. "I'm listening."

Ben Moshe nodded. "Follow me now—Moses's copy of the Book of Names was passed down to him from Isaac—one of Abraham's two sons—and was stored for years in the Temple Vault in Jerusalem. But when the Romans destroyed the Temple in 70 C.E., they carried off its treasure to Rome, and the Book of Names disappeared, along with the high priest's breastplate. And with that breastplate," the rabbi said softly, "went the gemstones of the Twelve Tribes of Israel."

David glanced at the stone on the desk, his brain roiling with questions. But he bit them back, listening as the rabbi continued in his low creaky voice.

"The copies belonging to Abraham's other son—Isaac's half-brother, Ishmael—passed to the sons his concubines bore him, and those papyri were lost to the desert sands. So for centuries, all copies of the Book of Names were lost. However, in recent years, archaeologists have discovered fragments in Egypt and other places in the Middle East which they believe are copied from Ishmael's papyri. Aided by historians and mathematicians, they're attempting to piece them together. These are the experts I contacted to compare your pages against the various fragments safeguarded in Israel."

David struggled to digest the enormity of the rabbi's theory. "Have they found more than one copy of Adam's Book?"

"We believe so. Papyri written in Aramaic, Coptic, and Hebrew have been discovered—"

"I would have thought only Hebrew."

"No." Ben Moshe shook his head. "Since Ishmael was Abraham's son by his non-Jewish handmaiden, Hagar, his descendants' copies were written in ancient Arabic languages. And although identical passages have been found in many papyri, no one has yet assembled one complete text. However," his eyes gleamed, "some of us feel we are close."

David leaned forward. "So there are ongoing archaeological digs?"

"Oh, yes." The rabbi's voice sharpened. "Unfortunately, we're not the only ones searching for the missing fragments. Others are racing to assemble the entire manuscript so that they can be first to translate all the names—only these are evil people, David. Enemies of God."

Baffled, David dragged a hand through his hair as the rain began to thrum more rapidly against the window. "Who?"

"The Gnoseos."

David looked blank. Rabbi ben Moshe walked around his desk, steepling his hands together at his chest. His face looked grimmer than David had yet seen it.

"The Gnoseos are a secret society descended from an ancient religious cult—the Gnostics."

David stared at him. "How ancient?"

"Predating Christianity. The Gnoseos are one of the few remnants of Gnosticism still existing—a sect even more vibrant and secretive than they were centuries ago."

David had heard of Gnosticism. He remembered Dillon mentioning it one Saturday when they were discussing the broader roots of religion over bagels and cream cheese.

"Hedonists, aren't they?" David searched his memory as thunder clapped outside. "They consider humanity to be trapped in evil bodies, right?"

"Yes. And that every soul has the ability to tap into some innate knowledge—a ladder, as it were—in order to elevate high enough spiritually to break free of the body."

"And what then . . . reach heaven?"

"Not exactly, David." Ben Moshe sighed. "The root of their name is *gnosis*—the Greek word for knowledge. The Gnoseos believe that with enough knowledge they can vanquish God. And they have resolved to do precisely that."

David had a dozen questions, but before he could ask the first one, there was a knock at the door and Rabbi Goldstein poked in his head.

"Rabbi, excuse me. Yael HarPaz has arrived."

"Good, good. Send her up, Tzvi." Ben Moshe returned to his chair. "I hope you won't mind, David. I've invited an antiquities expert to join us—a brilliant Israeli archaeologist from Safed. She arrived from Israel this morning."

"Look, Rabbi." David threw up his hands. "This just gets more and more complicated. I don't want us to get off-track. My stepdaughter's name is in my journal, and I'm worried. If you know— please just cut to the chase and tell me why so many dead people want me to remember their names!"

"We're getting to it, David. Please be patient. You must begin to comprehend that you are a part of something much bigger than you can imagine. I understand you have a Ph.D. in political science and are renowned in your field. I assure you that I am as knowledgeable in my field as you are in yours. And so is Yael HarPaz in hers."

Before David could answer, a woman appeared in the doorway. She was tall and slender, in a long gauzy black skirt, ivory shell, and fitted silk blazer. She strode into the room with purpose, carrying a copper leather tote. He was struck by her exotic cheekbones and generous mouth, frosted with the barest tinge of pink. He guessed she was about thirty, and from her coloring—long coppery hair twisted into a loose knot and a tawny complexion—he guessed she was a Sabra, a native-born Israeli.

"Yael HarPaz, this is David Shepherd, the man I told you about."

The woman flashed David a straightforward, appraising glance and set down her tote. They shook hands, her silver bracelet jingling. "Shalom."

Her voice, with its rich Hebrew accent, was as sleek and attractive as the rest of her.

"You've come a long way on my account. I don't really understand why."

"I came for the stone. Did you bring it?"

David was surprised by her authoritative tone. He paused before turning back to the desk, then picked up the stone and studied it. "So you also believe this is from the high priest's breastplate?"

"May I?" Yael's dark green eyes sparked as she took it from his hand. Before David could say anything, she began turning it from side to side, as the rabbi had done.

"Naphtali," she said with excitement in her voice.

The rabbi smiled.

"All right." David drew a breath. "Let's say for argument's sake this is one of the stones from the breastplate. What about the others? Are they accounted for?"

"We have four others secure in Jerusalem," Yael told him. She glanced at the rabbi, waiting for him to speak.

"I have another here," he told David. "Levi's stone, an amber."

Even as he said the words, he moved toward the bookcase and pulled down the volumes that masked the safe. "This one surfaced in a Sephardic synagogue in Detroit. A Tunisian Jew bought it at an outdoor market in Cairo seventy years ago and had no idea what it was. His son emigrated to the United States and a month ago he showed it to his rabbi, who contacted me."

The rabbi pulled out the worn satchel and reached inside. He withdrew a velvet drawstring pouch from which he plucked a stone identical in size to David's agate. When he set them down side by side, David's breath caught in his chest. Not only were the agate and the amber stones identical in size, they were identically cut. Even the Hebrew script was undeniably from the same hand.

Everything was happening too fast. The stones, the names, the names on the stones, Crispin, Stacy, his journal. He tried to marshal his thoughts, even as the rabbi spoke again.

"I intended to carry the amber to Israel next week, but your visit has saved me an urgent trip. It's imperative that these two stones reach the safety of Jerusalem—before any harm befalls them. Yael?"

As ben Moshe picked up both stones to hand them off to the archaeologist, they slipped from his arthritic fingers to the floor and rolled under the desk. David knelt to retrieve them.

But he saw something under the desk that stopped him cold.

"What the hell?" There was a small silver receiver stuck to the bottom of the desk.

"Are you taping our conversation?" he asked, an edge of anger in his voice. Scooping up the gems he surged to his feet.

Alarm flicked across Yael's face.

The rabbi spoke quickly. "What are you talking about?"

Even as he finished the question, Yael sank to her knees and peered under the desk. She ripped the bugging device from the wood, her face fading pale beneath her tan.

"They know," she said, meeting the rabbi's horrified eyes.

"Quickly." Ben Moshe latched the satchel with shaking hands. "Take these things and go—"

Just then a loud noise sounded from the floor below. For a moment David thought it was a car backfiring, but then they heard a scream.

"Rabbi, run! Get out!" Rabbi Goldstein's voice gurgled from the main floor. Then more shots rang out and screams filled the building.

"David, hide the stones!" Ben Moshe pushed the satchel into Yael's arms as heavy footsteps pounded up the stairs. "The fire escape! Hurry! Take everything—I'll explain later, God willing—but you must leave *now*."

The rabbi rushed to bolt the door as David shoved both gemstones into his pants pocket. He threw his journal back into the duffel and slung it over his shoulder. Yael was already thrusting the window upward.

"You first." David grabbed the rabbi's arm and pulled him toward the fire escape, but the older man shook free.

"No, David, *you* first. Now." Ben Moshe's tone was calm. "Yael, get him to Safed. *He knows the names.* He knows the names of the Lamed Vovniks."

She was already throwing a leg over the windowsill. "Come on," she ordered David.

"Go!" Ben Moshe pushed him as the intruders began battering against the door.

His adrenaline pumping, David ducked his head and climbed onto the fire escape. Rain slashed at his face. Yael was halfway to the street, yet he hesitated and reached a hand back for the rabbi. But as Ben Moshe struggled to position himself on the windowsill, the door burst open and shots rang out. With a grunt, the rabbi toppled, blood dripping crimson from his beard, splattering across David's hand.

"Run, David!" Yael screamed as horror rocketed through him. He hurtled down the fire escape to the street below, nearly slipping on the wet metal. He glanced up for an instant to see a huge man with blond hair kick the rabbi's lifeless body aside and take aim.

David ducked as a bullet pinged the brick beside him. He bolted after Yael as another shot rang out and the blond charged down the fire escape.

They ran through the driving downpour and rounded the corner, Yael nearly colliding with a woman battling her way down the street with an umbrella and an armful of groceries.

"Watch out," the woman yelled, but Yael had no breath to apologize. She catapulted between two buildings and David followed, gaining on her as she plunged across the street, dodging traffic as horns blared at them. Suddenly, a gunshot blew out the rear tire of a UPS truck, sending it careening straight toward David.

He threw himself forward and landed sprawled on his side against the curb. Yael grabbed his arm and he scrambled to his feet. The blond man was barreling toward them, gun in hand, and people were scattering.

"This way!" David tugged her toward a bus discharging passengers ten feet away. They scurried around piles of bagged garbage and forced their way up the steps, wedging past others trying to get on. David caught a glimpse of the blond through the rain-smeared window—he was running hard now, straight for the bus.

The doors hissed closed. The blond took aim.

"Everybody down! There's a maniac with a gun back there!" David yelled. An old woman screamed.

"Move it, man, *now!*" he shouted at the driver.

Other passengers spun to look out the window.

"No shit, man!" a black kid listening to his iPod yelled. "Get outta here!"

Swearing, the driver swerved into traffic. A bullet screamed into the bus's back end as it lumbered away from the curb, sending tall sprays of water in its wake. The giant windshield wipers raced to keep pace with the torrent of rain dousing the city.

"Call your dispatcher," Yael directed the driver breathlessly. David saw there were tears on her face. "Tell him to send an ambulance to the B'nai Yisroel Center on Avenue Z. A man's been shot."

She looked at David, but neither of them spoke as the bus rumbled through traffic. They both knew it was too late. Rabbi ben Moshe was dead.

Dazed, David wondered if he looked as pale and shaken as she did. His heart was still thundering in his chest. He couldn't wrap his mind around what had just happened.

His grip tightened on the rain-soaked satchel even as his other hand checked his pocket.

The gemstones were still there. And Stacy's name was still in his journal.

"He emptied the goddamn safe! Everything's gone!" Enrique shouted, as Gillis hurtled back into the room from the fire escape. Gillis stared at the barren cavity gaping behind the bookcase.

Shit. Sirens were already screaming. There was no more time.

"The journal's not here? What about the gemstones?"

"Shepherd and the Israeli woman must've got away with both." Enrique had already torn through the rabbi's desk and dumped out the contents of each drawer onto the floor. Suddenly, he spotted the stack of faxed pages beside the computer. David Shepherd's name and fax number were scrawled across the top. He snatched them up.

"Hey, what do you make of this?"

He thrust the papers at Gillis, whose face relaxed as he scanned through the list of names.

"Got something, Sanjay," he barked into the microphone of his cell phone's headset. "The pages Shepherd faxed from his journal. We're bringing them over now with the computer."

"Aren't the cops there yet?" Sanjay demanded. His voice no longer sounded steady and bored. It sounded alarmed. "Get out."

Even as he spoke, Enrique hoisted the computer, ripping the cords from the power strip on the floor. He sprinted toward the stairs. Gillis took time only to grab the stack of floppy disks from their bin on the desk, and to whip out his lighter. He watched the flame for a split second before touching it to the tumble of papers on the floor, relishing how close he was now to the world to come.

He took the stairs two at a time, as the scream of sirens grew closer.

By the time the police cars squealed to the curb, the white bakery van was half a block away, nothing but a pale, insignificant blur in the driving rain.

And Sanjay was already e-mailing his initial coded report to headquarters in Sicily where Eduardo DiStefano bent forward at his computer, poring intently over each and every word.

CHAPTER NINE

Meredith leaned forward in the bleachers, her shoulders tensing. She watched as Stacy wiped the sweat from her forehead and bounced the ball twice at the free throw line.

Come on, baby, she thought. *Sink it.*

Stacy squinted at the basket and then lobbed the ball toward the backboard as if it was the easiest thing in the world. For a moment silence hung over the middle school's packed gym. Even Meredith held her breath as the ball arced through the air, then cheers erupted as it swooshed through the net.

Grinning, Stacy spun around to slap fives with her teammates. There were only five seconds left in the game—not enough time for her opponents to sink a basket.

"That's my girl!" Meredith yelled from the bleachers as the buzzer blared. Stacy was already in line with her teammates, shaking hands with their opponents.

Glancing at her watch, Meredith considered her options. The game was over early. Len wouldn't be calling her from Stockholm for another hour. Plenty of time for her and Stacy to grab some Chinese on the way home.

"I'll get the car while you shower, sweetie."

"Okay, Mom, but I'll be quick—I'm starving."

"Why don't we go to China Palace? It's just around the block," Meredith called as she headed across the court toward the exit.

Stacy ran for the locker room. It felt great to strip out of her sopping uniform and plunge under the water. She didn't even bother to dry her hair after she washed it, she just pulled it into a damp ponytail and reached for her jeans and the hot pink t-shirt David had bought her last summer when she'd visited him in D.C. The same day he'd bought her the yellow message bracelet she wore every day as a reminder to always "Aim High."

It was only because of David that she was such a good basketball player, she thought as she dressed. He'd started her shooting hoops in the driveway when she was five and barely able to wrap her hands around the ball. He'd taught her to dribble when she was eight, and they'd practiced every night while her mom made dinner. Stacy smiled, remembering how David would yell for her mother to come cheer her whenever she beat him at a game of Horse. Of course, she knew now that all those times, he was letting her win.

She loved how they'd raced to load the dishwasher every night after dinner so there'd be time for her to get in her hundred free throws before it got dark.

Then, when it was too dark to see the net, they'd sit on the patio, all sweaty, alongside Mom, cooling off with big blue bowls filled with bananas and ice cream, watching the first stars peek out. David had called it "twinkle time."

Running toward the door, Stacy slung her gym bag over her shoulder and tried to push the memories away. *Face it. Now Len is your stepdad. And he isn't into basketball—or ice cream.*

Len was into squash and soy lattes.

Suddenly, as she pushed the double doors open, the ground seemed to tremble beneath her feet. All the girls screamed.

Oh, God, was that another aftershock? Yesterday she'd woken up to the vibrations of a 3.6 earthquake rocking her bed. It turned out to be nothing too major, luckily, just a little wiggle.

Good thing she was almost used to them by now. When she and her mom had first moved to Santa Monica her heart had pounded in her throat every time there was a little tremor. Now she was more like a native Californian, letting them roll on by.

But lately, there'd been so many disasters in the world, she'd started worrying that a big earthquake might come, too. Everyone said it was only a matter of time before the big one hit the West Coast. It was scary to think about.

Scary—like that sniper in Toronto. How many people had he killed already? Just this morning Mom had switched off the TV in disgust, saying she couldn't take one more news report about all the horrible things happening in the world.

But Stacy kept worrying about them.

Just for a day, why can't you try to be like Mom and block out all this bad stuff? she asked herself, hurrying toward the car in the late afternoon sunshine. *Try thinking about chicken lettuce wraps. And hot and sour soup. And ginger ice cream.*

She was so engrossed in her thoughts that she didn't notice the man reading a newspaper in the Dodge Caravan idling at the front of the parking lot. She hadn't noticed him in the back row of the bleachers either.

She climbed up into the Explorer and buckled her seat belt, her stomach growling with hunger.

"I need food!" She slid an Alicia Keys CD into the player and turned up the volume as Meredith put the SUV in gear.

Stacy Lachman was a cute kid, Raoul LaDouceur thought. Too bad she was about to meet with some very foul play.

He folded the newspaper and tossed it to the floor. He pulled out of the parking lot and kept a good three cars behind Meredith

Lachman's Explorer. The woman was as oblivious as her kid. He'd been tailing them for the past two days, making a log of their routine, and getting comfortable navigating the streets of Santa Monica. And those two didn't have a clue.

The only tough part about this assignment was the damned smog. It was far worse than the raw stinging throat he got from the fucking olive trees.

He'd have to remember to stop at Walgreens for a new inhaler tonight, before he ran this one dry. By necessity he always carried a current prescription with him—along with his guns, ribbed Trojans, and an international cell phone.

When the Explorer pulled into the China Palace lot, Raoul did the same, parking a short distance away.

He felt a wheeze coming on and took a puff from his inhaler as he watched Stacy Lachman and her mother head inside.

His instructions had been general—make this one look like an accident or an abduction. He'd decided abduction would be cleaner. So Stacy Lachman was going to vanish. The same way his target in Sierra Leone had vanished four months ago. This time, he'd dump the body in Death Valley on his way to Vegas. It would be months before anyone found the bones.

Not until his stomach protested did Raoul realize he was hungry. He stepped out of the car and ambled into the dimly lit, red and black restaurant.

The Lachman kid and her mother never turned a head as he slid into the booth catty-corner from them. He placed his order, then watched the girl, so adept with her chopsticks. Stirring two packets of sugar into his oolong tea, Raoul smiled.

Eat up, Stacy Lachman. You'll be dead by tomorrow.

Unless the fucking smog gets to me first.

CHAPTER TEN

"Bolt the door," Yael ordered as David followed her into Room 736 of the Riverside Tower Hotel. She plopped her tote and the rabbi's satchel on the desk near the window, and pulled out her phone.

"I need to make a call—"

David grabbed the BlackBerry from her hand. "First you're going to tell me who the hell we're running from."

"There's plenty of time to explain once I've made the call. Give it back!" Her voice was cold, her green eyes even colder.

"Who was he? Gnoseos?"

Yael scowled. "Their assassination squad. They're called Dark Angels. Please—I have a contact here and if you allow me to call him, you and I just might get out of the country alive."

"Get out of the country? How? I don't even have my passport."

"That's the least of your worries. Now give me that phone."

She grabbed it from him and David turned away. He tossed his soaked duffel onto the luggage rack and caught sight of himself in the mirror over the dresser. His hair was plastered to his head. His skin had turned a sickly gray. Probably from shock. No wonder. His mind kept replaying the image of ben Moshe slumped across the fire escape.

He and Yael had jumped off the bus at the next stop. Somehow, they'd managed to hail a cab in the pouring rain and headed toward the Hudson River, silent, soaking wet, and shivering from more than the storm.

Who knew if they were safe even now. Was the blond hulk after the gemstones? Or the journal?

Ben Moshe had said they were searching for the names.

And one of them is Stacy's.

David yanked out his cell phone and listened in frustration as Stacy's line rang four times and then dumped him into voice mail.

"Hi, Munchkin." He tried to sound natural, but his voice sounded strained. "Give me a call as soon as you get this, okay? Just checking in to see how you're doing."

He tried Meredith next and swore aloud when her recorded message began.

"Call me, Mere, it's urgent. I need to talk to you about Stace. Right away."

Not that he knew what he was going to tell her when she called back. How do you tell someone their kid's name might be on a list of people who are turning up dead? He needed to get some answers from Yael HarPaz before Meredith or Stacy called back.

Pacing to the desk near the window, he unlatched the rabbi's satchel. As Yael spoke in rapid-fire Hebrew behind him, he scanned its contents—a Hebrew prayer book, a looseleaf binder, a small bronze coin embossed with a figure eight.

David looked closer. No, not a figure eight—a pair of snakes.

He noticed two laminated cards on the bottom and picked one up, staring at its strange, intricate drawing. *What's this?*

It was a diagram. Ten different colored molecules connected by intersecting lines. It reminded him of a molecular formula on a prescription insert. Or something he'd built as a kid with his wooden Tinkertoys.

As he heard Yael end the call, he dropped the diagram back into the satchel and wheeled to face her.

"Now I'd like that explanation."

She spoke coolly. "Where do you want me to start?"

"The names in my journal. Why are they written on all the ancient papyri the rabbi told me about?" The words poured out of him. "Whose names are they? What do they have in common?"

"They are the people who keep the world in existence. Rare and special people. And they are being systematically murdered by the Gnoseos."

A cold terror drenched him. The names he'd Googled—he'd been right. All those accidents weren't really accidents.

Stacy.

God, where *was* she?

"My stepdaughter's name is in that journal." His voice cracked. "Are you telling me she's in danger?"

Yael swallowed. A hint of compassion flickered in her eyes.

"I'm sorry. I didn't know. Yes, she is in danger. All of the Lamed Vovniks are. Is she in D.C.?"

"No, on the opposite coast. Santa Monica." David gritted his teeth. "Are the same people after her? These Dark Angels?"

She nodded, her expression grim. "They are highly trained and relentless killers." She drew a breath. "If they have her name, they'll find her. She needs protection immediately. I'll call Avi back—"

"No." David's jaw was set. "I've got someone I trust. He's the best there is. He'll protect her, and he's less than an hour from her by plane."

Yael bit her lip, then shrugged. She peeled off her soaked silk blazer and shivered. The color still hadn't returned to her face. "Very well. I'll brew some coffee while you make your arrangements."

David punched in Karl Hutchinson's number, one he knew by

heart. It had been three years since he'd seen him, but they talked every few months. He prayed Hutch would answer.

"*Hola!*" Hutch's familiar voice told him to leave a message after the tone. David's chest constricted.

"Hutch, it's me, I'm in New York and I've got an emergency. I think Stacy's life is in danger. I need you, buddy."

David's head felt like it was going to explode. He gulped down a deep breath, and then another. *Focus.*

He focused on Yael as she handed him a cup of coffee. "Now will you tell me everything that's going on?"

"I'll try. Sit down, David." She looked at him appraisingly. "This isn't going to be easy for you to accept. Or for me to explain."

David folded himself into the desk chair and set down the coffee cup.

He remembered what ben Moshe had shouted to Yael as she climbed onto the fire escape.

There was no way he was getting on a plane to Israel—not without Stacy.

His gaze leveled on the long-legged woman seated on the bed across from him.

"You can start," he said quietly, "by telling me about the Lamed Vovniks."

CHAPTER ELEVEN

"Are you familiar with the Talmud?" Yael watched him steadily.

"Generally. Ancient rabbinical commentaries on the Old Testament, right?"

"It's more than that. The Talmud is *the* main body of Jewish religious writings—everything there is to know about Jewish law, history, philosophy, moral teachings—even legends." Yael took a sip of her coffee.

"Sixty-three tractates, all written between the third and sixth centuries by the most learned of Jewish sages—men who spent their entire lives arguing, analyzing, and defining every aspect of Jewish law. Within the Talmud lies the explanation of the Lamed Vovniks."

"Keep talking." David struggled to control his impatience.

"According to Rabbi Abbaye—one of those learned sages—in every generation the world must contain thirty-six righteous people who are blessed by the *Shekhinah*."

"Who?"

"God's feminine aspect." She met his eyes.

"Jewish tradition teaches that only by the inherent merits of these thirty-six does God continue to keep the world in existence."

David shook his head. "Hold on—you're telling me that there's only thirty-six righteous people in the entire world?"

"Actually, there are about eighteen thousand," she said with a flicker of a smile. "But the Lamed Vovniks are special individuals, people whose souls reach the highest spiritual level. Their goodness is so powerful, so inherent, that they're capable of complete spiritual unity with God while on earth."

His brows lifted in disbelief. "You're saying they have a hotline to God? Look, I've always known Stacy was a sweet-hearted kid, but, c'mon—"

"The mystics say that the Lamed Vovniks walk among us undetected. At least thirty-six in every generation, always unknown, even to themselves. So anyone who claims to be one is definitely not. They're humble and do good in quiet ways, avoiding credit or praise. The Hasidic rabbis tell tales of Lamed Vovniks who arrived as strangers in a town, saved it from disaster, and then vanished without fanfare as quickly as they'd appeared."

Yael's hands were clenched around her coffee cup. "If all the Lamed Vovniks in a generation were to die, the world would cease to exist."

Thunder split the sky. They both glanced at the window, where rain sheeted down upon a city already drowning.

"Don't you see, David? It's already started. Haven't you wondered about all the horrors multiplying around the world, one after the other? Do you remember a time when the turmoil was so intense, so relentless? The Gnoseos, David, they are destroying the world. By destroying the Lamed Vovniks."

David's head began to pound again, in syncopation with the drum of the rain. He pushed himself from the chair, crossing to the window. He focused on the swell of rainwater gushing along the street. As he watched, lightning arced off the building across from him. Its upper windows shattered even as thunder exploded like a bomb. David jumped back as the reverberations shook beneath his feet.

The earthquakes in Turkey, the explosion at the port in Dayyer, the terrorists in Melbourne. The hurricanes spinning one after the other in the Atlantic . . . the mudslides in Chile. . . .

No. Impossible. He spun toward Yael. Her clear green eyes were somber in the dim hotel room. "David, we need to get you to Israel—to Safed, a sacred and mystical city."

"I'm not going anywhere except to Santa Monica."

"Safed, David. The answers are there. It's in the light—in the air. And even secular scientists like my father and I can't deny the mystical aura that seems to beam from the stars there. The Kabbalists in Safed need your journal, your *mind.* They have scraps of papyri dug from the sand, fragments of the ancient book containing the names of all creatures—including the secret names of the Lamed Vovniks. But you, David, have their names, too. They're in your head."

"If Stacy's one of them—" he broke off, his stomach roiling with fear. *If they even exist.*

She thrust her hand through her hair, sweeping the burnished waves from her face. "We cannot count on your Hutch to get to her quickly, especially since he has not returned your call. I'm sending in a backup team. My contact Avram Raz has access to the best of Israeli security and intelligence. His name fits his work."

"What is that supposed to mean?"

"Raz means 'secret' in Hebrew. But every Hebrew letter also carries a numerical value. And the letters that spell Raz have the same numerical value as the Hebrew words for 'light' and 'stranger.'"

"I'm still not following you."

"Avi Raz is a man who brings secrets and strangers to light," she said, opening her phone. "That should tell you enough about his occupation—and his qualifications."

David clamped his lips together. He needed to hear from Stacy *now.* His cell rang just as Yael began speaking quickly in Hebrew, and he snatched it up, praying he'd see Stacy's name across the display.

Hutch.

"David, what in hell's going on? Tell me what I can do."

"Get to Santa Monica—I need you to protect Stacy and Meredith. You remember the house? Get them out of California. A backup team's coming—I'll need you to call me with your location once you're all safe."

"Jesus, man, what are we dealing with here?"

"I think Stacy's on a hitlist, Hutch." David could scarcely believe what he was saying. "Some religious cult is after her. I need you there yesterday, pal."

When he snapped his phone closed, David found Yael watching him. No trace of sympathy softened her eyes.

"Avi hand picked two Mossad agents who are flying in to LAX tonight. As soon as Hutch gets word to us, they'll meet up with him and take over. She'll be all right, David. You have to trust me on that."

As another crack of thunder shook the windows, she pushed herself off the bed and advanced toward him. "In the meantime, you and I must get to Safed as soon as possible."

"Not going to happen. I'm going to my daughter. She's my only priority."

"She'll be protected, David. But there are a lot of other people who won't be. Think about it—after what happened today, you're on the Gnoseos radar. If you go to Stacy now, you could lead them right to her."

David's temples throbbed. He could still hear the gunshots in his head.

What if Yael was right?

"You can help her more in Safed than anywhere else. The sooner we get there the better, but someone needs to overnight your passport." Her eyes locked with his.

"Who can you trust?"

CHAPTER TWELVE

Floating on her back was the most peaceful feeling in the world. Stacy closed her eyes and basked in the caress of the sun, sighing contentedly at this near-perfect afternoon. She'd won today's game, her fortune cookie had promised an adventure, and best of all, David was going to talk her mother out of dragging her along on the "family honeymoon."

Now if only she could block out the sound of her mom making those mewing noises on the phone to Len. It was nauseating.

If I wasn't so comfortable, Stacy thought, *I'd paddle over to the pool deck and crank up the music.* But she didn't want to move. . . .

From the window above, her mother's laughter shot up ten decibels. *Who am I kidding?* She slipped off the raft into the tepid water, her face scrunched in exasperation. *Who can relax when their own mother is embarrassing herself like that, and loud enough for all the neighbors to hear?*

Sloshing from the pool, she padded toward the chaise lounge where she'd dumped her phone, her sunscreen, and her towel. Her can of Coke had grown warm in the sun but she swigged it anyway as she spun up the volume on her boom box.

There. Way better. Now she didn't have to listen to—

Coke shot from her nostrils as she was grabbed hard from behind. The can went flying and she struggled for air as a rough-skinned hand smashed against her nose and mouth. She was choking, gasping, fighting for breath and trying to scream all at the same time, but even though she managed to wrench her lips slightly apart nothing audible came out.

Terror punched through her as with one hairy arm her attacker hoisted her clear off her feet. Her chest felt like it was going to burst from lack of air as he began running with her like a quarterback streaking for the goalpost.

Wild with panic, she realized where he was headed. In ten strides she'd be inside the strange van parked outside the garage.

Eva Smolensky grunted as she tugged the Dyson down the stairs. She was a tiny bird of a woman, barely a few inches taller and not much wider than the vacuum she pushed into Dr. Shepherd's office. Flicking on the overhead light, she clucked her tongue at the stack of newspapers that had piled up since she'd cleaned last Tuesday. She figured as long as Dr. Shepherd had called and asked her to let Father McGrath in this afternoon, she'd clean the house a day early, leaving her Tuesday morning free to visit her newest grandchild.

But, boy oh boy, she wasn't as young as she used to be. Eva hadn't cleaned this late at night since her kids were little and she'd waited until they went to bed to pick up around the house. And picking up after Dr. Shepherd wasn't exactly easy. He was a very nice young man and all, but he was a slob, just like her son-in-law, Henry.

Eva shook her head. Well, at least he'd called early enough. She'd have most of his house in order before Father McGrath got here and picked up whatever Dr. Shepherd needed.

Peering out the window for a glimpse of the priest, Eva massaged the small of her back. She was getting too old and creaky to clean houses, but she still kept her favorite customers. For now.

Next year, who knew? Maybe she'd finally retire.

There was no sign of that handsome priest yet, so she trudged back to the vacuum and bent over, pushing the plug into the wall. No matter if he came to the door while she was still vacuuming—she'd told him the front door would be unlocked in case she didn't hear the bell over the vacuum and washing machine.

As her finger hovered on the vacuum switch, a buzzer sounded. The dryer. With a sigh, she shuffled to the laundry room and the waiting load of permanent-press shirts. Those she had to get on hangers right away, before they wrinkled.

The washing machine thudded into its rinse cycle as she opened the dryer door. *Now why couldn't someone invent a washer and dryer that cycled on the same schedule? Would that be too much to ask?* Suddenly, Eva heard movement in the hall. Father McGrath. He must have slipped in right before she looked out the window. Now how had she missed him? Maybe she did need a hearing aid like her daughters kept telling her. . . .

Hmmph. She scurried to the hall, more than happy to spend a few moments with her favorite priest. Not only was Father McGrath easy on the eyes, but he had that warm and gentle manner about him. Every time she saw him, she came away feeling she'd been in the company of angels.

She peered around the hall. Strange. He wasn't there.

"Father McGrath?" Eva sang out. She padded to the kitchen and glanced around, then doubled back to the hall and squinted up the staircase.

Odd. She could swear she'd heard someone in the house. "Father?" she called again.

There was only silence.

Puzzled, Eva started toward the office.

But she never got there.

Dr. Shepherd's pin-striped pale blue shirt was still piping hot from the dryer when it was flung over her head and its sleeves twisted around her crepey throat.

She fought for air like a marionette dangling at the end of her strings, but she was with the angels a full minute before her body was stuffed in among the shirts wrinkling inside the clothes dryer.

Stacy's eyes pleaded toward her mother's open bedroom window. *Mom*, she wanted to scream. *Mom!* But she couldn't scream, she couldn't even breathe. Her nostrils, her throat were on fire, and pinpricks of light began to dot her vision.

She struggled to wrest free of the man's grip, twisting the same way she did to wrench the ball from an opponent. It wasn't working. He was too strong. The van's open hatch yawned like the mouth of a monster. *Don't pass out*, she told herself, then on a surge of adrenaline she forced her mouth open as widely as she could and bit down like a Doberman on the fingers crushed against her lips.

Instinctively the man released his grip and yelped. Stacy gulped air and twisted free of his grasp. She threw herself forward even as he lunged for her.

"*Help! Rape!*" Her bare feet pounded toward the street. *Thank God!* Mr. Atkins was taking Reckless for his after-dinner walk.

The border collie began barking and Mr. Atkins was staring at her. Then he was suddenly dragged forward as the leashed dog lunged for the Lachman's driveway.

The van's engine roared to life behind her and she dove out of the way, toppling into the jacaranda tree as the van squealed past her and careened into the street.

"Stacy! Who was that? Are you all right?" As Mr. Atkins and Reckless reached her, Stacy let out another scream.

"Mom!"

CHAPTER THIRTEEN

A muggy twilight settled over Capitol Hill. Dillon McGrath let himself out of the house on D Street and hurried to his Acura. He slid behind the wheel and fitted the key into the ignition, but didn't turn it. Instead, he pulled out his cell phone and a handkerchief, swiping at the perspiration beading along his upper lip.

"Dillon, do you have it?"

David sounded more anxious than Dillon had ever heard him. That was more than understandable, Dillon thought, considering he'd seen ben Moshe die right before his eyes.

"Sorry, David. I couldn't find it. It wasn't in your top bureau drawer, or in any of the drawers, as a matter of fact. I even searched the desk in your office. No luck."

"Look again. It has to be there." Alarm resonated in David's voice.

"I scoured the place, believe me. It wasn't. Eva wasn't there either—she left the front door unlocked for me." With a flick of his wrist, Dillon brought the car engine to life.

There was silence at the other end.

"David?"

"Someone got there first. Before you." David's voice shook with frustration. "Someone took my damn passport."

"No, no, I don't think so." Dillon gripped the steering wheel, tension winding through him. "The place didn't look like it had been ransacked. Everything was in order. Except the vacuum cleaner. Eva forgot to put it away."

"That's not like her."

"So what should I do?" A car whizzed past, scattering dry leaves in its wake. "Do you want me to call the police and report your passport missing?"

"No. Forget the police. I'll find another way."

"David—the agate." Dillon cleared his throat. "You still have it, don't you?"

"Yes. As well as an amber stone. Ben Moshe gave me Levi just before . . ." His voice trailed off.

In the dark car, Dillon closed his eyes. "I hope you realize the power you're packing."

"I haven't had much time to dwell on it."

"I wish there was more I could do, David. As it is, I've got to leave the country for a bit. If you need me in the next few days, leave a message with my office. I'll be checking in regularly. But . . ." He hesitated.

"Be careful, David. I'm not liking the feel of this."

David grimaced. "Tell me about it."

As David snapped the phone shut, he glanced at Yael. Her hair fell across her cheeks like a copper curtain as she bent over the rabbi's loose-leaf notebook.

"My passport's gone, Hutch hasn't called back, and I don't know where the hell my daughter is. So how is *your* day going?"

Sinking down on the bed, he pressed the heels of his hands into his eyes.

Yael looked up. "That's how."

She pointed to the muted television, where images of death and rubble wrought by the earthquake in Turkey flickered across the silent screen.

"We're not the only ones having a bad day," she said.

Dillon waited until he'd stopped at a traffic light before dialing another number.

For days he'd been ruminating about the gemstones. Now it was time to take action.

"You're sure Bishop Ellsworth is there?" he asked without preliminaries. "I'm on my way to Reagan International as we speak."

He listened for a moment as the light changed and an impatient horn sounded behind him. "Excellent. I should be landing in Glasgow early tomorrow evening. I'll come directly to you."

Chapter Fourteen

"I know Avi Raz can get you a counterfeit passport, but it could take him a few days." Yael fretted, pacing back and forth in front of the window.

David emerged from the bathroom, rubbing his face with a damp towel. "I've got a better idea. I know how to get a genuine passport by tomorrow morning."

"How?" She paused, staring at him.

"Sometimes it pays to be the son of a senator."

If Judd Wanamaker was even in the country.

He made the call.

His father's closest friend was now the American ambassador to Egypt. They'd been allies in the Senate and had worked tirelessly championing the national wetlands preservation bill they'd co-sponsored—to the chagrin of developers and logging interests. Their families had also formed a bond. The Shepherds and Wana-makers vacationed together one year at Niagara-on-the-Lake and an annual tradition was born. It had continued for almost two decades, right up until the time David's father dropped dead on the Senate floor of a heart attack.

"We're in luck," David told Yael. "He's right here — on business at the UN. He insisted on meeting us for dinner. There's a Japanese place only three blocks away with a private room where we can talk freely. We're meeting him in an hour."

"That gives me time to look through the rest of this." Yael carried the rabbi's satchel over to the bed and, one by one, began removing its remaining contents. She arrayed them across the flowered bedspread next to the notebook, shooting David a questioning look.

"Did you find anything of interest when you checked it out earlier?"

She's observant as well as attractive, David thought, suddenly surprised he'd even noticed.

"Actually I did. A few things I didn't understand. What about you? Anything important in the rabbi's notebook?"

She settled on the bed beside the satchel before she answered, tucking her legs beneath her. "Some details he's researched about the Gnoseos. How they're obsessed with secrecy, just like the ancient gnostics. It's why so little is known about their beliefs and practices. They pass their traditions down by word of mouth only and still use secret talismans and symbols to identify one another."

A frown furrowed along her forehead. "He was deeply worried. He wrote of his fear that the Gnoseos are close to achieving their goal. He also wrote something else."

David waited, watching her expression soften.

"The rabbi wrote of his faith in God. His belief that God would reveal the way to defeat the Gnoseos."

David had never experienced faith like that. He wondered what it would feel like to believe with such conviction. *His* soul had been stirred by critical thinking and careful analysis of political systems and how they function—not by sermons, prayer, or Bible stories. But now, here he was, trying to find logic in the inexplicable.

For a moment the only sound was the rain drumming against the windows. Then David plucked some sort of colorful card from the bedspread. "Did he make any reference to this?"

"A tarot card." Yael reached for it, her brows knitting.

"Is that what it is?" David looked surprised. "I thought consulting palm readers or Ouija boards—anything occult—was forbidden to Orthodox Jews. I had a college suitemate once who was Orthodox—he kept nagging one of our Jewish friends to quit reading her horoscope every day, insisting that the Torah forbade divination."

Yael raised her brows. "That's true, but your friend was misguided. Astrology has never been equated with divination. You should see the floors of ancient homes and synagogues that we've excavated in Israel—especially those from the first to the fourth century. I can't begin to count how many I've seen adorned with elaborate wheels of the zodiac."

"Seriously?"

"Oh, yes. Ancient Kabbalists believed that everything in the spiritual realm is reflected and transmitted to our physical realm on earth through the cycles of the stars and planets. They taught that the stars and planets are an integral part of God's great design. That everything in the heavens is mirrored on earth."

Yael studied the card in her hand. The face of it was a brightly colored drawing of a tower—a mighty spiraled fortress from which people were tumbling head first into a moat. Behind them, lightning crackled across an inky sky, setting the uppermost tier of the tower aflame. On the back side, there was a simple drawing of intertwining snakes and the number 471 in the lower left-hand corner.

The Tower

"I can't imagine why Rabbi ben Moshe would have this card." She sounded puzzled. "I'm no expert on the tarot, but I can tell you that it was derived directly from the Kabbalah's Tree of Life. I'll show you."

Nothing surprises me anymore, David thought as Yael picked up another card, the small laminated drawing he'd noticed earlier. She pointed to the interconnected molecules.

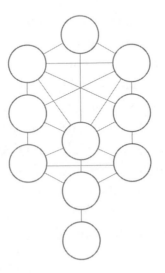

"This is the Tree of Life," she told him. "The central framework of Kabbalah."

"So that's what it is. I thought it was a drawing of molecules," David admitted.

She shook her head, trying to hide a small smile. "It's a symbolic tree, of course. Each of these ten circles—or *Sephirot*—represents an attribute of God, an attribute humans can emulate. Kabbalists meditate on them as stepping stones along their path to spiritual enlightenment. You know that I'm a scientist, too, David, not a mystic—but I'm in awe of the concepts, the mystery, and the beauty of what this tree represents."

David glanced at the card, impatience beginning to chafe at him. The circles still looked like molecules. And he didn't see how any of this was tied in with protecting Stacy.

"But what does it have to do with the tarot? Or the Gnoseos?" he asked tautly.

"I don't know of a connection to the Gnoseos, but the tarot deck was patterned after the Tree of Life. A nineteenth-century French occultist named Eliphas Levi was the first to explore the similarities. It's like this—" Yael bit her lip, choosing her words carefully.

"In a nutshell, the Sephirot represent all of creation—past, present, and future. Imagine each of these circles, David, as a 'vessel' filled with divine light or energy. The mystics say that God created the world from them—pouring such strong light into these 'vessels' that they shattered into shards. The shards scattered, sprinkling that divine light throughout the universe to form the world."

"The Big Bang?"

Yael narrowed her eyes. "Not exactly. May I go on?"

Her pained expression reminded him of his beleaguered third-grade teacher, Mrs. Karp. But Yael HarPaz was much prettier.

"Go on." David flexed his shoulders. The tension in his neck was starting to get to him.

"Okay, the scattered shards," Yael continued. "The mystics say that each of them was concealed by a shell which hid their light, and that our task as human beings is to crack open those shells, to bring God's light into the world again."

She pushed herself off the bed and began to pace once more.

"Don't expect to understand much of this, David. Kabbalah is extremely complex. Believe me, my knowledge is superficial at best. It takes years of in-depth study just to scratch its surface. Which is why, in the past, it was always kept secret."

"I guess the Kabbalists have something in common with the Gnoseos," David mused.

"Secrecy, yes. Also an intense yearning for a divine connection." She stopped pacing and turned toward him. "But the Kabbalists' views of the world and of humankind's purpose in it is radically different from the Gnoseos'. Kaballah teaches of the potential for creating light and goodness in the world. About our job as human beings to repair the world, not to destroy it."

"Finally. Something I remember from Hebrew school—*tikkun olam*. The obligation to repair the world, to make it better."

"Exactly." Yael leaned a hip against the desk. "Here's another difference. The Gnoseos start teaching their children at a very early age that the material world is evil. Kabbalah, on the other hand, has traditionally been taught only to married men over forty who'd spent years studying the Torah."

"That would have left Madonna out."

Her lips quirked. "And a lot of others who've appropriated it as a pop religion. You can't separate Kabbalah from Judaism, from the study of Torah. They've always been intertwined."

"Well, I'm not forty yet and I'm not married anymore, but I still want to know how this tree is connected to the tarot."

"Patience isn't your strong suit, is it?"

"Not when my daughter is in danger."

Yael shoved her fingers through her still-damp hair. "We're almost there." She thrust the card into his hands.

"The ten Sephirot—the circles—represent levels of spirituality. The twenty-two interconnecting lines running between them are the paths Jewish mystics follow to elevate their spiritual consciousness."

David rubbed his temples. A slight headache had begun to throb at the back of his skull. "Got it."

"Okay—ten sephirot, twenty-two paths—and twenty-two letters in the Hebrew alphabet. There also happen to be twenty-two cards in the major arcana of the tarot. The number ten is important in the tarot deck, too—What's wrong?"

David was kneading his temples. He looked like he was in pain. "Are you okay?" she pressed, moving toward the bathroom to fill a glass with water.

David had the strongest impulse to close his eyes. This headache was consuming him. He forced himself to check his watch.

It was nearly time to meet Judd. Why hadn't he heard from Hutch? He saw Yael holding out a glass, looking at him with concern.

"Headache," he muttered, then suddenly he stumbled from the bed. In two strides he reached his duffel and yanked out his journal. *Percy Gaspard.*

Seizing a pen from the desk, he flipped frantically to the back section of the journal and scrawled the name in the next blank space.

"Percy Gaspard." His voice was barely audible. Yael crossed to him and peered over his shoulder at the newest name in the journal as David scribbled the date after it.

"I'll call Avi, have him run it against those we've transcribed," she said quickly. "He'll cross-reference it to see if he's still alive."

Or dead. Or a current target . . . David thought.

"While I'm at it," Yael spoke with the phone to her ear, "I'm telling him to get going on your passport—in case your father's friend doesn't come through."

David staggered to the bathroom and splashed cold water on his face. "We have to leave," he muttered, returning to the room. He stuffed his journal inside the duffel, then scooped up the rabbi's belongings from the bed and threw those in, too.

"We're taking all this with us, just in case." Pulling a deep breath, he grabbed the door handle. "Ready to face the deluge?"

Yael shrugged into her green silk jacket, barely dried. "Too bad Noah's not waiting outside with his ark." She stepped briskly past him through the open door.

CHAPTER FIFTEEN

Judd Wanamaker looked like a country doctor. He was a sparse-haired, stout man with a neatly trimmed gray beard and a Santa Claus nose dominating his earnest face. David's father had always said that if Judd ever lost a bid for reelection, he'd have a great second career as a New York cabbie because he drove like a fiend with a death wish, had a million stories to tell, and never tired of sharing them.

"You have to order the *sanma shioyaki*," Judd insisted the moment introductions were completed and they were seated in the private tatami room one floor above Yotsuba's main dining area. Yael settled against the curved wooden back of her floor mat plump with rice straw, and crossed her legs beneath the low table. She picked up the menu decorated with an embossed four leaf clover.

"Salt grilled jack mackerel. And they serve it with freshly grated daikon. The best I ever ate. Ted Kennedy introduced me to it five years ago and it was so fantastic I came back the next night for more."

"Judd's always been as enthusiastic about food as he is about politics," David told Yael, as the waiter bent to set water glasses before them. "And about his wife."

He turned back to his father's friend. "How *is* Aunt Katharine? Still raising more money than anyone else for the National Symphony?"

"Setting records even as we speak. I think fundraising is even more political than politics, and Katharine is a natural. You really should consider the mackerel," he told Yael, setting aside his menu.

"I'm afraid that's a little too adventurous after the day we've had, Ambassador Wanamaker." Yael offered a wan smile. "I think I'll stick with the *kitsune udon.*"

Judd regarded her sympathetically. "And what kind of a day was that, Ms. HarPaz, besides a very wet one?"

"A very harrowing one."

She looked remarkably self-possessed, David thought, for a woman who'd arrived in the country only this morning, had seen a man murdered, been shot at, pursued, and was now dining with an American ambassador. He wondered what else she'd been through in her life that had given her such mettle.

"I think we should order first," David suggested with a glance at the hovering waiter.

For the first time, concern entered Judd's eyes and he gave a nod.

Suddenly the lights dimmed, then powered back on. David felt his nerves tighten.

They settled on an array of appetizers and main courses, and only after the waiter exited, sliding the shoji doors closed behind him, did David's tension begin to ease. The brown-out hadn't been a harbinger of a power failure.

"I wouldn't involve you in this if it wasn't necessary, Judd." David cleared his throat. "But I need to leave the country tomorrow and my passport has turned up missing."

"I see." Judd searched David's face. "Business or pleasure?"

"Business." The word came out more curtly than David had intended. Judd's eyes sharpened with concern.

"Sounds urgent."

"I wouldn't impose on you if it wasn't."

"It's not an imposition, David. I'm more than happy to help you. There'll be some paperwork involved, you'll need to meet me at the UN first thing in the morning, but it shouldn't be a problem getting you emergency clearance."

"How long will it take?" Yael interjected, unwrapping the linen napkin that covered her chopsticks.

"I'll make a phone call after dinner and you should have it in your hands by noon."

"Thank you, sir." Filled with gratitude, David addressed him in the formal manner he'd been taught as a child. That made Judd grin.

"I daresay your father would have done the same for one of my brood."

"How are Katie, Ashley, and Mark?" David asked as the waiter returned, setting down a wooden tray overflowing with an artistic array of sushi rolls and sashimi.

David took a bite of a California roll, but it could just as well have been Styrofoam. His appetite was nowhere to be found. Hoping Judd wouldn't notice, he moved the food around his plate with his chopsticks as they fell into an easy patter of conversation about family, careers, marriage. He saw Yael listening quietly as she picked at her bowl of wheat noodles and fried tofu, commenting occasionally, but for the most part observing.

Then Judd inquired about Stacy, triggering a sudden tense silence.

"I haven't spoken to her in a few days." David tried to conceal his anxiety. "She's a bit rattled since Meredith remarried."

Judd was no fool. He caught the flash of uneasiness clouding David's eyes for a brief millisecond before he regained control.

The furrows in Judd's brow deepened. "There's some trouble here, isn't there, David?" he asked quietly. "I can read you like my own children. Is Stacy ill?"

"No. She's fine," he began, then as his chest filled with pain, he shook his head. "She's in danger, Judd. And there's a lot of it to go around."

The ambassador set down his chopsticks and fixed David with the intent stare that had cowed many a witness in a congressional hearing. "What are you saying?"

"You don't want to know. I don't even understand it myself."

"Try me. If there's something I can do, anything, you know I will."

David and Yael exchanged glances. The tiny shrug of her shoulders freed him to follow his own instincts.

He looked directly into Judd's questioning face.

"Have you ever heard of a religious sect called the Gnoseos?"

Chapter Sixteen

Two hundred fifty miles outside of Santa Monica, and Stacy was still shivering. The dark night enfolded the open road, lit only by the distant flare of wildfires in the hills as the rented Jeep Grand Cherokee barreled east on I-40 beneath the shadow of the Black Mountains.

Hutch glanced in the rearview mirror. In the backseat, Meredith cradled her daughter in her arms. Stacy's sobs had subsided as they'd left city traffic behind and lost themselves in the hum of the highway. Now she was settled in against her mother, no longer jumping at every white minivan that sidled alongside them.

What kind of maniac went after this kid in her own backyard? Hutch wondered.

Or was David the one they were after—was someone trying to get to him through his stepdaughter?

It was like some kind of weird déjà vu. How many years ago had he guarded David—and now this girl, who meant as much to David as if she'd been his own blood, needed his protection too.

Meredith stirred in the backseat. "How much longer to Flagstaff?"

she whispered and he realized Stacy had fallen asleep against her shoulder.

"Three hours and counting. Need a bathroom break?"

She hesitated. "Not yet. Let's get across the state border first."

"Comin' up." Hutch glanced again in the rearview mirror but it was too dark to see Meredith's expression. When they'd zoomed away from the house in Santa Monica it had been one of pure terror. "Why don't you try to catch a few winks and I'll wake you when we hit the first decent rest stop in Arizona."

"No thanks. I doubt I'll ever sleep again," she muttered.

"You will, I promise. Where I'm taking you, no one's going to find you."

Hutch was a big man, tall, with the shoulders of a bull. He was a former Navy SEAL, trained to fight and protect. Quiet confidence oozed from him and she knew she ought to feel reassured. But she didn't. The night held menace, and her enemy had no face.

Chills prickled her arms and she tightened their grip around Stacy.

Blearily Meredith stared into the flickering headlights on the other side of the interstate, praying Hutch was right, that no one would find them. Today had started off so unremarkably and now everything was changed. She felt like a different woman. Like a fugitive, filled with terror. Not for herself, for the one person who meant more to her than anything in the world.

"I'm going to try reaching David again." Her hand slipped to her purse for her phone.

"Good luck." Hutch accelerated to pass an eighteen-wheeler. "For some reason it keeps dumping into voice mail."

"You'd think he'd be checking it." Her voice held a waspish note.

"Something tells me David's doing the best he can right now," Hutch said calmly. "He'll call."

When he does, Meredith thought, her lips clenched with barely contained tension as she flipped open her phone, *he'd better explain why someone is after my daughter.*

Chapter Seventeen

Judd Wanamaker gave a low whistle when David stopped talking. He stared from David's taut face to Yael's pinched one and gathered his thoughts before breaking the silence.

"This sounds like science fiction, David. Lamed Vovniks, secret cults, superceding God."

"Don't forget annihilating the world." Yael slanted an even glance his way.

Judd sighed. "If you weren't Bob Shepherd's son, I'd be hard-pressed not to laugh in your face and walk away. But under the circumstances . . ." His shrewd gray eyes pierced David's. "I don't know what to make of this."

"Judd, I know it sounds insane, but the danger is very real. The Gnoseos and their Dark Angels are very real. We were nearly killed today." David gripped the edge of the table.

"If you don't believe the Gnoseos are trying to end the world," Yael interjected, "why don't you step outside and look at the streets. This is no normal rainstorm. Have you ever seen the streets flood like this? All around the world, everything is amiss. Off center. It's not a coincidence."

"Maybe I should phone the President," Judd quipped. It was half-challenge, half-joke.

David pulled his journal from his duffel. "Maybe you should read him this."

He pushed the red leather notebook across the table. Judd reached into his breast pocket and pulled out a pair of reading glasses. Silently he opened the book and scanned the pages.

"It's a list of names."

"Special names, according to the rabbi," David said. "Remember when I fell off that roof with Crispin Mueller and Abby Lewis? When I died for a moment in the hospital that afternoon, I had a mystical experience. I saw the owners of these names; they spoke to me and told me to remember them. They're the people I told you about—the ones Yael insists the Gnoseos are trying to wipe out. Somehow I've been given their names, Judd. The rabbi told me these are the names of the Lamed Vovniks."

David reached over and reclaimed his journal, his hands closing hard around it. "These names match up with those Yael and her father deciphered in ancient papyri found in the Middle East."

Yael leaned forward. "The papyri have been authenticated. They're fragments of the legendary Book of Names first recorded by Adam."

Judd looked startled. "As in Adam and Eve?"

"Now you're beginning to understand," Yael said softly.

Judd frowned. "Do you realize what you're saying? . . ." He turned toward David, his gaze piercing. "What does this have to do with you leaving the country?"

"David needs to meet with the mystics in Safed," Yael answered before David could speak. "He might hold the key to unraveling the Gnoseos' plan. We believe David has special knowledge which no one else on earth possesses. Archaeologists are nowhere near assembling the complete text of Adam's Book."

She glanced over at David. "And if he stays here," she said slowly, "the Gnoseos will find him and kill him."

Find. Kill. Suddenly, David peered at his watch. Why hadn't he heard from Hutch yet? Or Meredith or Stacy?

He checked his cell phone. *He'd missed four calls.* "Excuse me a second," he muttered as he retrieved his messages.

"Oh, God." The words blurted hoarsely from his throat.

Yael and Judd both froze.

"Someone tried to grab Stacy. She got away—she's with Hutch—Meredith, too."

"David, no." Judd pushed back his chair and stood up, his brow creasing in consternation. "Is she all right? Did they go to the police?"

"Hutch says she's okay. The police came right away, before Hutch got there. He's taking them to the cabin." David pivoted toward Yael, his jaw clenched. "When will the team Avi sent get there?"

"Tomorrow. Give me their destination and I'll call the team for an estimated time of arrival."

She unfolded her legs and came smoothly to her feet, moving to a corner of the screened room.

"I'll be at the UN first thing in the morning for the passport," David said tightly. "Whether you buy any of this or not, Judd, I need it." His gaze locked with the other man's.

"You'll have it. I . . . I don't know what to make of this, David. I'm a man of faith. You know that. But . . ." Judd Wanamaker clasped his arm. "How can any of this be true? It seems to me—"

"*No!*" Yael's cry interrupted him. "That's impossible!"

Her fingers were clamped around the cell phone as she listened, and tears sprang into her eyes. When she clicked off, she moved woodenly toward them, her face white as the rice left on their plates.

"That was Avi. The team's plane went down. Both engines exploded over the Atlantic."

David's stomach plunged.

"El Al engines don't just explode," she said raggedly. "Not on their own and not both at once."

CHAPTER EIGHTEEN

With their heads lowered against the downpour, Yael and David struggled up Parkside toward the Riverside Tower. Not an unoccupied cab in sight and the puddles were now ankle deep. A savage wind slapped at them as they dodged across intersections, ignoring the traffic signals, desperate only to escape the fury around them.

Other pedestrians likewise ran, fighting to win the battle against the buffeting winds so intent on making a mockery of their umbrellas. The few vehicles on the street sprayed water as their tires churned the rising puddles.

David and Yael had gone less than a block when he spotted signs for a flower shop and a Duane Reade drugstore and then—from a basement entrance—in flickering purple neon: TAROT READINGS.

He snagged Yael's arm. "I have an idea," he yelled over the rain. "This way."

They dashed down the half-staircase and through the door painted with an unblinking crimson eye. A crystal wind chime pealed their arrival. The room in which they found themselves smelled oddly of vanilla and garlic. Several folding chairs surrounded a table centered in the room, a dusty chandelier gleaming dully above it. Pots of ferns, lucky bamboo, and sword-shaped sansevieria flanked the corner display case, where amulets twinkled beneath soft accent lights. A rickety bookcase on the opposite wall leaned to one side, crammed with a jumble of books.

Then a curtain of beaded gold threads shimmered and parted—an old woman appeared. She was tiny, in an ankle-length black skirt and embroidered purple tunic, and her graying hair hung down her back in a thick braid. David would have put her in her seventies, but her skin was smooth and dewey and her exceptionally small hands were unmarred by veins. The cataracts clouding her pale umber eyes betrayed her years though, as did her eyelids, thin and crinkled as crepe.

She moved toward the round table, which was draped with a long satin cloth. An unlit candle and matches huddled in its center. Without fanfare, she scooped up a deck of tarot cards.

"Welcome. I wasn't expecting visitors on such a rainy night. Which of you would like a reading?"

Me. If only I believed you could tell me if Stacy is all right, David thought grimly. Not knowing was torture, but he had to push that worry aside for now.

"We're here for information, actually." David pulled out a chair for Yael and then took the one beside her.

"The cards contain a great deal of information," the old woman said, offering the deck. "Who would like to shuffle?"

Instead of accepting them from her, David riffled through his duffel and yanked out the rabbi's tarot card.

"I'm more interested in what you can tell us about this."

With a look of annoyance, the woman set down her deck and settled into a chair across from them. She took the card from him with a shrug, studying the tower illustration for a moment before flipping the card over.

"It's a Tower card. What else do you want to know?"

———

"Got 'em. I know the area."

James Gillis snapped his fingers at Enrique, lying across one of the double beds in their Lower East Side motel room. At once, the Puerto Rican sprang off the bedspread, snatched the van keys from the bureau, and strode to the door. Gillis was still talking rapidly into his cell phone as the door thudded shut behind them.

"We're on it." Gillis raised his collar against the deluge. "Enroute as we speak."

He briefed his partner as they hustled for the van.

"We got damn lucky. Got ourselves a second chance. They just left Yotsuba. Over near Riverside Park."

Yael scooted her chair closer to the table. "We need to know what the images on this card mean."

The tarot reader pushed the card at her and met Yael's eyes.

"The Tower card is a message card from the higher arcana. It's the most ominous card in the entire deck."

"Ominous in what way?" David asked.

Her gaze shifted to his intent face. "It points to death, destruction, fear, and sacrifice. In other words, something's about to change."

She jabbed a ragged fingernail over the figures tumbling from the tower. "It's spelled out right here—a mighty fall leading to the revelation of an ultimate truth." She leaned back and out of nowhere a pure white cat leaped into her lap. David hadn't even noticed it in the room until now.

Her fingers stroked its fur as she spoke. "Kabuki, you've come to inspect the visitors."

David shifted in his seat. "Is there anything else?"

"How much time do you have?" she asked with a smirk. The cat sprang from her lap as she rose and shuffled to the bookcase. She scanned the shelves, then pulled out a fat volume and brought it back to the table.

Her fingers deftly found the page she sought. "Here." She began to read, squinting, holding the book close to her clouded eyes.

"The warrior planet Mars rules the Tower card, which makes it a card about war." Her lips pinched around the word.

She continued reading from the book in a singsong. "A war between structures built of lies. And"—she pointed to the lightning bolt shattering the turret on the card's tower—"a blinding flash of truth."

She set down the book and peered at them. "When someone gets this card in a reading, I warn them to expect a shocking revelation. Something powerful enough to bring down a king—or to shatter a system of long-held beliefs."

A *system of long-held beliefs.* The sashimi churned in David's stomach. *Would you call the civilized world a system of long-held beliefs?*

Don't start buying into this woo-woo stuff, he told himself. As the old woman started to speak again, a crash of thunder reverberated. Sudden blackness clamped over the tiny room, leaving them breathless during the moment it took the tarot reader to strike a match and light the fat candle in the center of the table.

"That's better," she murmured calmly, as a wisp of vanilla scent trailed upward from the candle flame.

David glanced around, anxious for the power to come back on. It didn't.

Beside him, Yael's face shone ghostly and tense in the flickering candlelight. But her voice was strong as she abruptly changed the direction of the conversation.

"Does the book say anything about a connection between the tarot and Jewish mysticism?"

"Of course. Kabbalah." The old woman nodded in the dimness. "Some sources say they're related, and some say they're not. There are numerous similarities, to be sure."

She pushed the book toward David. "The power's not coming back on so quickly. Your eyes will find it easier in the candlelight than mine."

"We already know about the numerical connection between the cards and the Hebrew alphabet," David told her as he flipped past illustrated pages to the index. "The twenty-two cards in the major arcana, the twenty-two letters in the alphabet."

He felt the cat slink around his leg, rubbing the length of its torso against him. "Kabbalah—here we go," he said. Turning to the middle of the book he began to read aloud.

"The tarot deck mirrors the Kabbalistic Tree of Life. Just as there are ten Sephirot, there are ten numbered cards in each suit of the tarot's minor arcana. There is another fascinating connection—the four mystical worlds in which the Tree of Life exists—earth, air, water, and fire—are reflected in the tarot's four suits—pentacles, swords, wands, and cups." David glanced up to see the candle flame flickering in the old woman's irises as she smiled.

"If you want even more connections, I'm sure you can find countless charts in the New York City Public Library," she said. "On the other hand," she added with a snort, "you'll also find a plethora of books claiming the tarot has nothing at all to do with Kabbalah. That the Knights Templar took it from the Saracens."

She tilted her head sideways. "Then again, there's a strong contingent which insists that the world's very first tarot deck was introduced in the mid-fifteenth century by the Gnostics."

A jolt of electricity shot up David's spine.

"Is that so?" He picked up the Tower card. "Can you see anything here that's particularly relevant to either Kabbalah or the Gnostics?"

She snorted again. "Of course. One could hardly miss it." The woman shot him a patronizing smile as she took the card and flipped it over, holding it closer to the candle's wavering light.

"This—the double *ouroboros*."

"That's Greek, isn't it?" Yael peered at the two serpents swallowing each other's tails, their bodies forming a figure eight.

"Of course. Greek for tail-eater. To the Gnostics, a single wingless snake swallowing its tail represents the sun or the world. But a double snake like this is called the Great World Serpent—the gnostic symbol of the eternal cycle of death and rebirth."

"Death and rebirth. Destruction and renewal," Yael said as David's stomach went queasy from the tempura and the cloying veil of vanilla. Yael leaned toward him, dropping her voice. "Exactly what the Gnoseos plan to accomplish on a worldwide scale. By killing the Lamed Vovniks," she whispered. "Are you finally starting to believe me?"

The rain seemed suddenly to intensify, sending hail clattering like bullets against the door.

Lost in thought for a moment, no one heard the two sets of foot-steps skulking down the back stairs of the shop.

David sat wondering why Rabbi ben Moshe had kept this tower card locked with the High Priest's gemstone and the other items in his safe.

The old woman was the first to break the silence. She returned the card to David, scrutinizing his face in the dimness.

"You have so many questions. Perhaps your answers wait in the cards." With a hopeful smile, she held the deck out toward Yael.

"Go ahead, dear. Shuffle them. I'll tell you what they have to say."

Yael shook her head, rising abruptly from her chair in the same instant that David caught movement behind the beaded curtain. Not the cat—a hulking figure with pale hair.

Intense danger crackled through him. "Go!" he yelled, shoving Yael toward the door. She flung it open only a split second before two figures charged into the room.

The blond man threw the old woman against a wall. A beefy His-panic raised his gun. It blazed fire as a bullet sang past David's ear, but he was already outside, bounding up the steps after Yael. They dashed into utter darkness, followed by the old woman's screams.

The city was black, completely black—drenched and deserted and filled with thunder.

Thank God for the darkness, David thought as he grabbed Yael's hand and they raced blindly up the street, hampered by the drag of the deep swirling puddles.

"This way." As splashing footsteps gained on them, Yael veered left suddenly, pulling him with her. They ducked down the stairway of a brownstone. Crouching in water nearly to their knees, they struggled to control their rasping breath. Fear gouged through David's stomach as they huddled in the opaque darkness like two rats in a gutter. He slipped a hand inside his pocket, reassuring himself that the gemstones were still secure.

Just above them, at street level, heavy footsteps pounded past, splaying water off unseen shoes into David and Yael's eyes.

They held their breath, cold with fear, waiting. Waiting . . .

A full minute passed before they exhaled and tentatively crept up from their hiding place. Quickly they forded the street, hugging close to the buildings on the other side, grateful for the cover of darkness as they wove their way back to the hotel.

"How did they find us?" Yael whispered, finally daring to speak once they slipped inside the Riverside Tower.

"Maybe there's more of them than we know about. They could be all over the city." Cautiously, David felt his way down the pitch black hallway until he found the indented surface of an exit door. "Good thing we're not on the top floor," he muttered as they trudged blindly, single file, up the stairs.

Descending footsteps. They froze, relaxing only when they heard a woman speaking in soft, bracing tones to a whimpering child.

Pressing themselves against the wall, they let the pair pass and then continued their climb in silence.

David's sodden duffel seemed a hundred pounds heavier as they crested the next landing. He felt like he was carrying the weight of the world.

And if everything he'd learned today was true, he was.

———

Dillon stared out into darkness so inky, he couldn't tell if he was looking at the sky or the ocean. Most of his fellow travelers were asleep in the airliner's dimly lit cabin, but he felt wide awake. And in need of a double Glenmorangie.

The last time he'd seen Bishop Ellsworth, they'd been at a conference in Rome set to coincide with Easter week. The bishop had sought him out, taking several minutes to praise Dillon's latest book. But Ellsworth had spent *more* time talking about the project *he'd* launched in his diocese—a Saturday morning bible breakfast for at-risk boys.

Dillon's eyes narrowed as he leaned back in his seat, picturing the ruby ring Ellsworth had worn that day, remembering how it glimmered in the sunlight on the piazza as he gestured enthusiastically.

At the time, Dillon had no idea of the history behind that gem. It would be years before he discovered its importance. And it wasn't until David brought a similar one to his attention that he realized what he had to do—starting with convincing David to go to Brooklyn.

Everything was coming together now.

He searched deep within himself for something he'd long ago subjugated—the anger that had consumed him as a scrappy kid in Boston, the cold rage he'd felt when his father belted him, when his mother fled the room. He needed to feel that rage again now. To use it.

He was prepared to use every means necessary to see this battle through.

Chapter Nineteen

Hutch set the pot on the burner and ignited the gas beneath it. He still preferred to perk his coffee the old-fashioned way, and always threw in a few extra measures of grounds no matter how many cups he was brewing.

As the TV blared bad news from the shelf in the corner, he cracked eggs into a skillet and tossed in some chopped bacon. But his mind wasn't on the food. It was on the two guests sharing the spare bedroom at the back of the cabin.

He'd carried Stacy in during the dead of night and told Meredith to call him immediately, no matter the time, if they needed him. He'd heard the girl call out in her sleep several times throughout the night, but Meredith's voice had always followed, calming her. It was nearly noon, and he hadn't heard a sound from the guest bedroom in the past two hours.

He'd thought David would have been in touch at first light, but he hadn't called. Hutch had been hitting redial the entire morning without reaching his friend, and now CNN was telling him why.

". . . the five boroughs and parts of New Jersey remain without electric power today, following the unprecedented thunderstorm that dumped more than eleven inches of rain along the East Coast last night. Lightning strikes hit the central power station, causing havoc similar to the August 2003, power grid failure. Yesterday's storm also knocked out cellular communication, and officials tell us that even once the power is back on, it may take weeks to pump the flood water from the subway system. . . ."

The voice droned on as Hutch dumped his eggs onto a plate. Until David bailed out of New York, there was nothing to do but sit tight, protect Stacy and Meredith, and keep Meredith from freaking the kid out even more than she already had.

"I smell smoke."

Hutch wheeled at the sound of the girl's voice. She stood in the kitchen doorway, her shoulder-length hair tousled and her eyes still red from crying. She wore the same gray sweatpants and t-shirt she'd worn in the car.

"The wildfires are far away, honey. It's just the smoke that travels. What can I get you for breakfast? Eggs? Or are you a cereal lover?"

"I want to talk to David," Stacy said tremulously.

So do I, thought Hutch.

"When he called yesterday asking me to go get you, he was in Brooklyn. A real bad storm hit the whole of New York yesterday."

Hutch nodded toward the television, where images of New Yorkers trying to negotiate flooded city streets played across the screen. "It's blown out all their power, Stace, and even the cell towers there aren't working. We'll have to sit tight and wait a while for David to get in touch with us."

"I don't understand what's going on." Her voice was small, and Hutch saw that the fear had crept back into her eyes. "There's wildfires here, and floods in New York. So weird."

Stacy went to the window and stared at the smoke rising from the distant orange glow along the horizon. She turned back to Hutch with tears brimming in her eyes.

"Hutch—I can't stop thinking about all the animals caught in the fire. Can any of them escape?"

Hutch cleared his throat. "Sometimes they can."

"What about the other times?" She fell silent for a moment. "I don't know why God lets that happen."

Looking into those hazel eyes was like looking into clear pools of pain. Raw hurt etched the girl's innocent young face. He wished he had an answer for her.

"I don't know as much about God as maybe I should," he said at last. "But I sure know a lot about cooking eggs. Scrambled, poached, or sunny side up, young lady?"

Stacy swallowed hard and pressed the back of her hands against her damp eyes. "Scrambled, I guess." She turned back to the window, her gaze fixed on the glow in the distance.

"How long do you think it'll take them to put out the fires?"

Chapter Twenty

It had taken David every bit of two hours to walk through the crowded streets to Judd Wanamaker's office. All of New York seemed to be on its sidewalks, huddled around radios, hunting for food or for a working ATM—not to mention looking for some hint of when power and normalcy would be restored.

David hurried along in their midst, keeping a wary eye on those around him, his senses on full alert until he reached the safety of the UN—only to find the building dark and in lockdown.

He stood outside cursing at his useless cell phone. And it didn't help that the hotel's phone system was down. No matter how many times he'd tried to reach Judd or Hutch, it had been impossible.

Frustrated and angry, David could only hope Stacy was safe with Hutch. With a knot tightening around his heart, he wondered if he'd ever see her again.

There was nothing to do but head back to the hotel. He hadn't gone more than a few blocks though, when the lure of pastries arrayed in a bakery storefront drew him inside. The shop was packed, lit only by daylight.

"They're all yesterday's," the clerk announced when he reached the counter. "Everything's on sale, three for the price of one. When they're gone, so am I. Can't bake a thing until we get some juice back."

David bought a half dozen muffins, several slices of biscotti, and a two-liter bottle of warming Coke, then ducked back out into the sodden streets. Though the water had receded overnight, road traffic was still eerily sparse. He glanced warily around as he continued to the hotel, still wondering how their attackers had found them last night.

There had to be a thousand tarot readers in New York—how had the Dark Angels known they were there? It had been a spur of the moment decision.

Unless we were followed from the restaurant. From inside Yotsuba. If the Dark Angels had spotted them dining with Judd, Wanamaker could be in danger too.

And there was no way to warn him—any more than there was a way to warn the remaining Lamed Vovniks of their own danger. He couldn't even be sure that he knew all of their names—or if some were still locked in his head.

For the first time he felt a real pull to get to Safed. His only weapons against the Gnoseos were the names in his head, in his journal. He didn't have Yael's knowledge or contacts, or Rabbi ben Moshe's wisdom, he had only the reverberations of an experience that defied rational explanation. If the city of Safed was as sacred and mystical as Yael claimed, it might shake loose the voices of those souls who had begged him to remember them.

His strides lengthened. He was glad for the chance to walk, to loosen his muscles, to clear his head. It seemed like ages, not just five days, since he'd beaten Tom at squash. He couldn't believe how his life had turned inside-out since then.

Now he was a fugitive, holed up in a steamy hotel room, incommunicado, and going insane. The hotel room seemed to be shrinking by the moment, yet Yael hadn't complained once. She'd been more than willing to stay put this morning while he ventured out for his passport. Meredith would have been climbing the walls while kvetching that they were closing in on her.

Hutch must have his hands full, he thought, scanning the stairwell before he began the climb. *If he has them.*

He has to have them.

The sound of voices from the other side of the hotel room door stopped David cold. He leaned closer, heard a male voice, and thrust the card key into the lock. He shoved open the door and found himself staring down the barrel of a gun.

CHAPTER TWENTY-ONE

VILLA CASA DELLA FALCONARA, SICILY

The prime minister's butler stepped onto the terrace where Di-Stefano and his wife tarried in their silk lounging robes over their usual breakfast of small cookies and espresso.

"*Scusi, Signore e Signora.*" He turned to the prime minister with a slight bow, his tone apologetic. "A young man from the village has begged to see you. He is most insistent. He claims his mother worked in the kitchens here when you were in the army and I do remember the woman. It is his belief that you are the only one who can help him."

DiStefano snapped his newspaper closed and set it beside his plate as his wife sipped her espresso. "You may show him in, Carlo," he said with a shrug.

Mario Bonfiglio burst onto the terrace, urgency etched in his swarthy face. The muscles of his laborer's body were bunched cords of tension, reminding DiStefano of a mountain cat primed to pounce.

"*Mi dispiace*—I am sorry, *Eccellenza*, I would not come to you if I were not so desperate. The police, they do nothing, know nothing. My fiancée's family and I live in daily torture." He swallowed thickly and continued, sweating beneath the keen gaze of the prime minister and the cool inspection of his wife.

"Your fiancée?" The prime minister prompted.

"*Si*, my Irina, my love, my heart. We were to marry last week. But she disappeared. Her father sent her on an errand to the post office and she never returned. We have searched, signore—the farms, the fields, everywhere. The police shrug and do nothing. They laugh and tell me she probably eloped with someone else. I know this is not true, my Irina and I were sworn to each other. We could not wait to get married and start a family."

"What is it you think I can do that the police can't?" The prime minister regarded him quizzically.

"You could order the police to investigate her disappearance, Eccellenza—and to notify the surrounding towns. It's been three weeks since she vanished and we've lost precious time. Please, if you order them, they will help us look for her." He stretched out his hands, beseeching the prime minister's wife as she set down her cup.

"Signora, you know what love is like. It is glorious and painful all at the same time. I need my love back. Something terrible has happened to her. She would never leave me."

Mario searched the woman's face for sympathy, compassion. He saw only the coolness of her steely blue eyes and upswept golden hair. She set down her napkin and rose with a smile as thin as a razor blade.

"Ah, but sometimes love is fickle, young man. And sometimes love flees. Perhaps your Irina does not wish to be found."

Anger flashed in Mario's face. His eyes burned like two obsidian coals, but he restrained himself from speaking with disrespect.

As Flora Dondi swept past him and into the house, he turned the power of his gaze to her husband. "Never," he said in a low tone. "Never would my Irina leave me willingly."

"I am sorry for you." The prime minister leaned forward and Mario was relieved beyond words to see the concern on his dignified face. "If you will write down your name and your fiancée's and her father's and the date she disappeared, I will demand the police investigate fully—and leave no vineyard or village unsearched." DiStefano held out a pen and called for the butler to bring paper.

"You did well to come here, my son," he said, after Mario scribbled the information and gratefully pushed the paper across the tablecloth.

DiStefano stood to offer his hand. Mario pumped his benefactor's beefy palm with joy. Hope surged through him and he silently thanked the Madonna for giving him the courage to come here.

"Bless you, Signore. Bless you." He nearly toppled a chair as he spun from the terrace and toward the butler who ushered him out.

DiStefano plucked up the paper and glanced at the thickly written words. A moment later he pulled a silver monogrammed cigarette lighter from the pocket of his robe. He glanced for a moment at the double ouroboros engraved upon it before he ignited the flame and incinerated Mario Bonfiglio's hopes.

CHAPTER TWENTY-TWO

David's hand clamped the barrel of the gun as he tried to twist it aside. But the gunman had an iron grip, belying his short stature. Before he could pull the trigger, David thrust a shoulder into the man's broad chest, knocking him off-balance. They went down together, grappling for control of the gun as the bakery bag went flying and David's duffel slammed into his back.

"*Lo Avi!*" Yael shouted in Hebrew. "No, don't shoot, it's David!"

David's fist paused in midair as her words registered. *Avi.* The adrenaline that had been charging through him at the sight of the gun ebbed, but his heart was still racing.

Shit. He relaxed his hold on the weapon and heaved himself to his feet. His opponent staggered up, also scowling.

"What the hell kind of greeting is that?" David demanded, glaring at the short, wiry-haired Israeli before him.

"In my line of work, it's the way we stay alive," the man rejoined in calm, accented English.

Yael bolted the door and picked up the bakery bag. "If you're done trying to kill each other, can we catch David up on what you've told me?"

Avi extended a hand. "You handle yourself well." The Israeli had reddish hair, sideburns, and the darkest eyes David had ever seen. There was a toughness in his stance and Ashkenazic features, an air of confidence and strength.

"Self-preservation makes a quick teacher," David rejoined.

"Did you get your passport?" Yael asked him.

He shook his head. "I never got to see Wanamaker. The UN's in lockdown. Power's still out everywhere."

"So I've noticed." She dabbed at the perspiration filming her face. The room had to be at least eighty degrees.

"But there is some good news, David. Avi has a passport for you. I don't know how he manages," she added with a small smile at the other man, "but he always does."

David caught the admiration in her tone and it annoyed him for some reason he didn't understand. He had to admit though, the passport the Israeli handed him was perfect. Totally indistinguishable from the one he'd left in his bedroom, the one that had disappeared.

"Sign it."

Imperious, isn't he?, David thought as Avi handed him a pen from the desk.

"Now all we need is for JFK to reopen," Yael said.

"And for the damned cell phones to start working again." David tucked the signed passport into his duffel. "Did your second team reach my daughter yet?" he asked Avi.

The Israeli took a seat in the room's only chair, next to the table where he'd set down his gun. "Not yet. They should reach Flagstaff sometime early tomorrow. My last communiqué said that Newark was closed—it seems the power failed in New Jersey first—so they had to take the longer route, from Tel Aviv to London and then to Phoenix, at least a twenty-one-hour trip."

David's heart contracted with frustration. "And then they still have to make the drive to Flagstaff?"

"Yael told us your man out there is pretty competent."

"Very." But David was wondering if Hutch could fend off a descending flock of Dark Angels. *They don't know where Stacy is,* he reminded himself. But then, he'd thought they didn't know where he and Yael were either. He took a turn around the stifling room, feeling as if his veins were going to explode.

"David." Yael seemed to have been reading his thoughts. She touched his arm. "Your job right now is to complete your book of names—and ours. We don't have all the names. There are numerous fragments of Adam's Book still missing, buried in the caves and the desert. But if those same names are locked in your brain, we can get them out."

"It's the only way to defeat the Gnoseos," Avi added, his dark eyes boring into David like a laser. "We have to keep as many Lamed Vovniks alive as possible. And only you can tell us who they are."

David stared at the floor. All he wanted to do was get out of New York and get to Stacy. But he couldn't chance leading danger right to her. He felt sweat dripping down his ribs and it wasn't from the sweltering room.

Yael continued softly, as if sensing his dilemma.

"Once you're in Safed, the mystics can help you remember everything you were told. You need to try to focus. That's your best way to help Stacy. The world hasn't come to an end yet, David, so you have to keep believing that your daughter is still alive."

There was a short silence. Avi broke it, picking up the bakery bag, rustling the paper as he pulled out a chunk of crumbled blueberry muffin. Popping it into his mouth, he passed the bag to Yael.

"What about Percy Gaspard?" David challenged, staring down at Avi. "What did you find about him?"

"Very little so far. Only one has turned up—a male born in Montreal in 1939. That's all the information our sources gathered before the power fizzled. By now they might know more. I'm leaving here and driving to Pennsylvania, or as far as I need to go to reach civilization, otherwise known as a city with a working cell tower. We should have a lot more to go on once I've reestablished contact with my colleagues."

"Then you should get going," Yael suggested.

Avi nodded, rising from the chair. "One more thing," he said, walking toward David. "The gemstones. I'll be taking them now."

"Why?" David demanded.

"They'll be safer with me, even if you two get to Israel first. They are vital to the Jewish people, and they've been stolen from us for too long." He glanced at Yael. "Did you tell him that we suspect the Gnoseos' elite Circle has already captured several of the gemstones?"

His gaze flashed back to David. "They'll stop at nothing to get their hands on them. They've coveted the gemstones almost as much as the thirty-six names because of the stones' innate power to tip the balance."

David flashed back on Crispin all those years ago—holding the agate aloft, promising David and Abby they wouldn't fall. How had Crispin known the stone was magical? And how in the world had he gotten his hands on it?

"Explain that last part to me," David spoke tersely. "About tipping the balance."

Avi pulled his damp khaki shirt away from his chest. "The sages taught of the stones' mystical properties. Each gem in the high priest's breastplate bears the name of one of the twelve tribes, and its color is the same as the banner which flew outside that tribe's camp. The high priest wore the breastplate whenever he entered the Holy of Holies. Do you know why?" Avi answered his own question before David could venture a guess.

"Because it represented the Jewish people, reminding God of the twelve tribes, invoking His mercy. And there's more," Avi said.

"Do you know how a Ouija board works?" Yael interjected. As David nodded, she went on. "The high priest's breastplate was like ancient Israel's Ouija board, a way of communicating with God. When the Jewish people found favor with God, the stones would shine brightly. When Israel was at war, and the stones glowed, it was an auspicious sign of victory."

"Here's an example for you." Avi holstered his gun as he spoke. "Yael mentioned the Ouija board. Here's how it worked in Biblical times. People would bring the high priest questions to ask God. After Aaron voiced them, he would stare into the stones on his breastplate and meditate on God's various names. While he did so, the letters on the stones would glow radiantly, spelling out God's answer."

David went still. He remembered the moment when he'd found the stone after the snow thawed. It had glowed so brightly it hurt his eyes. He'd thought it was a reflection from the sun. Now, as Avi's words sank in, he withdrew both stones from his pocket and studied them.

An agate and an amber. Napthali and Levi. They looked so ordinary. They weren't glowing now, and yet, what if . . .

"I'll take them back myself," he said, closing his hand around them and meeting Avi's eyes.

"No, you won't—" the Israeli began, but David cut him off.

"If we're talking mystical happenings, I think I have a bit more experience than you do. I found this stone, and based on everything I've been hearing, there's probably a damned good reason for that. Not to mention that Rabbi ben Moshe entrusted both of these to me just moments before he was murdered."

"I think he's right, Avi." Yael stepped between the two men. "He found Napthali shortly after the fall that led to his vision. It lay *waiting* for him. I don't believe that's a coincidence. It's been in his possesion all these years. He was meant to hold on to it," she insisted. "Perhaps for some reason we don't yet know."

Avi stared from one to the other, his mouth clenched in a frown. At last he shrugged. "I suppose you could be right. Fine, then."

He extended his hand to David. "As soon as the power returns, I will let you know about your stepdaughter—and about Percy Gaspard. Pray that the airport reopens within twenty-four hours. Time is not on our side."

CHAPTER TWENTY-THREE

Alberto Ortega was displeased. And that had Raoul LaDouceur pissed off.

It wasn't often Raoul lost his cool, but he was sweating and furious as he peeled away from the Sofitel in the yellow Firebird convertible he'd rented earlier from Avis. His first impulse had been to simply ditch the white van, but he'd thought better of that after realizing it would disappear more neatly back at LAX in the National lot. And now he had a new set of wheels under a different name. The cops would never connect him to Stacy Lachman.

But Ortega's rage still boomed in Raoul's head. *He's not pleased! Does he think I am?* Raoul fought his need to floor the Firebird. Instead, he spun the radio volume full blast to clear his head.

Tonight should have been a cakewalk. That kid ought to be in Death Valley by now, crying to the coyotes. *Hell. Another day . . . two, at most,* he told himself . . . *and Ortega's stinking breath will be off my neck. The state of Arizona isn't big enough for the kid to get away a second time.*

More and more, old Ortega was reminding him of his grandfather. Demanding, ungrateful. In Ortega's younger days, back when he'd been secretary-general of the UN, he had been quick to praise, quick to promote Raoul up the ranks of the Dark Angels. Now that the end was near, he was becoming as cantankerous as a sour old woman.

After all of the enemies I've dispatched for him, all it takes is one little hiccough to set him off with threats and warnings. As if I, the most accomplished and successful of any Dark Angel, could be denied passage into the Ark! Now, when the Ascent is imminent.

They were only waiting for the Serpent to complete his work, to zero in on the final two names.

So why is Ortega badgering me? How can I kill them before the Serpent tells me who they are?

This one—the girl—wouldn't pose a problem. What happened tonight was a fluke. He glared at the bloodied bandage angled across the back of his hand. She had sharp teeth for such a soft little mouse. But all she did was buy herself a few more hours.

And she would pay for them.

His phone beeped, signaling an incoming text message.

Ortega again, from that palace of his in Buenos Aires. Well, he wouldn't be enjoying it for much longer, the sly bastard. Raoul knew Ortega had only hastened back to Argentina for one reason— to gather his wife and children and bring them to the Ark.

He scanned the text message.

Change of scenery. I desire to inspect the specimen personally. Bring it to safe harbor, unscratched.

Raoul stiffened at the change in plans. Now they wanted the girl alive? What value could she possibly have, unless she was dead?

Unless they're going to award the kill to someone else.

His mouth curled into a scowl as he sped toward the Arizona border. He'd just see about that.

Chapter Twenty-four

Rabbi Tzvi Goldstein's widow was a delicate, fawnlike woman who'd collapsed into herself in grief. She looked barely past her twenties, yet had borne her husband seven children in as many years. The youngest, a girl of only five months, could not yet know the significance of the deliberate tear across the top left corner of her yellow cotton jumper. Nor could she know that she would never again see the face of her father looking down upon her as he blessed his children at the start of each *Shabbos*.

Sarah Leah Goldstein and her children sat in near darkness in their modest apartment. They were perched all in a row like little birds, on a sofa from which the cushions had been removed. On the console table behind them, a large memorial candle burned within a red glass. Due to the storm, it was the only light in the room. Alongside it was a stack of prayer books the men used during their twice-daily services at the home.

It would be so for seven days, while Tzvi Goldstein's next of kin abided the laws of mourning.

Upon news of her husband's murder, Sarah Leah had taken a scissors and snipped the collar of her blouse and then made a similar cut on the garments of each of her children. For these seven days, called *shivah*, all the mirrors in the house would be covered, the family would sit on low stools or cushionless couches, and Tzvi's father and brothers would refrain from shaving.

Other family members and friends came in a constant stream, sustaining the family with food, prayer, and the comfort of their presence. David and Yael felt like intruders in this sea of close-knit support, yet they both knew that this incursion was necessary.

When Sarah Leah's niece took the baby from her and urged her to go to the dining table for a glass of juice, Yael touched her arm.

"Mrs. Goldstein, Professor Shepherd and I were with Rabbi ben Moshe when the attack occurred," she said softly. "We don't wish to burden you further, but if you could give us a few minutes of your time, perhaps it will help discover who was responsible for your loss."

The widow peered at them with pain-filled eyes. "Come with me."

She led them to a small study brimming with books. Waning daylight slanted through the blinds, revealing a modest, comfortable room smelling of pipe tobacco and furniture polish.

"My husband, may he rest in peace, spent many hours here studying and working."

Helplessly she glanced around the room as if seeking something that was no longer there. "How can I help you?"

David drew the tarot card from his duffel. "This was among the items Rabbi ben Moshe gave me for safekeeping. Do you have any idea why he had it or where it came from?"

She recoiled as he held it out for her inspection. Her eyes darted to his face. "Death follows that card."

She swayed and Yael grasped her arm to steady her.

"What do you mean by that?" Yael asked, shooting David a startled look.

"My husband told me about that card. Rabbi Lazar of Krakow sent it to Rabbi ben Moshe, of blessed memory, only two weeks ago. He hoped Rabbi ben Moshe might know who might have ordered two thousand identical copies of this card." Her mouth trembled as she struggled to continue. "And who might have then killed a man for the printing plates."

"Killed *what* man?" David asked, stunned.

"The printer—the printer in Krakow." Sarah Leah moistened her lips. "His young son was in the back room changing ink on the press when it happened. His father was teaching him his trade. Tzvi said the boy heard arguing between his father and a man who spoke Polish with a thick foreign accent. He remembered the voice because the man had come in only two days before, offering to pay double if the printer could finish the job within forty-eight hours. The man wanted him to print two thousand of these cards."

David sucked in his breath. "So there are 1,999 more. . . ."

"Do you know what they argued about?" Yael asked.

"The customer demanded the printing plates. The printer refused, saying he'd never heard of such a thing. The man was angry, he kept insisting, and then the printer made an excuse to go into the back room. He sent his son home, wanting to shield the boy from a nasty exchange. The boy was barely out the back door when he heard a gunshot—he turned back, only to see flames shooting from the windows."

Sarah Leah shook her head sadly. "The poor boy tried to get back to his father, but the fire was too hot. All that paper, ink, and chemicals—it was ferocious."

Her skin looked gray. "Rabbi Lazar said the printer was a good man—like my husband. . . ." Her voice trailed off.

David felt a wave of sorrow. He could identify with that little boy's sense of helplessness. "Do you know how Rabbi Lazar got this card?" he asked gently.

"The printer's boy had a fascination with snakes. When he helped his father trim the printed cards, he was mesmerized by the intertwined snakes on the back. The printer, like most, always kept samples of each job for his records. When Rabbi Lazar paid a shivah visit to the printer's family, the boy came forward. He was shaking as he told Rabbi Lazar that he'd snuck the card from his father's files." Her mouth twisted. "The poor child felt responsible for his father's death, thinking he was being punished for having stolen the card."

"What a heavy burden for a child," Yael murmured. "And one he shouldn't have to bear." Her voice grew harder. "Had that customer known the boy was in the back room, he would have killed him, too, in order to keep the cards secret."

Secret. David was fitting the pieces together. "That's why he killed for the plates—so the cards could never be traced or reproduced."

"Will this help you find my husband's killer?" Tears glimmered in the widow's eyes. She blinked rapidly in an attempt to stem them. "Do you think this same customer followed the card from Poland and killed Rabbi ben Moshe and my husband to get it back?"

"Something like that." David's fingers tightened on the card. "It's all related, but it's a lot bigger than just one man."

There was a silence as Sarah Leah pressed her hands to her throat. Suddenly a baby's cries pierced the stillness in the study.

"I think Bayla's hungry," the niece said, appearing in the doorway with the howling infant.

"I must go." Sarah Leah gathered up her infant daughter and began rocking her.

"Thank you for your help, Mrs. Goldstein," David said as the woman gave them a sad smile and followed her niece from the room.

He and Yael threaded their way back through the crowded living room. Just as Yael placed a hand on the doorknob, a low thrum of electricity droned through the apartment and, an instant later, the living room lamps blazed to life.

"Let there be light," David muttered, feeling as if the awful limbo he'd been living in had just been lifted.

The moment they stepped outside, he and Yael both tried their cell phones, but found neither working yet.

"We'll use the hotel phone to make our flight reservations." Yael was already striding to the intersection in search of a cab.

"If the lines aren't still jammed." David matched his strides to hers and started to slip the card back into his duffel, then jerked it out again, noticing something.

Why hadn't he seen it before? There, behind one of the bodies falling from the tower, was a drawbridge. It was cracked in two, collapsing into the moat. The falling body had almost obscured it, so that it looked more like a rampart, but it was a bridge.

Suddenly he realized he'd seen a drawbridge just like that before. Stood upon it in London earlier this year, looking out over the Thames at the spectacular views of the city by night. The same evening he'd dined with Tony Blair, a small party had insisted on bringing him to one of the private rooms inside the Tower Bridge which spanned the Thames. The view had been astonishing. And the fact that the public could rent out the banquet facilities for special occasions and business conferences had been even more surprising.

Staring at the tarot card, David studied the artistic rendering of the bridge's architecture. The similarity to the Tower Bridge was striking, the same Victorian style, the combination of bascule and suspension, the masonry . . .

It wasn't a precise rendering, but still . . .

London Bridge is falling down.

The childhood refrain sang in his head. Even though he knew it referred to a different bridge, not the one near the Tower of London, the words kept spinning across his brain.

London Bridge. Falling down. The figure falling in the card . . .

The Tower card. The Tower Bridge?

David felt chilled. Was the card a warning? Were the Gnoseos planning to launch some kind of attack on London? Or *from* it?

And why would someone want two thousand copies of the same card . . . warning or no?

"Here's a taxi—come on!" Yael called, as a cab screeched to the curb before her.

David loped toward it as she ducked inside, his brain whirling in too many directions, all of them crisscrossing to form a roadmap he couldn't yet follow.

CHAPTER TWENTY-FIVE

The familiar ring of his cell phone bleated as the cabbie blared his horn at a bus swinging into his lane. *Finally!*

"Hey, pal," Hutch's voice boomed in his ear. "I've got someone here who's been waiting to talk to you."

"Not as long as I've been waiting to talk to her." David's heart leapt and stayed airborne as he listened to Stacy's small clear voice.

"David, Mom said you tried to warn us that a man was going to hurt me. How did you know?"

He closed his eyes, at a loss for words. How could he explain it to her, when he couldn't explain it to himself?

"David? Are you there?"

"I'm here, Munchkin. I can't tell you the whole story right now, but you need to do everything Hutch tells you. Stay inside, stay right by him. No wandering off."

"That man could come back?"

"Him, or someone like him." David grimaced as he heard Stacy start to cry.

"I'm scared. Why can't you come here with us?"

Her plea tore him in two.

"I wish I could, sweetheart. I'd give anything to be with you right now. But there's some place else I need to go, some place far away. It's very important—and it has to do with protecting you."

"How f-far? . . ." she began, her voice quivering. And then he heard Meredith demand the phone.

"David, what the hell is going on? What did you get yourself mixed up in? Do you know someone nearly choked her to death in our own backyard and tried to throw her in the trunk of a car?"

David opened his mouth to answer, but Meredith steamrolled on.

"Do you know we are in fucking Arizona, holed up in the middle of nowhere with wildfires burning all around us? I can't reach Len and we're supposed to be going on our damned family honeymoon! What the *hell* have you gotten us into—"

"Meredith, let me talk to Hutch." David gritted his teeth.

"Not until you tell me what you've done. You put *my* daughter in danger, and I have a right to know."

"Meredith, it's the end of the world, ok? I'm trying to stop it. Now let me talk to Hutch."

There was a sharp intake of breath. He could just picture the fury—the disbelief—on her face. "It's the end of the world. He wants *you.*" Her voice dripped sarcasm.

"What's the deal, pal? Your backup team hasn't shown yet."

Hutch again. A voice of reason.

"That's because they're dead. Someone blew them up over the Atlantic, but another team should be there any time now. Think you can hold the fort?"

"Can a bear crap in the woods?"

"Listen. I'm leaving the country as soon as I can book a flight out. Just for a few days. Your backup team is Israeli. Make sure they say a few prayers in Hebrew before you let them in the door."

"Like *"Hava Nagila,"* shalom and oy?"

"Smart ass. Those aren't prayers." David closed his eyes as the cab made a hard right turn, narrowly missing a bicycle messenger. "I'm trusting you with everything, Hutch. You know that, right?"

"Like I know my own blood type."

David shoved his cell back in his pocket.

"She was crying," he said.

Yael's hand touched his, resting lightly on his fingers. "David, I'm sorry. It's awful."

Her touch was gentle as a feather, yet warmth flowed from her fingertips. It seemed to melt a little of the cold dread inside him.

"With any luck, we'll get onto a flight leaving JFK tonight," she said.

Luck. Was that all it came down to? Luck? Wishbones? Four leaf clovers?

God only knows, he thought darkly as the Riverside Tower came into view.

GEORGETOWN UNIVERSITY

Tom McIntyre jumped from his chair, nearly toppling his coffee mug across the quizzes he'd been grading as two uniformed police officers charged into the office.

"Are you David Shepherd?" The younger officer advanced toward his desk and waved a search warrant in his face.

What a cocky SOB. Tom's hackles rose instantly. *With those pink cheeks, the regulation crew cut, and the show-off physique of a lifeguard. And the eyes,* Tom noted. *Pure cop.*

"No. Tom McIntyre," he said, ignoring the search warrant. "What's this all about?"

"Do you know where David Shepherd is?"

"Why do you want to know?" Tom met the cop eye to eye. He couldn't imagine any scenario in which the police would come looking for his office mate, especially with a search warrant. David's best friend was a priest, for God's sake, and his father had been a U.S. senator. How much more of a straight arrow could he be?

"When did you last see him?"

Tom hesitated a second, trying to gather his thoughts.

"Uh, several days, I guess. Monday or Tuesday of last week . . . I can't really remember."

"This is his office, isn't it?"

"Yes. And mine. Look, why don't you tell me what this is all about?"

"Murder." The second cop finally opened his mouth.

Tom hoped his shock didn't register on his face.

"David Shepherd's housekeeper was found murdered in his home, Professor McIntyre," the second officer continued, his voice as gritty as his appearance, with his square jaw and aggressive stance. "We need to ascertain that Professor Shepherd is all right."

Officer Cocky took over. "We can't get an answer on his cell phone. Would you know if this is the correct number?" He pushed a slip of paper under Tom's nose.

It was David's number all right.

"That's it." Shaken, and trying not to look it, Tom moistened his lips, his mouth suddenly dry. "He went to New York for a few days—on personal business. As you know, the power's been down there, the phones, everything. That's probably why you didn't get an answer."

The young officer studied him evenly. "Probably."

The second cop had already begun riffling through David's desk drawers. He yanked up the framed picture of Stacy and showed it to his partner, who nodded in recognition.

"Do you know who she is?" the second cop demanded.

"Yeah. That's his stepdaughter."

Tom gave them Stacy's name and Meredith's. His stomach rose into his chest as the police asked where they lived.

"Listen, I've got to tell you, David Shepherd would never kill anybody. I mean, he plays a mean game of squash, but that's as fe-rocious as the guy gets." Against his instincts, Tom sank back down into his chair.

"Professor," Officer Cocky began, condescension dripping from his tongue, "we aren't accusing your roommate of murdering anyone. We just want to talk to him, okay? Make sure he's not a victim of foul play himself. So if you know where he is, it would be in his best interests, and yours, to share that with us."

"All I know is he went to New York." Tom hated the fact that David could regularly beat him at squash and could outclimb him. Granted, there were times he secretly itched to see David take a fall. But he didn't wish this on him. Officer Cocky looked like he was champing to earn his stripes. *Or to put David in some.*

For the better part of an hour, they tore through David's desk, files, bookshelves, even the test papers in the top drawer.

When they were done they handed Tom a card with a case num-ber and their contact information. The cocky one left Tom with the strong "suggestion" that he call them immediately if he heard from David.

He waited until he was sure they'd started down the stairs before he closed the door and went for his phone.

CHAPTER TWENTY-SIX

Officer Scott Conrad typed the date on the APB in between bites of a ham and cheese sandwich he'd grabbed from the University deli on the way back to the station.

His partner, Lou Minelli, had returned to the victim's house to interview her adult daughter once again. Conrad wished him luck. They'd gone together to fill out the initial report and he'd had to stifle his impatience as the daughter sobbed so hard she was almost incoherent.

By her account, Eva Smolensky had left a stew simmering in the Crock-Pot before she left for Shepherd's house. The daughter's dinner. The bereaved was a thirty-year-old CVS photo clerk. Mother had called daughter at work, letting her know she was going to clean Shepherd's home and not to wait dinner for her. That was the last time the cleaning woman's daughter heard her mother's voice.

Conrad liked this case. He liked it a lot. He'd like it even better when Dr. Shepherd was sitting across the interrogation table from him.

Eyes narrowed, his fingers drummed the keyboard.

Attention all police departments and agencies. Be on the look-out for subject wanted in the questioning of a homicide at 233 D Street NE, Washington, D.C.

Looking for Professor David Shepherd, white male, thirty-three years old, six foot two, 188 lbs., brown hair, hazel eyes, no distinguishing characteristics. DOB: August 15, 1973. Residing at 233 D Street NE, Washington, DC.

Conrad slugged back a swallow of Dr Pepper and wiped his mouth with a flimsy paper napkin. He scanned the computer screen for typos, then continued.

Subject said to be in New York City. May be traveling by plane, train, or rented vehicle. Please detain and immediately contact the Washington, D.C. Police Department.

Officer Conrad hit the SEND key, dispatching the All Points Bulletin to the New York City Police Department and to the Transportation Safety Board for immediate distribution to all New York and New Jersey airports.

Once the communication centers there circulated the APB, Conrad told himself, it would simply be a matter of time.

Chapter Twenty-seven

"David—" Yael's voice was sharp with apprehension as she looked at his stunned expression. "Who was that? What did they say?"

He shook his head in disbelief, his mouth opening and closing in sync with the clenching of his jaw.

"Tell me what's wrong," she demanded, jumping up from the chair where she'd been watching CNN coverage of one disaster after the next. She stopped before him, wondering what had turned his complexion to ash.

"Eva's dead."

"Who's Eva?"

"My housekeeper. Someone murdered her—in my house."

He closed his eyes a moment and saw the baggy-lidded eyes and tired smile of the diligent woman who'd scoured his house once a week for the past seven years.

He opened his eyes and looked straight at Yael. "The police are looking for me."

"Oh my God." Her face tightened. "When did they find her?"

"I have no idea. That was Tom McIntyre—we share an office at Georgetown. They came with a search warrant and tore apart my desk. They know I'm in New York." Nausea churned in his stomach.

"This means we can't wait for morning—we have to get to the airport right now and get you through security before your picture is plastered all over JFK."

David stared at her blankly, still too overcome with shock to think clearly. "First I have to check in with the police—"

"No." Yael pushed him into the chair. "Think about it, David. Whoever killed Eva might have been there looking for *you*. If you contact the police, they won't let you leave the country until they make an arrest."

He knew she was right. Still, he wavered.

Yael was already gathering up her toiletries, her movements swift and sure. "We're going to have to spend the night at the airport. I'm taking a quick shower while you pack."

When the bathroom door had shut behind her, David paced the room, his thoughts racing.

It's my fault for asking Eva to meet Dillon there, he thought. *But Dillon had said she was gone before he got there. And the vacuum cleaner hadn't been put away. . . .*

Because she was dead already, David realized. He stopped pacing, staring blindly out the window.

So why didn't Dillon find her body?

Sweat dripped from his armpits. Dillon and the killer had probably been there within moments of each other. Dillon's the one who might be able to help the police. . . .

But Dillon's out of the country, he remembered.

His stomach dropped. Dillon was his best friend. He could have been killed along with Eva. *Because they were after me?*

He strode to his duffel and tossed it on the bed, then rolled up the shirt he'd worn yesterday and stuffed it in. As the flickering image on the television caught his eyes, he grabbed the remote and canceled the "mute" command.

"The wind has shifted here in Arizona," a long-haired female correspondent reported. "A hundred thousand acres have already burned and now the fire has changed direction, advancing on Flagstaff, heading away from the backfires intentionally set behind it. This is a tremendous blow to the efforts of firefighters who have battled around the clock for the past thirty-six hours. The sheriff's department is advising residents to be prepared to evacuate should that become necessary. This is Dana Landau, reporting live from Flagstaff."

Terror slammed him. Meredith had shouted something about wildfires, but he'd paid scant attention.

Hutch will have to move them, and David knew what that meant. Hutch had taught him years ago, while guarding his family, that being on the move upped the danger quotient.

Suddenly, he needed to hear Stacy's voice again. One more time before his plane left the runway tomorrow morning.

There was something he hadn't told her. Meredith had grabbed the phone away before he'd had the chance.

One more time, before he left the country, before the world ended, he needed to make sure Stacy knew how much he loved her.

Yael turned on the shower full blast and thought about David being wanted by the police. *His brand new passport is worthless.*

As she waited for the water temperature to stabilize, she leaned against the counter and considered their options. She'd known Avi for fifteen years and for fifteen years she'd listened to him boast about his unlimited ingenuity.

It was time to call him on it.

CHAPTER TWENTY-EIGHT

Staring down from the hotel window at the freighters on the Hudson, tension seared across David's shoulders. It was déjà vu all over again. Hutch, Meredith, and Stacy weren't answering their cells.

He'd muted the sound again on the TV, but still the images of raging wildfire and black smoke blazed across the screen.

The backfires weren't helping. Nothing was. He could only hope that Hutch could dodge the path of the fire.

He heard Yael switch off the bathroom faucet, but another part of his brain heard Stacy screaming his name in terror.

No. He switched off that nightmare tape and reminded himself that Karl Hutchinson was the best at what he did—no one could get by Hutch to hurt Stacy and Meredith, not even a Dark Angel.

"None of them are picking up," he called to Yael. "I've got a bad feeling about it." He turned from the window and stopped cold.

Yael stood at the foot of her unmade bed. Her terry cloth hotel robe hung half-open, her green eyes looked translucent with fear.

Beside her, the blond monolith pressed a four-inch hunting knife to her throat.

I never heard a thing.

Up close, David realized the guy was just a kid—a massive kid. Broad as a football player with a face like a gung-ho ROTC cadet. There was something off with his eyes. They were pale blue, almost colorless, and as empty of emotion as a pair of Ping-Pong balls. *He looks like a cross between a college linebacker and a contract killer.*

"Let her go," David said. He licked his lips. The two gemstones in his pocket suddenly burned like hot coals, scalding against his thigh. He stared at the vein in Yael's throat pulsing mere millimeters from where the blade pressed against her skin.

How do you reason with a Dark Angel?

"I'm sure the two of us can reach some sort of agreement if you don't hurt her," he began, taking a slow step forward. "First of all, you have to let her go."

"I'll think about it—*after* you give me your little red book."

He knows about my journal. David was stunned. *We thought he was after the gemstones, or the rabbi's satchel.*

Drawing a breath, David sized up the hulk. *Take your time. Get your footing. He's no older than one of your students. And from the way he's sweating, just as insecure.*

"Why don't you tell me who you are, and what this is all about?" To his surprise, his voice emerged an octave lower than usual.

"I'm just a messenger boy, Professor." He gestured with his chin. "Set your phone down on that table and tell me where that book is. I'll also take everything you acquired from the rabbi."

David's gaze locked with Yael's. Pain pulsed through his temples. He wanted to tell the kid to fuck himself, but he bit his tongue, forcing himself to stare down his adversary.

There has to be something in there, behind those veiled eyes. But how to reach it? Maybe if I offer him one of the gemstones, he'll leave Yael alone.

It was as if she heard him. "Don't do it, David." Her voice was almost as panicked as the chaos clamoring in his own head. "He's going to kill me no matter what. Get out of here—*now*."

The hulk smiled thinly and pressed the blade harder against her flesh. He nodded toward the unmade bed. "You poked her last night. Looks like it's my turn to poke her today."

Yael gasped as the knife nicked her throat. Blood spouted from a tiny puncture.

"See why bodies are so inconvenient," the hulk said with disdain. "So messy. Bothersome. And such a barrier to spiritual ascension." He drew the knife a quarter of an inch across Yael's throat, and she winced as blood began to trickle toward the collar of her robe. "Move it, Professor. Or would you like to see more?"

"Bastard," Yael spat between her teeth, and with one backwards thrust slammed her foot into his shin. David lunged. The room tilted as he grabbed for the knife. Writhing desperately, Yael twisted free, but with one punch, the monolith sent her flying into the paneled closet doors. Then he spun toward David. A perfectly aimed karate kick to the stomach sent David crashing to his knees.

He couldn't breathe, couldn't even remember how. He felt as if his lungs were collapsing and on fire all at the same time. Nausea roiled in his throat as he clutched at the headboard and pulled himself to his feet.

All three of them spotted the amber on the floor in the same instant. It had rolled from David's pocket and now winked like a tiny sun beside one of Yael's kitten-heeled sandals, its ancient carved letters dark with mystery.

Even as the blond's thick arm shot out, Yael dove for the stone. David seized the metal luggage rack and slammed it down on the man's head with a sickening crack. The Dark Angel thumped to the carpet like a felled elephant.

"Yael, are you all right?" David gulped at the air that was slowly feeding oxygen back to his brain.

"I'll be better once we get out of here," she said, tying her robe. She pressed a shaking hand to her throat, wincing at the feel of blood. "What about you? Anything broken?"

"Probably," he grimaced. "If I ignore it, I'm sure it will go away."

With a weak smile, she scooped up the gemstone and handed it to him.

David slipped it back inside his pocket and heard the soft clink as it fell against the agate still hidden there.

"Let's find out if he has anything we can use before we get out of here," he said, kneeling beside the fallen man.

The New Jersey driver's license identified the hulk as James Gillis.

"That ID might be fake. If we could get it to Avi he might be able to find out who sent this putz," Yael murmured, riffling through Gillis' back pants pocket.

"You sure rely on Avi a lot, don't you?"

"We go back a long time." She searched through the rest of the wallet. "He was recruited by the Mossad the same year as my husband."

"Husband?" David asked, investigating the bulge in Gillis' knee-length sock.

"We were only married three months when he was killed on a mission. We'd delayed our honeymoon. . . ."

Sympathy welled within him. But before he could give voice to it, she changed the subject, eyeing the small caliber handgun he'd just pulled from Gillis' sock.

"I wouldn't recommend trying to get that past security. Give it to me."

Swiping a hand across the sweat pouring down his forehead, he watched her empty the chamber and hide the bullets under the mattress. Then he checked Gillis' other leg and found a tarot card in the second sock.

"Well, look at this. It's identical."

Yael moved closer to examine it. "The number on the back is different," she pointed out.

She was right. This one was marked 1,098. *We'll have to figure it out later,* David thought. Right now he needed to restrain Gillis before he came to. He wanted answers.

Quickly, he ripped the sheet from his bed.

"Yael, get a glass of cold water from the bathroom."

She gave him a long look, then disappeared while David tied one end of the sheet tight around Gillis' arms, binding them behind his back, then did the same with his legs.

"Ready?" Yael held the glass of cold water over Gillis' head.

"Do it."

Gillis didn't so much as flinch, even when David slapped at his dripping face. "Wake up, blondie." But Gillis' eyelids never blinked.

Yael dropped down beside him and pressed her fingers to his throat. "His pulse is weak. He could be out for a while, and we don't have the luxury of waiting."

David stuffed the man's driver's license and the tarot card into his duffel as Yael dressed. She slung her tote over her shoulder as they took one last look around the room. On the TV screen, Turkish rescue workers carried more broken bodies from the earthquake's rubble.

Gillis groaned once, but didn't move. David started toward him, but Yael grabbed his arm. "We don't have time. David, please."

He knew she was right. It might take hours to get Gillis to talk. And in the meantime, police bulletins would have airport security interested in talking to *him.*

He opened the door cautiously and glanced down the hall. Empty.

But he had no way of knowing about the beefy Puerto Rican leaning against a wall downstairs in the lobby, his gaze glued to the elevators just in case Professor David Shepherd and Yael HarPaz managed to slip past Gillis and tried to check out.

"So much for modern technology." Disgustedly, Hutch pushed the sunglasses up on his head and regarded the burly clerk in

Charlie's Convenience Store while Stacy pondered the array of candy piled on wooden display shelves.

"Yup." The clerk worked over the ball of tobacco jammed in his stubbled cheek. "Those wildfires are sure doing a number on us. Mother Nature, she'll trump technology every time."

"This is preposterous. You're telling us there isn't a single working cell phone in Flagstaff?" Meredith demanded. The impatience in her tone earned her a low grunt from the clerk. Stacy looked at the pine-beamed ceiling and rolled her eyes.

"That's what I'm telling you, ma'am—not if ya got AT&T, Verizon, Cingular, and such. Not a one of 'em that bounces through the main tower here's got any signal whatsoever."

"And all of the land lines are jammed with people trying to get through," a sun-browned man hoisting a six-pack called from the beer cooler. Stacy stared at his black boots, which were a work of art with intricate stitching and elaborate tooling.

Hutch wasn't paying attention to the man. He was keeping an eye on both Stacy and the front door, as well as the road with its outcroppings of scrub and rock beyond the parking lot. No one had followed them from his cabin in Walnut Creek. Not even the backup team, due any time now. He had no idea how he was going to meet up with them, but there was no choice—they had to get out of the path of the fire.

"And what if someone has an emergency?" Meredith's voice rose, sounding shrill in the small store, which smelled of stale coffee and Pine-Sol.

"The whole world's got an emergency, Mom," Stacy muttered, her cheeks flushing the color of the lettering on her gray sweatshirt. "Haven't you been watching the news?"

The clerk smirked and moved off to ring up some soda pop and chips for the two young boys waiting at the cash register.

Hutch weighed his options. There weren't any. They'd have to try to hook up with David and the backup team once they reached a secure location.

"Come on, ladies, let's get a move on. We'll find some other place where we can call Grandma and wish her a happy birthday."

Stacy's gaze flicked to him for an instant, then dropped as she caught on. *Poor kid.* Every now and then she probably forgot what this little adventure was all about. For a thirteen-year-old she was pretty grounded, but still, all this had to take a toll. He'd watched how furiously she'd scribbled in her diary this morning, curled in the big high-backed chair where his grandfather used to sit and read him *Cattle Rancher* magazine. In a short time, he'd realized that Stacy was intense and empathetic, a sweet, scared kid who had no idea she wore her heart on her sleeve for all the world to see.

Meredith slapped a pack of Marlboro Light 100's on the counter along with a ten-dollar bill as Hutch lowered his sunglasses and preceded Stacy to the door.

"Go ahead, I'll be right there," she called after him.

As Hutch escorted Stacy to the Explorer, his eyes scanned the road and the rough open land sloping away from the store. He saw nothing unusual, but he kept a light hand on the girl's shoulder just the same.

Raoul LaDouceur smiled. The bodyguard was precisely in his sights. Three more minutes and he'd have the girl in his trunk, sleeping chloroform dreams as they sped toward the private plane waiting for their arrival.

"Hold on there, ma'am." The sun-browned man grabbed Meredith's arm and yanked her backwards, just as she reached for the door.

"Take your hands off—" Meredith's face drained of color as she saw the gun in his hand.

"Stacy! Run, baby!" she screamed.

But even as she screeched the warning, the man catapulted past her, firing his gun so rapidly it sounded like fireworks. It took a moment for her to realize that shots were also exploding from another direction.

"Get the hell down, lady," the clerk yelled from the floor. At the same moment Meredith saw Hutch hunched on the ground, a gun in his hand, and Stacy scrambling out from under him, sobbing.

"Run!" Meredith bolted outside, shrieking. "Run, Stacy!"

A bullet blew the pack of Marlboros from her fingers. She stumbled, then tore off toward the Explorer. At the same time, the sun-browned man serpentined through the parking area, firing in the direction of the rock outcropping a hundred yards away.

"Help him, Mom, there's so much blood. You have to help Hutch." Her face white with terror, Stacy crouched beside Hutch as the sun-browned man suddenly wheeled, running toward them.

"Don't kill us," she begged. "Please, don't kill us."

He dropped to one knee and grabbed Hutch's right hand, easing the gun from it and setting it beside Meredith. "I'm on your side, ladies. Garrick Rix, Hutch's backup," he said, checking for a pulse.

He slapped Hutch's face, without reaction. "Come on, shithead, don't crap out on me now."

Rix unthreaded the belt from his jeans and tossed it at Meredith. "He's going to die unless you twist this around his leg as tight as you can, and hold it there until I get back. And no matter what happens, don't move from this spot. I hope I wounded that son of a bitch out there, but there's no guarantee. I'm going to make sure he's not waiting to pick us off one at a time, and then we get the hell out of here. Your job in the meantime is to keep Hutch from bleeding to death."

Chapter Twenty-Nine

Stacy grabbed the leather belt and twisted it, ignoring the blood seeping across Hutch's jeans. Dimly, she was aware that Garrick Rix had left them. The shooting had stopped, but the sound of it still roared in her ears. She felt sick to her stomach, but if she allowed herself to give in to it, Hutch might die. It was already her fault that this had happened to him.

"Please don't die," she choked out, staring down at the man, whose face was the color of the gray modeling clay she used in art class.

"Stacy, let me." Meredith was shaking so hard her teeth clinked against one another as she gently tried to pry the leather from her daughter's clenched fingers. "Get under the Explorer *now*."

Stacy's fingers tightened on the belt. "I'm staying here with you and Hutch. I can help."

"Stacy, they're after you. Get under the—"

A gunshot rang from the outcropping. Stacy whimpered.

"Do you think Hutch's friend got shot?" Tears streamed down her cheeks.

Sounds like somebody did, Meredith thought, her heart pounding, but before she could answer, the clerk's hoarse whisper reached them from the store.

"Get back in here, you two. I can hold 'em off with my rifle. Run!"

"He's bleeding too much. I can't leave him," Meredith called back in a low tone. "Stacy, go on now," she urged frantically, her hair straggling over her eyes. Hutch's sticky blood warmed her knees. "Crawl back into the store, baby. I'm begging you. I promise I'll take care of Hutch."

Stacy was torn between obeying her mother and protecting her. She couldn't seem to stop crying. She couldn't seem to move. And then it was too late.

Garrett Rix crawled on his belly, his gun trained on the swarthy man less than twenty yards ahead. He'd been hit, but adrenaline was keeping the pain at bay. He just needed one shot, one good shot.

The man moved closer. The son-of-a-bitch was smiling like a man who'd just turned over a royal flush. Rix tried to blink the sweat out of his eyes, to raise his arm a little to the left. He spit out the blood gathering in his mouth so he wouldn't choke on it and give himself away. *He thinks he's got me like a squirrel in a stew pot. But I've got another shot in me, one more shot.*

The blaze of fire blinded him as his finger squeezed the trigger. The world turned red. Then black.

Raoul kicked the gun from the man's lifeless fingers and shot him once more through the head just to make sure he stayed dead.

Without any wasted motion, he sprinted to the Firebird, feeling jaunty for the first time in days. Death always put a bounce in his step.

The sound of tires spitting gravel split the air as a yellow Firebird convertible fishtailed around the outcropping and came to a stop. It purred at right angles to the Explorer, effectively cutting off any path of escape.

The storekeeper fired, but his shot missed the convertible's front tire and ricocheted off the bottom of the passenger door.

Stacy recognized the man who stepped from the Firebird.

"Mom, it's *him!*" she sobbed, and dove for the SUV.

Grabbing Hutch's gun, Meredith struggled to aim it. But her arms were trembling uncontrollably and she'd bitten her lower lip so hard she could taste blood. The man wasn't paying her any attention. He was fiddling with something on his belt.

She watched, numb, as he brought his arm back and threw something toward the store.

Shoot him, now! Shoot him, a voice inside her screamed. She squinted her eyes and pulled the trigger, toppling back onto Hutch from the kick of the gun. At that instant, a deafening explosion lifted the store from its foundation and flames burst from the windows.

Shock froze her for a full second. Then she was on her feet, trying to get off another shot.

"Give me . . . the gun." Hutch's voice was barely audible. "Just drop it," he whispered, "like you're giving up."

She sank to her knees and let the gun fall into Hutch's open palm. Her eyes found Stacy's as her daughter stared back, shivering under the Explorer. *Stay there, baby* she prayed silently. *Stay right there.*

Coughing, the dark-haired man turned his back on the inferno and moved toward Meredith with long, sure strides. As he came to a halt less than six feet from her, terror throbbed through every cell in her body. Yet all she could see was the oddness of his eyes. They were two different colors—one brown, one blue.

She was so fixated on them she never saw Hutch raise his arm. She only heard the shot and saw the man with the strange eyes reel.

For an instant, hope surged through her. *Again, Hutch. Shoot him again. This time in the heart.*

But the man moved with remarkable speed, even as blood stained his right shoulder.

"No!" Meredith cried, as he fired four times across the length of Hutch's body. "Oh, God. No!"

"Stacy!" the man barked.

The sound of her daughter's name on his lips chilled Meredith to her core. She'd never imagined such evil.

"Leave her alone!"

"Shut up. Now!" The gun was pointed at her head. "Stacy, if you don't come out here like the good little girl we know you are, your mother's going to be as dead as your bodyguard."

"Don't listen to him, Stacy!" Meredith screamed.

Wind whipped smoke and glinting ashes from the burning store. The man coughed, then aimed the gun lower, at her heart. But at the last second, he jerked his aim inches to the left as he pulled the trigger. The ground beside her exploded in a spray of rock and dust.

"Mom!" Stacy shrieked and came scrambling out from under the Explorer to throw herself across her mother.

"Leave us alone!" Meredith sobbed. "What do you want from us?"

"I want *her.*" He pointed the gun at Stacy. Then flipped it in his hand so he was holding it by the barrel, and sprang at Meredith like a panther.

The last thing she saw before he cold-cocked her were those indifferent, mismatched eyes.

The girl threw herself on her mother, sobbing. It took Raoul no longer than six seconds to uncork the vial of chloroform and soak the square of cloth he pulled from his pocket. This time, the sharp-toothed little mouse would not make so much as a squeak.

CHAPTER THIRTY

7 . . . 6 . . . 5 . . . the elevator whooshed downward. As it neared the fourth floor it slowed for a halt. David pulled Yael closer in case they needed to get out fast. They tensed as the doors slid apart, but the sharply dressed businesswoman who stepped on dragging her luggage barely gave them a glance.

He felt Yael relax beside him as the car resumed its descent. Suddenly his hand shot out to press the button for the second floor.

"I almost forgot, honey. I told your parents we'd stop by their room."

Yael flicked him a puzzled glance. "Oh . . . they aren't meeting us in the lobby?" Even as she uttered the words, she exited beside him, waiting until the doors closed before she spoke again.

"What was that all about, *honey?*"

"It suddenly dawned on me—Gillis doesn't travel alone. His partner could be staked out in the lobby."

Yael's eyes narrowed. "Good thinking. I suggest the stairs."

David glanced back and forth, pondering the exit signs posted at opposite ends of the hall. "Do you remember if we turned left or right to find our room last night when we came up the stairs?"

"Right . . . I think."

"Then we go left. That's the staircase farther from the front door."

Yael hitched her tote higher on her shoulder. "Let's hope there's a back exit," she muttered as they started toward the stairwell.

Stealthily they made their way down. David took a breath before he inched open the first floor exit door.

So far, so good. The hallway was empty. Glancing to his left, he spotted another corridor branching off it and they hurried toward it.

But it was just an alcove, with dining chairs stacked to the ceiling alongside a door marked EMPLOYEES ONLY.

"In here." David shoved open the door, but Yael spun around at the sound of quick footfalls in the hall behind them.

A dark-skinned man bore down on them—running like a wolf after a rabbit. Gillis' partner, the Hispanic who'd shot at them yesterday.

"Go! Hurry!" Yael pushed him through the door and slammed it shut behind her.

David grunted as he rammed his shin into the legs of a banquet table stacked on its side. "Shit."

They were in a storage area littered with long tables, more stacks of chairs, podiums, projector equipment, even a piano.

David skidded to the piano. "Help me with this!"

He braced his palms against its side, leaning in with all his weight. It didn't budge. Yael ran to its opposite side, and together they succeeded in shoving it several feet toward the door.

"Come on! Again!" Perspiration dripped down David's temples. His face flushed red with exertion. Yael was wincing, her fingers splayed across the rich wood. This time they managed to shift it nearly to the door.

"Once more," he grunted, bracing himself for the effort.

At that moment, the door moved toward them, thudding against the piano. Sudddenly hairy fingers gripped the edge of the door and a shoulder rammed against the wood.

"Now!" Yael screamed.

David shoved, every muscle straining. The piano lurched against the door and slammed it into the jamb, trapping the thick fingers. From the other side they heard an inhuman howl, followed by the desperate slams of shoulder against barricade.

"Come on!" Grabbing Yael's hand, David zigzagged past the banquet furniture and a chest of china into an adjoining room—a huge stainless-steel kitchen, where a red-coated bellman munching a sandwich dropped it at the sight of them.

"Excuse me, sir." He jumped toward them, palm out, as several startled cooks looked up from their workstations.

"I'm sorry, sir, but this area is off-limits to guests—"

"Where's your back door?" David shouted.

The bellman looked too astonished to reply, but the Asian cook who'd been chopping onions gestured sideways with his chef's knife.

They followed the blade, just as the bellman started in the direction of the Hispanic's howls. "What the . . . hell . . ."

"Don't open that door—he's got a gun!" Yael shot over her shoulder. "Call security!"

"What is this?" the sous chef asked, grinning. "Reality TV? We being punk'd, man?"

Outside, David and Yael found themselves in the brightly lit service entrance. They tore around the building to the street side and ran until they finally spotted an empty taxi.

Just as it slid to a stop, Yael's cell phone rang.

"JFK," David panted as he slid into the car, leaving the door open. "But wait for the lady."

He caught his breath as Yael climbed in, her phone to her ear.

"Getting out of that hotel was the easy part," she gasped at last as the taxi jerked into traffic. She leaned toward David to whisper in his ear. "That call was our first step toward getting you past your Homeland Security."

CHAPTER THIRTY-ONE

Hpynotized by the screen, the Serpent worked all through the night.

By dawn, the last two names still eluded him.

He attacked the formulas again. His dirty-blond hair had gone unwashed for two days, and his armpits reeked with sweat as his fingers flew across the keyboard. His mind raced faster than the CPU at his command.

For days he'd forgotten to bathe, to eat, even to use his cane. At one point he'd shoved back his chair and sprung up without it, only to tumble to the floor.

Cursing, he'd struggled back up, grasped the damned cane, and smashed it full force against one of his treasured sculptures.

He was growing to hate the numbers, the graphs, the overlays of transcriptions. Instead of reflecting his brilliance, they now seemed to mock him, hiding their secrets, refusing to part the curtain of mystery. There had been no more breakthroughs, but then, neither had any more papyri fragments been found, none since the summer of 2001.

Everything I need is here. It *must* be here. I'm so close.

We're so close.

And it's all hanging on me. The downfall of God. The end of the world. The victory of the Gnoseos.

They'd tried so hard, so many times. His people's history never failed to move him.

He thought of the first time they'd come close to wiping out the Hidden Ones. How the imbalance it caused in the world had triggered the eruption of Mt. Vesuvius, destroying Pompeii. And of the hero, Attila the Hun, who brutally slaughtered so many in the fifth century he was dubbed the "scourge of God."

The Gnoseos had rejoiced at the plague, the Black Death that killed nearly half the people in Western Europe in the fourteenth century. They'd prayed it would spread throughout the world.

The Inquisition in Spain under Torquemada, and the Armenian massacres, had killed many of the Hidden Ones, but never enough of them, never thirty-six within a generation.

There had been so many moments of hope—the Yellow River bursting its banks in China, killing nearly a million people in 1887. The sinking of the Titanic. Communism—and the Khmer Rouge— the movement that massacred millions in Cambodia.

In many lands and in many times, slavery was their tool— suffocating hope, drowning the human spirit, destroying those with pure souls as if they were vermin.

The Nazis also did their part—and for a time his great-grandfather had led the Circle of his generation in a valiant campaign to bring down the world. They'd come so close.

But we are closer now, he told himself, *closer than at any other time in history.* He thought of the Ark, of the provisions newly stockpiled in that subterranean stronghold, and of the two thousand faithful awaiting the signal—the signal to enter their new world, the signal that could only come once *he* completed his task.

Two more names. Why couldn't he find them? What was he doing wrong?

He tried a different algorithm, altered another sequence, ran another equidistant letter skip.

Garbage. The screen showed him only garbage.

He bit his tongue until it bled. Stupid blood, what does it matter? Patience mattered.

His youth, locked in the darkness, had taught him about patience. He'd always known the light would come again. *And it will come again now,* he thought. *Light and answers. Patience.*

But it was difficult to practice patience when the Circle was pressing him. Even his father seemed distant, disappointed, as the days dragged on. How much more would he despise me if he knew the truth—all of it?

I cannot fail. I will not.

He needed to clear his mind. To go back to the stillness of that dark peaceful place, to hear the sound of nothing.

The answer was within him. He possessed the power to ascend, to reconnect with the Source. It was intuitive—he'd been taught that since the day he received his amulet.

His hand sought out the gold medallion hanging around his neck. As his fingers traced the double ouroboros carved in its center, he pictured the world cracking in two. Head bowed, he chanted the ancient meditation over and over until he slid to the floor in a trance.

> *Foul earth, sphere of illusion,*
> *I curse your shackles,*
> *Despising the evil flesh that imprisons my mind.*
> *Like a candle flaming upward, I seek the Source,*
> *Striving toward the heavens,*
> *To merge with my Divine.*

It was late morning when he opened his eyes again, his mind still, his shoulders relaxed for the first time in weeks.

Suddenly, he knew what he'd overlooked. A subtle variance of the ELS skip, but it could change everything.

And it did.

This time, after only an hour of churning through the server's myriad data files, there was finally something new across the top of his screen.

He scribbled down the letters, and ran the variance again. Each time, the results were identical.

It was a name. A name he hadn't culled before.

Jack Cherle.

Two minutes later, he shot the name across the network. It wouldn't take long to give the Dark Angels what they needed to know.

If Jack Cherle was currently alive, he wouldn't be for long.

Without stopping to shower or to eat, the Serpent plunged back into his work.

CHAPTER THIRTY-TWO

Queen Mary 2

Jack Cherle threw open the doors to his balcony and watched the moonlit Atlantic roll by. There were two full days remaining before the ship reached Southampton and he intended to savor them both.

This was the trip of a lifetime. His wife had often daydreamed of taking a cruise on the QE2, but the ship's successor, the *Queen Mary 2*, was a ship beyond anything either of them could have imagined.

He loved watching Yasmin sigh with delight over the high tea every afternoon that came complete with musical accompaniment. Loved hearing the excitement in her voice as she announced it was nearly time for their onboard course from Oxford. Loved holding her close on this balcony every evening after they'd overeaten meals to die for.

He'd decided to splurge for this trip to mark their thirtieth wedding anniversary. They were treating all three sons and their wives and children to six nights at sea, followed by a week in London. Yasmin could scarcely contain her joy. This was the first family vacation they'd taken since their oldest went off to Cornell.

Their life in St. Louis was comfortable, but their time off from their busy pediatric practice was spent on children other than their own. Each year, Jack and Yasmin packed their sunscreen, shorts, and sandals, took their preventative vaccinations, kissed their grand-children good-bye, and flew off, as part of Doctors Without Borders, to a different region plagued by war and disaster.

Jack thought about the malnourished children they'd treated last summer in Darfur, and the five colleagues who'd been murdered a mile away from them in Afghanistan the year before. Here, looking out from the balcony at the endless expanse of inky sea and sky, Jack could almost forget about the chaos in the world. Almost.

Still, it tugged at him. They'd almost canceled this trip after the recent tsunami in Japan. If not for disappointing their children and grandchildren, and the fact that they'd booked their passage a year ago, they'd have taken off for Asia. Instead, he and Yasmin had compromised, changing their two return tickets so that they could fly to Tokyo directly from London, foregoing the British Airways flight home.

Some days Jack fantasized about the two of them simply packing up the practice and traveling the globe together for months at a time, tending to the most vulnerable children adrift in the world.

Maybe someday . . .

A knock at the cabin door drew him back inside. Yasmin was brushing her teeth so he opened the door to find their eleven-year-old granddaughter, Emily, grinning up at him, a beach cover-up draped over her pajamas.

"I need another goodnight kiss, Poppa. Timmy's driving Mommy crazy because he wants to order room service. He claims he's *starving*."

"Thank God your brother will never know what starving really is," Jack said, smoothing back Emily's long brown bangs. "That's

better. I can see your beautiful eyes now." He leaned down and
kissed his middle granddaughter's fresh-scrubbed cheek.

"We only have two days left on the boat," Emily sighed as she lingered at the door. "Don't you wish we could all stay here forever?"

Jack chuckled. "You don't really mean that, Em. You have plenty
of adventures waiting for you the rest of your life."

"I guess," she shrugged, then brightened. "So do you, Poppa."

"Of course," Jack began. Suddenly, a breath of ice wisped down
his back and vanished. *Now what was that?*

With a shiver he glanced at the open balcony door where the sea
flowed in foamy caps. But the sudden chill had gone.

Yasmin emerged from the bathroom and Emily ran into her
arms. By the time Jack walked her back to the cabin down the corridor, he'd forgotten about the odd sensation. He'd forgotten about
everything but the gentle roll of the sea and the precious days ahead
with his family.

PYONGYANG, NORTH KOREA

Half a world away, a computer secreted in a building owned by
the Central Bank of the Democratic People's Republic of Korea
pinpointed Jack Cherle's whereabouts. Within moments, a team of
three Dark Angels stationed in Wales set out to greet the *Queen
Mary* when it docked in Southampton.

CHAPTER THIRTY-THREE

JFK was jammed with travelers trapped by all the delays. Amidst the din of thousands of inconvenienced customers, ticket agents worked feverishly trying to rebook tickets and juggle passengers and flights. David was stuck in a line that snaked through roped lanes five deep as he waited to purchase a round-trip ticket to Israel. His nerves stretched taut as he wondered if the ticket agents up ahead were already on the lookout for him.

In another line, Yael looked calm and unfazed as she waited between a mother with two unruly children and a group of teenagers wearing soccer uniforms. They'd chosen separate lines as a precaution in case David was stopped.

He glanced again at the passport in his hand, marveling at the remarkable facsimile Avi had procured on short notice. But as he inched up in the line, he prayed that the harried airport employees didn't have his photograph taped beside their computers.

"Next."

The blond ticket agent, who looked so much like Kate Wallace he nearly did a double take, tucked a strand of hair behind her ear and regarded him through bloodshot eyes. "What can I do for you today?"

So far, so good. David requested a round-trip ticket to Tel Aviv via London. He knew the next flight, leaving the following morning, was the one Yael was booking too.

"Let's see, the next flight leaves at nine a.m. tomorrow. You'll arrive in Tel Aviv at five thirty-five a.m. There's only a two-hour layover at Heathrow. And," she added, still checking her computer screen, "you're in luck. Five seats left. Most people aren't getting their first choices today. Name, please?"

For a moment David's mind went blank. He felt his entire body going cold with terror. For a man obsessed with names, he was having trouble getting this one out.

"Alan Shiffman." He let out his breath slowly, hoping she couldn't hear the thumping of his heart as she typed his name into the computer.

"May I see some identification, Mr. Shiffman?"

David was appalled to see his hand shaking slightly as he slid the passport across the counter. The Kate Wallace look-alike peered at it closely, then handed it back.

"And will you be putting this on your credit card?"

"I'll pay cash."

Hotshot Avi Raz had gotten "Alan Shiffman" a passport, but neglected to procure him a matching credit card.

David had been stunned on the way to the airport when Yael informed him they'd be meeting a contact in the bar who was bringing him yet another passport. She warned him to behave naturally—as if they were three business acquaintances having a preflight cocktail.

Still, it had flummoxed him when their "acquaintance," a middle-aged woman with chin-length red hair and a toothy smile had suddenly exclaimed, "Oh, Alan, you dropped your passport!"

David was about to correct her when Yael kicked him under the table. As the woman slipped off the barstool and scooped a passport from the floor, David caught himself.

"You certainly don't want to lose this," the red-headed woman chuckled, handing him the open passport.

David saw it looked identical to the one Avi had brought him earlier, except for the name attached to his face.

Alan Shiffman.

That's who he was now. Alan Shiffman, whose passport had been issued seven years ago in Chicago.

He'd forced a smile, and downed the rest of his drink. "Thank you *very* much. I wouldn't get very far without this."

He couldn't imagine how Avi had pulled it off on such short notice, but he was grateful. Still, traveling under a false identity, especially out of the country, especially when you're wanted for questioning, had to be a crime of some magnitude.

David didn't want to think about the possible consequences. Right now he had to keep drilling the name Alan Shiffman into his head—as if there weren't enough names rattling around in there already.

Leaving the ticket counter, amazed he'd pulled it off, he spotted Yael sitting nearby, pretending to organize her tote. She rose from her chair as their gazes met, and started toward the security line. He followed at a short distance.

Alan Shiffman, he reminded himself, heading toward the first checkpoint, the passport gripped between his fingers. As he passed the entrance to the men's room, a deeply-tanned loudmouth in a Coors Light t-shirt, baseball cap, and leather flip-flops came barreling out. Cell phone to his ear, he nearly tripped over a tow-headed kid bent over the water fountain.

"Well, nail her ass then, man. Get yourself a lawyer and screw her before she screws you. I told you she was only out for—"

"Hey—" David spoke sharply, as Mr. Coppertone charged ahead, swerving so quickly to avoid knocking down a shuffling old man that he collided with a flight attendant dragging her carry-on behind her. She lost her footing and would have fallen, had David not lunged toward her and caught her elbow, dropping his passport in the process.

"Watch where you're going, buddy," he called out, scowling at the oblivious jerk's back.

"Here, you dropped this," the flight attendant said, stooping to retrieve his passport. She smiled up at him. "Good catch."

David's fingers closed around it. Dammit, he'd lost track of Yael. But as he quickened his pace he spotted her waiting for him twenty feet ahead. Her eyes briefly met his as he strode right past her. *She wants me in the lead*, he realized. *She's going to follow me through the checkpoints.*

He scanned the throng of passengers waiting to be screened and stepped up to the next place in line.

Two checkpoints to go. Two chances to be caught.

Jeff Fortelli slurped down one last cup of joe in the TSA lounge before clipping on his identification badge. His twelve-hour shift started in about ninety seconds. And even though his supervisor was an idiot who changed his mind about procedures every other day, Jeff knew that timeliness was important. Almost as important as a keen eye and a clear head. That, and a sense of discipline, were the hallmarks of any good security man.

Especially one with the TSA at a major international airport, he thought, hitching his dark pants up over his hips. JFK was one of the major crossroads of the world, although his supervisor and fellow screeners often lost track of that fact. Half the time they seemed more interested in rushing the passengers through than in conducting thorough screenings.

Hell, his buddies down in baggage told him all the time that the airlines bitched about how many bags didn't make it on the planes in time. They whined about what it cost them to deliver those bags, ordering the handlers to screen them faster, to get those bags on the planes on time even if it meant skipping screening a couple of them.

What kind of way was that to run security at a time like this?

Jeff tossed his Styrofoam cup in the trash and headed to the bulletin board as he did every night before he went on duty. He was diligent about keeping up with the security alerts posted there, memorizing the bulletins, looking for new names added to the no-fly registry.

Nothin' new tonight.

Then he saw the APB out of D.C. His thick shoulders bunched as he leaned forward and, with his thumb, traced an imaginary line beneath the subject's name.

David Shepherd. Wanted for questioning about a murder in his home.

Too bad there's no face to go with the name—yet.

He reread the APB, committing the subject's vital statistics to memory. An easy name to remember—David Shepherd.

Now if I was the one to ID that guy, I'd really have a leg-up on making supervisor. Gotta catch someone or something significant to make you stand out. And one of these days I will. And then, bada-boom, bada-bing. The Times *will be interviewing the most eagle-eyed and fucking indispensable screener at JFK.*

Jeff Fortelli's blood pumped with anticipation. Man, how he'd wave that front page story under his old man's nose. Show him that his second son was no slouch—even compared to son *numero uno,* golden boy Tony, who'd gotten his fool foot blown off in Afghanistan and won himself a Purple Heart.

Well, Pop, I'm on the front line, too. I'm the Homeland's first line of defense—right here, before anyone even reaches the X-ray machine or takes off their stinkin' shoes.

Fortelli punched in and strode toward the security gate, ready to take on the trail of endless, faceless passengers waiting to get past him.

Okay, David Shepherd. Come on down, and make my day.

———

As David advanced through the security line, he caught a glimpse of the first TSA screener. A young woman with short blond hair pulled back into a stub of a ponytail, her spiky bangs poking out of purple barrettes that clipped them back at the temples. David guessed she probably had a pierced tongue, too, but ditched the metal stud while she was on duty.

Not too threatening, he thought, watching her smile as she handed back each ID. *Not for a guy like Alan Shiffman.*

As those in front of him inched forward again, repositioning their carry-on bags, he glanced back to find where Yael stood in line. She was only seven spots behind him, directly in front of Mr. Coppertone, still jabbering away on the damned phone.

David moved forward once again, watching passengers ahead load their laptops and shoes and keys into plastic bins for the journey down the conveyor. His stomach started doing a funny little dance and he tried to school his expression into one of nonchalance.

Maybe I should have spent my time playing poker all these years instead of squash.

Just then he noticed a bull-necked man in his twenties stalking toward the head of the line. He wore a TSA uniform and the blonde with the barrettes lit up with a relieved expression that could telegraph only one thing. He was here to replace her.

Great.

There was something about the guy that reminded him of some of his most ambitious students. Something about the way he carried himself. He planted his feet when he took over for the woman. There was an aggressiveness in his stance. After scrutinizing the first documents handed to him, he passed them back with nothing but a brusque nod. *Not exactly your "have a nice day" kinda guy.*

Then something happened that set David's stomach plummeting. The man five spaces ahead of him handed over his documents and the screener examined them for longer than usual. But that wasn't what alarmed David. Instead of returning the man's passport and boarding pass, the new screener demanded a second piece of identification.

Alan Shiffman had only one.

He felt his palms slicking with perspiration and forced himself to take a deep breath as the man ahead fished through his wallet.

After a few seemingly endless seconds, the screener grudgingly handed back all of the man's documents, and waved him forward.

David tensed as the passenger hurried on. *We're about the same height and weight,* David thought uneasily. *Same hair color.*

He's looking for me.

David fought the urge to step out of line. It would only draw attention to him. There was no retreating. There was only one way — forward. He had to get through.

His pulse was buzzing in his ears when the screener reached for his passport. The man's eyes locked on his, the gaze cold and suspicious.

It seemed to take him forever to scrutinize the passport and boarding pass. But he made no move to hand them back. Instead, hiz gaze bored into David's face and he started to speak. David cut him off.

"I need to report something," he said in a low tone. "There's a guy about eight people back in line. He's wearing a Coors Light t-shirt — and a baseball cap. We were in the men's room at the same time. It might not mean anything, but he was acting kind of funny."

"Whaddya mean, funny?"

The screener's eyes seemed to X-ray his face.

"I can't swear to it — I could be wrong," David rushed on. "But I thought I saw him slip something shiny under his baseball cap. It might be nothing," he added quickly, "but I figured I should tell someone. These days, you just never know."

For a millisecond he saw the screener's eyes shift off him and down the line. Saw the slightest twitch in the center of his jaw as his eyes zeroed in on Mr. Coppertone.

"You did the right thing, sir."

Without another glance, the screener passed David's papers back and reached for the next set, his gaze flicking back and forth between the woman he was screening and the guy in the baseball cap.

David forced himself to continue at an even pace toward the X-ray machine and conveyor belt, his waistband damp with sweat. Only after he'd re-tied his shoes and was heading toward the gate, did relief pour through him hot as a shot of sake.

A few minutes later Yael sauntered across the concourse to sink down beside him in the bank of seats. A smile broke out across her face and trilled into a laugh.

"And just what, may I ask, did you tell that screener to make him take such fierce interest in the poor *shlub* behind me?"

CHAPTER THIRTY-FOUR

It made no sense. Not one iota. Drop everything and run out to Heathrow to collect his father? He could take a bloody car, couldn't he? For that matter, he could ask Gilbert to pick him up. But no. The e-mail was emphatic.

I need to speak to you, face to face, Crispin. Something has come to my attention and only you can enlighten me. Arriving at Heathrow at 9:47 P.M. Will be expecting you the moment I clear customs. Do not disappoint me.

He addresses me like I'm ten years old. It's clear he resents the impact I've had on The Circle. What I've managed to achieve in the past dozen years is far greater than everything he's contributed in his entire illustrious career. Here I am, within the grasp of greatness, and he's summoning me like a headmaster commanding a schoolboy.

The Serpent closed the e-mail with disgust and groped for his cane. *As you wish, father.*

A pity. Now he'd have to shower away the musk Chloe had left fragrant on his skin. The night before had been a long and adventurous one, a potent release from the pressure of hunting the names. As he soaped himself in the shower, the scratch marks she'd dug into his torso burned. He savored the spicy licks of pain and remembered all over again the way her lips curled back when she screamed his name.

Dear Chloe, one of the most feral women he'd ever bedded, and one of the most succulent. A shame he'd never see her again. This was the last interruption he'd allow himself, the last indulgence of the flesh before joining the others in the Ark and leaving Chloe and this evil world behind. Once he deposited his father at his club, there would be no respite until it was done. The last name, the last obstacle. The descent to the Ark.

By the time he floored his Ferrari in the direction of Heathrow, his annoyance with his father was rising in pace with his excessive speed.

Only you can enlighten me. For the first time, a tinge of uneasiness prickled down his maimed leg. He rubbed the gnarled muscles absently with the side of his hand.

He was ten minutes late pulling into the short-term car park.

Wasn't that too bloody bad.

CHAPTER THIRTY-FIVE

David's legs felt as if they'd turned to petrified wood by the time the plane rolled to the gate at Heathrow. He and Yael limped out onto Terminal 4 along with their fellow transatlantic passengers. Desperate to stretch their muscles, they welcomed the walk over to Terminal 1, where they would catch their connecting El Al flight.

He was surprisingly weary despite having napped on the plane after dinner was cleared away. And all he could think about was how much farther away he was from Stacy.

"Why don't we grab a Coke to wake us up," Yael suggested.

"I need to get some euros first—but I can't risk using my Visa card."

"There's a cash exchange downstairs on the international arrivals level."

After waiting in line behind half a dozen other travelers with the same idea, David stuffed his euros into his pocket, his fingers accidentally brushing the gemstones. As he did, an odd sensation came over him—as if a snake had slipped down the back of his shirt and was slithering over his shoulder blades. *Someone is watching me.*

The thought came out of nowhere. He straightened and wheeled around.

The man was standing perfectly still in the midst of a moving crowd. Even from a dozen yards' distance, his eyes were fastened on David as if no one else in the terminal existed.

It can't be. It's impossible.

Blood rushed through David's head. He felt off-balance. Teetering back in time. He was a boy again, young, unsure. Staring at someone older, stronger, far more confident. Someone daring him to risk his life. . . .

But it couldn't be. This urbane man with the lionine dark blond hair couldn't be . . .

Overtaken by a surreal confusion, David started toward him until Yael's voice broke through his fog.

"No, David, wrong way. That's the International Arrivals Meeting Place—the self-serve restaurant is the other way."

"It's him, Yael." David's voice was a croak. "My God, it's him!"

CHAPTER THIRTY-SIX

She followed his gaze. "That man with the cane? Who is he?"

Before David could answer, the crowd surged between them and David lost sight of him. When it parted, the man he'd seen was no longer alone. An older man had clapped a hand on his shoulder and the younger spun around to face his father. David recognized Erik Mueller instantly. He looked furious—even as his son gesticulated wildly, the older man didn't appear to be listening.

"Either that's a doppelgänger or it's Crispin Mueller with his father." David shook his head dazedly. "But that's impossible. He was in an irreversible coma."

Yael's eyes went wide. "That's the boy who dropped the gemstone?"

"I'd swear it. How bizarre is this? No one expected him to recover. My father checked on him two years—then four years—after the accident and he'd never left the private facility in Stockholm where his parents took him as soon as he was stable enough to be moved."

"I've learned not to believe in coincidences," Yael said in alarm, pulling him away from the cash exchange and into the moving crowd, toward Terminal 1. "Especially now."

"We have to figure out his connection to the gemstone. And to the Gnoseos," David muttered, glancing back. But he could no longer see Crispin or his father through the constantly shifting sea of travelers.

"I agree. But first we have to get out of here," she said, "before he finds a way to come and renew acquaintances."

Erik Mueller was already punching buttons on his cell phone as they peeled away from the car park.

"Are you certain that was David Shepherd?"

"Oh, that was him all right. If you'd have listened to me in the airport, you could have seen him for yourself. It was the same face I saw alongside Tony Blair's in the *Daily Mail* months ago. He's the same bloody jerk who knocked me off that roof, trying to save his little girlfriend, and stealing four years of my life in the process."

"Eduardo," Erik Mueller spoke rapidly into the phone, "David Shepherd and the woman were just spotted at Heathrow."

Crispin whipped his head toward his father. "Why are you telling DiStefano—?"

"Quiet!" Erik barked, holding up an authoritative palm.

Crispin gritted his teeth. Why did Shepherd's whereabouts matter to DiStefano?

His father's voice was affecting him like metal scraping glass. He burned to go back inside and hunt Shepherd down.

Anger, contempt, and a vile sense of unfinished business soured Crispin's throat. If it weren't for his damned leg . . .

His thoughts raced instead.

Who was that beauty on Shepherd's arm? His little girlfriend all grown up?

"Crispin, it's time you leveled with me." Erik snapped his phone closed as Crispin stamped on the accelerator. "Everything we've worked toward is at stake at this moment and I need to know the truth now. The agate that disappeared from our home nineteen years ago—did you take it?"

Crispin kept his eyes on the road. "My keen mental powers tell me that you asked this very question two weeks after I woke up from the coma."

"Are you telling me your answer is still the same?"

"Of course. But I'm still waiting for you to respond to *my* question. What interest is David Shepherd to DiStefano?"

Erik Mueller turned his head, studying his son. "It seems the stone has resurfaced."

Briefly, Crispin's grip on the steering wheel tightened. He hoped his father hadn't noticed.

"Has it? Then you know I had nothing to do with it."

"I know that the late Senator Shepherd's son is in possession of it."

Crispin's mind roiled. *David Shepherd has the gemstone?* "We're going back," he said, looking for a place to turn. "I'm going to find that son-of-a-bitch."

"No, you are not," Erik contradicted. "This is a matter for the Dark Angels. So let's stick to the subject. Curious, wouldn't you agree, that Shepherd has the stone? Especially since it vanished coincidental to our visit to his home—and to your accident."

So. Shepherd not only stole those four years of my life, but the gem hidden in our family since the twelfth century. And the thief's here. Now.

At that moment, Crispin knew with crystalline clarity that fate had put Shepherd in his path today.

This is not a bad thing, he told himself, struggling to regain his composure. *No, it's a fortuitous one. Shepherd was with me when the stone was lost, and now—just at the culmination of my work—he's going to return it to me. Only he doesn't know it yet.*

Crispin feigned surprise. "Curious? Why is that?"

"Because Shepherd is working with our enemies," Erik retorted angrily. "That's the reason I insisted you meet me today. He brought the agate to our most dangerous adversary, Rabbi ben Moshe, on the very day the Dark Angels assassinated him. Somehow Shepherd managed to escape with it—and with the entire contents of ben Moshe's safe—but not for long. The Dark Angels will find him. Especially now."

"What else did DiStefano have to say?"

"He just shared more details with me from the surveillance tapes in ben Moshe's office. Disturbing news. There's a new threat to the completion of our work. Shepherd's now collaborating with an Israeli ancient texts expert, a woman named Yael HarPaz. And somehow he's compiled a journal of names—names of the Hidden Ones."

Crispin had been changing lanes just as his father dropped that petite grenade in his lap. The implications filled him with such strangled rage, he didn't realize that the car ahead was coming to a stop until he was nearly in its back seat. Slamming on the brakes, he swerved a hard left to the shoulder as his father braced himself on the dashboard with a curse.

I've worked for more than a decade, years of mind-numbing computations to discover the Hidden Ones, and he knows the same names I've sweated blood to produce?

"*How?* Where is he getting the names? How many does he have?"

"Calm down before you kill us both. We don't have his journal yet—but we'll get our hands on it shortly. DiStefano believes he may have *all* of them."

Crispin slammed a fist against the steering wheel. "And just when were you going to tell me this?"

"I've only just found out about the journal. The gemstone is another matter. Have you still nothing to say in that regard?"

I'd say David Shepherd is not going to get away with ruining my life again.

But Crispin kept that thought to himself, refusing to answer despite his father's expectant silence.

"I see." Jaw set, Erik leaned back against his seat. "Well, there's more—DiStefano has also informed me that the existence of the journal necessitates a change in plans. The Dark Angels are no longer under orders to retrieve the journal and then kill Shepherd."

"And why not?" Crispin spat.

"The Circle wants him brought to the Ark alive. Because of the girl. Stacy Lachman. Surely you know the name."

"Of course I know the name. I gave it to the Circle not a week ago."

"Shepherd knows Stacy Lachman's name as well. They're very close—she's his stepdaughter. Even as we speak, Raoul is escorting her here to London."

"And Shepherd will attempt to rescue her." Crispin thought of Abby Lewis, the apple-cheeked girl young David Shepherd had risked his life to save from falling.

"The Circle is certain of it. And when he does, he'll be ours—as will his entire book of names. And once we've relieved David of the rabbi's amber, and the agate is back in our hands," Erik sent him a reproachful glare, "side by side with the emerald and the amethyst we've already moved into the Ark, the balance of power will tip even more strongly in our favor."

Crispin felt like he was struggling against a vast force. Here he was, so close to success, and now David Shepherd—the same bloody David Shepherd who'd sent him flying off that roof—was draining the focus away from his own accomplishments, his own unique power within the Circle.

For years, I've been the one toiling to make ultimate destruction possible. I've been the one The Circle has depended on to lead us to victory. Now, here comes Shepherd to knock my feet out from under me. Again.

Hatred pounded through him. A red haze sizzled in his brain.

"I have to get back to my computer," he said thickly. "I need to finish my work *today*."

"You won't be finishing it in Marylebone. DiStefano wants you to gather your things and shift your base of operations into the Ark. The time is drawing close. The Circle is beginning to move underground."

Finally, Crispin heard something that gave him pleasure. *Shepherd will be taken underground as well.*

"Perhaps I'll have a chance to get reacquainted with my old climbing companion."

"Most certainly. If the Dark Angels don't succeed in bringing him there, his stepdaughter's pleas will."

Full circle, Crispin thought, his spirit abruptly lightening. *After all these years, a reunion.*

CHAPTER THIRTY-SEVEN

Dawn broke with rays of opalescent light splayed across the leaden London sky, but Stacy Lachman never saw it.

Miles beneath the teeming city, she slept curled upon a cot, locked in a dimly lit chamber. The space was small, not much bigger than a pantry. It was devoid not only of windows, but of any furnishings aside from a ladder-backed chair, a tiny wooden bureau, and the cot upon which she lay in drugged slumber.

The room where Raoul LaDouceur had deposited her after a series of flights on a private jet was cold and damp despite the underground heating system carved into the bedrock.

She lay shivering beneath the wool blanket her abductor had flung across her shoulders before he strode from the room and bolted the door. It would be hours before the sedatives wore off. Hours before she remembered what had befallen her, before she awoke in fear and panic.

Her chest wheezed as disturbing images flickered at the periphery of her brain. With each memory, adrenaline screamed at her limp limbs to flee.

But she was so far under she couldn't even wiggle a finger.

A voice deep inside told her to be still. She obeyed, sensing she couldn't have moved an eyelash, even if she'd wanted to.

CHAPTER THIRTY-EIGHT

SCOTLAND, NORTH OF GLASGOW

The wheels of his suitcase clacking behind him, Dillon sprinted up the deep steps of the ancient stone abbey. Cornelius McDougall held open the carved wooden door in welcome. Cornelius was still erect and tall, but in the years since Dillon had last seen him, his red hair had grayed to a buff color and he'd grown a short, trim beard.

"There's a pint of Belhaven with your name on it." He greeted Dillon, taking charge of the suitcase. "We'll quench your thirst and then you can freshen up before dinner. We've a long night ahead of us."

Dillon took in the scent of the abbey, part candlewax, part incense, part damp musk rising off the ancient walls. It reminded him of the first summer he'd spent in the seminary and of his resolve to put aside the world to find God.

He wanted to ask news of the bishop, but that would wait until he and Cornelius had drained their first pint. It was a touchy subject, even between the two of them. Besides, there were the other monks to greet and the abbot who would welcome him to table.

He tried to control his impatience, to put aside his thoughts of the stone, though it had been all he'd thought about as his plane soared across the ocean. And even as he and Cornelius lifted their foggy mugs in a toast, it was the stone he thought of still—the stone he'd come for.

CHAPTER THIRTY-NINE

JERUSALEM, ISRAEL

David was transfixed by his first glimpse of Jerusalem. The sunrise glowing pale rose off the ancient stones was ethereal, otherworldly.

"Now you know why we call her Jerusalem of Gold." At his side, Yael seemed to be drinking in the radiance of the ancient city. Her face was alight, despite the weariness in her eyes. "They say that God sent ten measures of beauty to the earth, and He gave nine of them to Jerusalem."

Staring into the light-drenched holy city from the side of the road, David had no trouble believing it.

A few feet short of the city limits, Yael had asked the driver she'd hired in Tel Aviv to stop his car.

"Come with me, this will only take a minute." She opened the front door and motioned David out.

"Mind if I ask what we're doing?"

"Following a tradition. New visitors to Jerusalem should enter the city on foot." Taking his hand, she led him up the sidewalk and past the sign marking the edge of the city.

Tired as he was, a sudden energizing tingle came over David as he climbed the concrete sidewalk and crossed for the first time into the ancient city sweeping across the hills.

"Now we need to go pick up my father," Yael told the driver as the hired car sidled up alongside them and they climbed back into it.

They'd landed in Tel Aviv shortly before dawn, but David had barely glanced at the modern seaside city before the driver had whisked them away from it. All he'd noticed was that, even so early in the day, the air was hot and dry and he'd been grateful when the man greeted them with chilled bottles of water.

The drive up Highway 1 to Jerusalem had taken them past rocky hillsides studded with church spires, tumbled rock, cypress trees, and the burned-out wrecks of cars and trucks, which, Yael had explained, remained there as a memorial from the 1948 War of Independence. David didn't know what he'd expected to find in Israel, but despite everything he'd endured the past few days and his wrenching worry about Stacy, he was stunned by the astonishing vista before him.

Magically, this tiny country was a hypnotic blend of the ancient and the modern, a seamless combination of thousands-year-old stone architecture and modern high-rises, of Biblical sites juxtaposed with kosher Burger King restaurants, airy cafés, and chic shops.

He tried to take in as much as he could, staring up at King David's ancient tower as they drove through the Jaffa Gate and into the Old City, where Yael's father, Yosef Olinsky, had spent the night at his cousin's home. The professor of antiquities had taken the bus into Jerusalem two days earlier, and holed himself up in the Shrine of the Book—the white-domed building near the Knesset that was home to the Dead Sea Scrolls, other ancient documents, and archaeological artifacts. It was also home to the most recently acquired fragments of Adam's book, which Yosef had wanted to examine firsthand.

"Did your father say whether he's found anything significant in the latest fragments?" David asked, gripping the seat in front of him as the driver dodged pedestrians along David Street.

"Unfortunately, no. But he's reassured that we've done everything right so far. It's like working with a giant jigsaw puzzle," she explained as the driver turned onto the colorful main thoroughfare, the Street of the Chain. "In our work, few of the pieces ever turn up at the same time, or even in the same vicinity. The Antiquities Authority determines the age of the parchment. Then we search for similarities in ink and penmanship in order to match up fragments that come from the same scroll."

Yael winced as the driver slammed on the brakes to avoid hitting a cat darting across the cobblestone road.

Taking a deep breath, she continued. "In this case, my father wanted to examine the original ink on those new parchments. Sometimes subtle differentiations don't show up on the slides we work with in Safed."

David smelled the aroma of spices and cooked meat as they threaded their way through the city and he realized he was famished.

"Now my father is positive that we've correctly linked the latest fragments to the most complete scroll assembled."

"Sorry, I'm not sure what that means."

"It means that we could well find the names we need encoded in these fragments." Yael uncapped her water bottle and took a sip. "In case you haven't written every Lamed Vovnik's name in your journal."

She leaned forward. "Driver, around the next corner. Right . . . there. The red door." She turned to David with a quick apologetic smile. "Brace yourself. You're about to meet my father."

As David followed Yael into the narrow house and up a flight of dark wooden stairs, he thought of his journal with its pages of names. He was suddenly eager for Yosef Olinsky and his colleagues to examine it with their own eyes. If they succeeded in matching up all of his names with those they'd extracted from the scrolls . . .

Would it mean he *had* been given the names of the Lamed Vovniks? And that the Gnoseos were actually in the process of destroying the world?

A teenager ran from an apartment and clattered down the stairs, brushing past them with a smile. For a moment, his heart leapt. For a moment, she looked like Stacy.

Is she still alive? His heart settled back, heavier in his chest. He thought back to Stacy's bat mitzvah, to the ceremony and the rabbi calling her to the Torah as an adult Jewish woman for the first time. He'd used her Hebrew name, *Shoshana*.

So many names in the fabric of Judaism, he realized. *So many names in my head. Too bad I can't pull up at will the ones I need right now.*

Ahead, Yael was entering a small living room, its walls crammed with bright paintings large and small, crooked and straight. Tea was set on a hammered brass tray on the low table, and his eyes lit on the plates of cookies, olives, and sliced melon. Then his attention shifted to Yael throwing her arms around a big sunbrowned man with craggy features and large ears fringed by salt-and-pepper curls.

He had the keen gaze and erect posture of a general and David could picture him on the field as easily as on a dig.

"*Baruch ha ba*, David Shepherd. Welcome." Yosef Olinsky crossed the room with his leathery palm extended, but there was a scowl on his face.

"Please." He motioned toward the low-backed couch strewn with colorful cushions. "Sit for some breakfast before we set out. It's going to be a long and taxing day."

As David filled his small plate, Yael and her father spoke rapid-fire Hebrew to one another. Though he couldn't understand a word, he sensed tension between them.

Minutes later they were joined by a younger version of Yosef, wearing khakis, a loose linen shirt, and sandals.

"David, this is my father's cousin, Eli." Yael leaned in toward the young man with a kiss, then took a seat beside David.

"No olives?" Eli asked him with raised brows.

"I'm more accustomed to fishing them out of martinis."

Yael and both men laughed. "If you've any intention of surviving our desert heat, you'd do well to take up eating them for breakfast," Eli told him.

"In Israel we eat salty foods in the morning to make us thirsty," Yosef lectured. "This way we don't have to remember to drink plenty of water during the day. We just do it." He popped two green olives into his mouth.

"It's easy to become dangerously dehydrated here without realizing it," Yael said.

"So eat plenty of olives," Yosef said curtly. "You're needed in Safed—not in the hospital."

No wonder Yael is strong-willed; she has to be. David piled a handful of olives onto his plate.

They ate quickly and prepared to leave. As David thanked Eli for his hospitality, Yael's father riffled through his rucksack and shoved a small plastic box at David.

"Open it," he ordered, "and put it on."

Yael stepped closer to examine the gift.

David lifted the gold chain from the box and immediately recognized the pendant dangling from it. He'd received a similar one on his bar mitzvah years ago but had no idea where it was now.

"A *chai*." He looked quizically at Yosef, glancing up from the two joined gold letters—*chet* and *yud*—which spell chai, "life" in English.

"Life is the most important thing in Judaism," Yael's father said. "*Everything* is about life. The here and now. The sages taught us that if you save one life, it is as if you've saved the entire world. And if you destroy a life, it is the same as destroying the entire world."

Yosef's deep-set eyes locked with David's. A far deeper green than Yael's, they were somber in the morning light. "Now more than ever, that belief is true. For if the Gnoseos do succeed in snuffing out the lives of the remaining Lamed Vovniks, they end the world. Based upon what Rabbi ben Moshe and my daughter have told us, you can save them, David. But it must be soon." With that, he turned abruptly and headed toward the stairs.

Nothing like a little pressure. David's stomach clenched and the residual tang of olive burned bitter in his throat.

Yael sighed, watching her father's quick departure. She took the chain from David's fingers. "He's like that, don't take it personally."

Deftly, she fastened the chai around David's neck. And then he felt a different kind of pressure—her fingers brushing featherlike against his skin. He tried to concentrate on the heft of the metal as the *chai* settled against his chest.

At that moment a memory flashed into his mind. Something from the recesses of his childhood. He couldn't have been more than seven or eight. Clearly he could see his mother's father handing David his own *chai* to examine.

Life. And death. David felt the burden of both as, in silence, he and Yael hurried after Yosef down the wooden stairs.

The drive north took nearly three hours. The olive trick worked all too well. David was especially thirsty and a pile of water bottles mounted in the backseat.

But his tensions mounted as well as he tried repeatedly to reach Stacy, Meredith, or Hutch—to no avail.

The knot in his stomach began to ache as they trailed a tour bus snaking into Safed. It puttered up Jerusalem Street, which looped around the main hill of the three hills comprising the city. He knew little about Safed, only what Yael and Yosef had told him on the drive, but he'd been surprised to learn that along with Jerusalem, Tiberias, and Hebron, it was one of Israel's four holy cities.

Taking in the panorama of splendid hills rolling south toward the Kinneret—the Sea of Galilee—he marveled at the antiquity of Safed. *Founded in 70 A.D., a year before the Romans built the Coliseum,* David reflected. *A decade before Vesuvius destroyed Pompeii. And more than a century before the Mayans built their first temples.*

That would put its origin at five centuries earlier than the fall of the Roman Empire, he realized.

Yet, according to what Yael had told him, it wasn't until the sixteenth century that the Jewish mystics settled here. Many of them were refugees who'd been expelled from Spain during the Inquisition.

So while Shakespeare wrote Macbeth, Michaelangelo painted the Sistine Chapel, and Henry VIII chopped off Anne Boleyn's head, the mystics of Safed established Israel's highest city as the world center for Kabbalah study.

"Think of it as the Israeli Sedona," Yael had suggested. "Here we have the same kind of juxtaposition—a vital artists' colony, waves of religious seekers, and the pull of unseen mystical forces."

So, based on his visit to the red rocks of Sedona with Hutch years ago, David thought he knew what to expect. The Arizona rock formations were famous for their beauty and their mystical vortices. But as the car circled up the white-rocked city, that rose like graceful tiers on a wedding cake, he felt an entirely new sensation.

Unlike Sedona, earth-toned and grounded in the land and vortices shooting from deep within its core, Safed seemed to draw its aura from the heavens. Even the air seemed to glow with a pure light, resplendent as the heart of a diamond. He leaned toward the open window as they reached the summit, where Yael pointed out Citadel Park.

"That's the site of the Crusaders' first fortress. When they took the city, they drove the Jews from Safed. Later, others, including the Knights Templar, held the city until 1517, when Ottoman rule extended over all of Israel."

In the city's center, Chasidic Jews hurried along the streets, dressed in frocked coats and wide-brimmed hats similar to those worn by their ancestors in nineteenth-century Poland. Tourists in walking shorts, t-shirts, and baseball caps strolled from one art gallery to the next, most of them bypassing the medieval synagogues dotting the cobbled streets between trendy shops and cafés.

"The Gabrieli Kaballah Center is there—just ahead on the left."
Yael pointed toward a curved driveway. At its crest sat a long stone
building with arched windows, rising up behind a decorative fence.
Flowering cacti and other blooms peeked from between the short
metal spikes glinting bronze in the sunlight. With its umber-tiled
roof, the Center might have been a Tuscan restaurant rather than
an international center for mystical study.

As David passed through the gate after Yael and Yosef, his cell
phone rang, startling him.

He stared at the caller ID.

"Thank God! It's Stacy!"

Yael whirled toward him as he answered the call.

"Stace! Are you all right? Is—"

His heart stopped.

CHAPTER FORTY

Elizabeth Wakefield rose from her sumptuously appointed bed and gazed around the rented Bloomsbury flat with a satisfied smile.

The oversized cherrywood sleigh bed she'd dreamed of having since she was a child looked as sumptuous as a strawberry-laden chocolate rum torte in a bakery window, nothing at all like the boring, clean-lined bedroom suite in her home.

Her lover had admired every embellished pillow she'd chosen, every set of 800-count Egyptian sheets, even the cream and gold duvet, telling her that the bed in which they lay together was nearly as beautiful as she was.

Elizabeth knew she wasn't beautiful. Her chin was too pointed, her brown hair too bland, and her only distinguishing characteristics were her delicate long fingers and her dark hazelnut eyes. But *he* thought she was, and in this room she believed him.

He was married, of course. And rich. And powerful. And so was she. They'd met by chance at the Old Vic, both of them waiting for their spouses at The Pit Bar beneath the theater.

There'd been an instant spark between them. Up until that moment she'd never dreamed of having an affair. She was a serious
woman, a senior partner in the law firm her grandfather had founded.
Her marriage was solid and comfortable, her surgeon husband an
easy companion.

So she'd surprised even herself when she'd accepted the debonair
stranger's offer of a drink and, by the time they'd finished it, his invitation to dine with him a week later.

What could it hurt to have dinner with such a fascinating man?
Her husband was lecturing at the university that night anyway.

It was supposed to be only one dinner, but one dinner had
evolved into four years of stolen evenings, scintillating conversation,
and this private retreat, where they shared the sort of electrifying
sexual abandon only secret lovers can ignite.

Somewhere between the long weekend they'd snuck off to Lyon
and their midnight strolls along the beach in San Tropez, when she
was supposed to be attending an intellectual property conference,
she'd fallen in love with him.

How could she not? He was giving, gentle, and brilliant, she
thought, as she lit the slim gold tapers on the bedside table, and
sprayed the bed linens with lavender.

Her heart thrummed when the doorbell buzzed only a few moments later, and she quickly checked her reflection in the mirror,
adjusting the ruby pendant at her throat, smoothing the hem of her
short black sheath. She was smiling as she opened the door, but one
look at his face, and she knew something was amiss.

"What is it? You look sad."

He shook his head. "Not at all. It's only that I've been called away
to Geneva. I'm afraid I can't stay."

Disappointment stabbed through her.

"Come in, tell me." She took his hand and drew him inside, closing the door and leaning against it.

"Elizabeth, please. There's a car waiting downstairs. I only stopped here on my way to the airport to tell you in person." He glanced at his watch, regret creasing his brows. "I'll be gone several weeks."

"Several weeks?" For the first time, a sense of unease came over her. "That long?"

"I'm afraid it's out of my control."

"I see." And she did. He was hiding something. She knew him well enough to know that. "Well, then," she said with a small shrug, "that should give me ample time to prepare my brief for the Penobscot case."

He pulled her into his arms and pressed kisses all across her face. "I'm going to miss you, Elizabeth. Every moment."

"And I, you." She kissed him once more, then searched his eyes. "Safe travels, darling."

He hesitated. "I'll call you."

She knew in that instant he would not.

"Don't keep the driver waiting." She steeled herself against the pain grinding through her chest, and took a step away from the door.

She stood in silence for a moment after the soft click of the door latch, then straightened her shoulders and went home.

CHAPTER FORTY-ONE

Far beneath the city of London, far beneath the underground subway system first built in the 1800s, an intricate labyrinth of tunnels snakes its way through ancient bedrock. Forgotten by most, though once a vibrant part of the subway system, some of the shafts have slept silent and abandoned since the 1930s. Others are sealed off, still others are used today as giant storage bins. Many tunnels were reopened to serve as bomb shelters during World War II, then forgotten once more.

Few Londoners remembered the location of the steep spiral staircases corkscrewing down through the earth to the tunnels. And fewer still knew that beneath the Tower of London, beneath the River Thames, the tunnels' giant ventilation fans had begun to churn anew.

Eduardo DiStefano escorted his wife by the elbow down one of those winding staircases. He knew it was his duty to get her settled, yet he was seething to escape. He needed to find the Serpent. And quickly.

The Circle had gone to great pains to construct the underground chamber where he'd conduct the final stage of his research—but he was nowhere to be seen. The damn computer ought to have been humming like a symphony finding the last of the names, but it had yet to be turned on. No one in the Ark had seen him and Erik still hadn't arrived.

"You will become acclimated to living underground, *bella*. We must hurry—get you settled. The Circle is convening in an hour."

"Just show me the door, *caro*—I don't need your help unpacking, or getting acclimated."

Flora's heels clacked confidently against the metal. In fascination she gazed about at the majestic, yet primitive surroundings. Though Eduardo had been here many times and had told her of it, this was her first glimpse of the Ark.

Her children and grandchildren would be here tonight, arriving from Milan just after dark. How clearly she recalled teaching them the songs when they were children, preparing them to begin their journey toward reunion with their Source. What an adventure lay before them.

She smiled as she reached the first landing, and paused to catch her breath. In the Ark there would be singing every night—for as many nights as it took for all of the Hidden Ones to die so that the souls of the Gnoseos could float free. Free from the constraints of the body, free to ascend to the Source.

She could hardly wait to hear the voices resonate in song, their secret words protected by the density of stone and rock.

Eduardo thought she was nervous about leaving their hilltop villa, but no, there was nothing to fear. This was a glorious moment. All of the Circle would be here soon with their families.

"Just think, Eduardo." Her tone was breathless. "This is what we've aspired to for centuries." The jubilation in her voice echoed off the stones. "Finally—the Hidden Ones are on the verge of extinction. Our liberation is imminent."

The warmth of his hand caressed her shoulder as carefully they traversed the steps. "I couldn't have accomplished so much without you, bella. Your fervor has nearly surpassed mine. You have been my joy."

"There is more to come." She smiled at him, thrilling more with each step that this triumphant day had arrived within her lifetime.

She felt no pang for those she was leaving behind. She had, at the last moment, spoken to her brother—wretched fool—phoning him this morning from the villa. Alfonso had had no idea it was the last time they would ever speak. He wasn't Gnoseos and was of no use—she'd never even entertained the notion of initiating him and his pious Protestant wife into the Order. No one in her large Milanese family knew of her conversion, or of the secret practices she'd adopted soon after she'd married Eduardo.

They all assumed she'd become an atheist. Nothing could be further from the truth. She knew God existed, but she didn't love or worship him. She knew the truth now—He had created a world of illusion and evil. The real world was spiritual and that was the realm her husband and the Circle had opened to her.

The ancient practices Eduardo had gradually revealed to her had stirred something deep inside her, broken it loose and given it permission to grow.

Every week as she and Eduardo sipped the drug-laced liqueur that enhanced their spiritual state while they meditated, she found herself more deeply connected to the Source of her soul.

And more eager to challenge the Source's cruel subordinate deity—the demiurge—whom their people believed created all flesh and matter, ensnaring the souls that yearned to float free. Eduardo had freed her from the obsequiousness of conventional religion. Now, along with the elite of her sect, she was only hours away from liberating her inner spirit from this deceptive, oppressive, and evil world.

Ironic, she thought, as she reached the bottom of the staircase, that the Ascension would take place so deep underground.

She surveyed the mammoth reception area, knowing that neither stone, nor bedrock, nor steel could entomb their souls once the world was cracked in two.

God destroyed his world the first time with the Flood. Now it was the Gnoseos' turn.

Chapter Forty-two

"Sorry," the male voice taunted in David's ear. "Your little girl can't come to the phone right now."

He felt the blood draining from his face. "Who is this? Where's my daughter?"

"You know who this is, David," the man mocked. "You have something that belongs to me. And I have something that belongs to you."

David did know then. He didn't know how, but in the same way that the names had always come to him, this one did, too.

Crispin Mueller.

"What do you want, Mueller?"

He heard a savage laugh. The line beeped once and went dead.

"What's going on?" Yael gripped his arm as David stared open-mouthed at the phone.

"Mueller has Stacy," he croaked. "And I don't know where. The bastard hung up on me."

Furiously, he entered Stacy's phone number. His body felt like a block of ice as a busy signal bleated into his ear.

There was no doubt now. Crispin was a Gnoseos.

And Stacy . . . Stacy is a Lamed Vovnik. Just like the others in my journal.

He was numb. Numb with shock and the realization that Yael and her father were right. The Gnoseos were destroying the world.

What if they'd killed Stacy already? Panic pounded in his chest.

No. Crispin will keep her alive—until he gets the gemstone. Until I bring it to him.

Yael seemed to read his mind.

"He's playing with you," she said quickly. "He won't hurt her, David, not until he gets what he wants. But you can't—"

"Give the stone back to him? Why can't I?" Rage surged through him now. He grabbed the gold chai at his neck, his fist clenching around it so tightly the metal pierced his palm.

"Isn't life the most important thing? Isn't that what your father told me? Well, a child's life is most important of all."

"But the entire world, David?" Yosef asked, his hands spreading in an encompassing gesture. His face was ashen, but his tone was stern. "Is one child's life more important than that?"

"She's a Lamed Vovnik." David wheeled toward him. "If I save her life—just *her* life—I'll save the world. Isn't that what you said?"

His hands shook as he opened his phone again. "We saw Mueller in London. I'm going there tonight on the first flight I can catch. You can keep my journal," he told Yael. He grabbed it from inside his duffel and shoved it at her, ignoring the pain etched across her face. "Go ahead—study it, tear it apart. Do whatever the hell you want with it. You don't need me for that."

He waved his phone in the air. "How do I reach El Al? Tell me the number."

"David, come inside." Yosef spoke in a measured tone. "We'll make the reservation for you, but you need to think this through. Things are coming to a head. And quickly."

Staring from father to daughter, David couldn't believe the two of them didn't understand the bond that was driving him.

A million ugly visions collided in his head.

What happened to Hutch? To Meredith? Are they both dead?

Unable to deal with the nightmarish images, he pushed past Yael and her father, shouldering his way inside the Center.

A blast of cool air struck him as he bounded into the wide, sunlit foyer tiled in almond-flecked linoleum. Suddenly an old whisper seemed to echo in his ears.

The mountain only seems *insurmountable.*

David froze.

Hutch's voice, calm and encouraging at the base of Granite Mountain. *You climb it the same way you eat a T-bone, buddy—slice off one piece at a time, and never more than you can chew in one bite.*

A strange, forced calmness flowed over him, the same kind of forced calm he'd faked during his first few climbs with Hutch. Faked until the fear tearing up his gut was replaced by confidence. Taking deep breaths the way Hutch had taught him, he tried to let the simple clarity drown out his rage.

From the periphery of his hearing, he caught the sound of Yael's voice. She was calling the airline.

And Crispin Mueller is calling the shots.

David slipped the two gemstones from his pocket and studied them, ignoring Yosef as the older man brushed past him to speak to several men who'd come into the hall from nearby rooms.

The agate and the amber felt heavier in his palm now—and the light dancing off the cabachons hurt his eyes. He closed his fist around their brilliance, and thrust them back in his pocket.

I followed Crispin's lead once. Acted on impulse. I don't have to do it his way again.

This time, David thought, *I'll trust my own footing. And take care where I step.*

"What do you mean, all flights are grounded?" David stifled the impulse to grab the phone from Yael's hand.

"You don't believe me? You're welcome to try to convince El Al to fly during a security alert. Frankly, I doubt you will be successful."

David took a deep breath. *Rein it in,* he told himself.

"What kind of security alert?" he asked.

"Iran might be preparing to launch a nuclear attack." Her voice was tinged with fear. "Let's get to the television."

They hurried toward the Center's staff lounge, a room lined with long tables covered with paper linens, red chairs flanking them. It looked like any school lunchroom, but for the large screen television mounted on the back wall. They joined Yosef, watching the screen intently along with a dozen or so grim-faced, silent Israelis.

"They're blaming the United States and Israel for last week's tanker explosion at the port of Deyyer," a small-boned woman whose eyeglasses dangled from a chain around her neck told Yael.

David stiffened. The announcer was reporting that casualties now numbered three hundred. Had it been just days ago that he'd watched the television footage at the airport on the way to New York? He felt as if an eon had passed since he'd left D.C.

"And for this accident," a rotund leather-faced Israeli grumbled, "millions of innocent people should die? We need a miracle," he added fervently, under his breath.

"Rabbi, this is the man who might be able to provide that miracle." Ten heads swiveled from the television toward Yosef Olinsky. Ten pairs of eyes watched him put a hand on David's shoulder. "This is David Shepherd, Rabbi Cardoza. He has come to Safed with his journal and with two precious stones from the breastplate of our *Cohen Gadol.*"

As a collective gasp went around the room, Yael watched the tension twitch a muscle along David's jaw. She knew he felt trapped. She knew he felt helpless to save his child.

"Work with us, David," she implored quietly, as the rabbi came toward them extending a hand. "Right now, it's the only way you can help Stacy. As soon as the airport reopens, I promise you, you're free to leave. But for now, we need not only your journal. We need *you*. There may be other knowledge hidden within your brain. This is the city—the one city—where you need to be. For Stacy's sake— for the remaining Lamed Vovniks. For the world."

What choice do I have? David thought. Despair compounded his sense of helplessness, but he knew she was right.

He looked straight at the leather-faced rabbi, a man not much older than he, and grasped his outstretched palm. "Where do we start?" he asked tersely.

As they passed through the immense computer laboratory on the top level, Rabbi Cardoza gave David a short introduction to the Gabrieli Kabballah Center.

"This is where we study the papyri fragments that have been validated by the Antiquities Authority," he said, breathing hard from the climb up. "After the archaeologists uncover them, the Antiquities Authority in Jerusalem authenticates and dates them—then we scan digital copies into the computers to search them for hidden messages from *HaShem*."

"David is a secular Jew, Rabbi," Yael interrupted. "He may not be aware of the many names of God—such as HaShem—or of their power."

More names? Why am I not surprised? David thought. "And how many are there?" he asked aloud.

"Seventy-two," she answered without missing a beat. "*HaShem*, *Adonai*, *Elohim* are some of the more common ones. The *Shekhinah* is the name of God's feminine presence in the world. The mystics meditate upon each Holy Name, one at a time, picturing each in its Hebrew form."

Rabbi Cardoza smiled approvingly at Yael. "You've learned a great deal in your time here, I see."

He turned to David. "As mystics, we also believe that the entire Torah—with all the spaces between the words deleted—spells another of God's names."

"Unpronounceable, I assume?" David muttered.

The rabbi cocked an eyebrow at him, but refrained from answering. They passed through a large glass door to enter the library. Flanked by an expanse of arched windows, skullcapped men sat poring over photocopies of parchment sections spread like floating continents across long oak study tables. Others studied stacks of computer printouts on tables piled with books.

This is where they matched the names in my journal to the names they've already found in their fragments, David realized.

"You'll meet Binyomin and Rafi later," Rabbi Cardoza said, waving him forward to a secluded study nook. "But first we start in here. You saw the many books on our shelves. But there is only one I would very much like to examine right now."

Cardoza pulled a chair from a round table stacked with several piles of printouts and a dozen freshly sharpened pencils. "May I see your journal, David?"

David glanced toward Yael, and she handed the journal over.

Pulling his glasses from a breast pocket, Rabbi Cardoza lowered himself heavily into a chair. "Sit, everyone. Make yourselves comfortable. We have much to discuss and very little time."

Page by page, he thumbed through the journal, quickly comparing it against a printout he pulled from the top of the stack. *What is he looking for?* David wondered, chafing with impatience.

Minutes went by, and still the rabbi bent over the journal, immersed in the names. By the time he finally snapped the book closed and peeled his glasses from his face, David felt ready to bolt. But Cardoza's next words kept him pinned in his seat.

"This journal may be even more significant than Rabbi ben Moshe thought."

Startled, Yosef leaned forward, his brows darting together. Yael didn't move, but drew in one surprised breath.

"How?" David demanded. "Have you found the missing names?"

"No, we'll need to feed the entire contents of your journal into the computer for that. However, on first glance I see something curious about the way the names have come to you, Professor—"

"David. Please."

"David, then. On all of the duplicate fragments we've uncovered, the names are always listed in the same order. Yours are not. So, why are those in your journal written in a *different* order than those hidden in Adam's Book of Names? Perhaps," he held the book aloft, "your journal holds the key to a breakthrough we desperately need."

"You think there might be an encoded message in David's book," Yael whispered excitedly. Cardoza rested his hands across his stomach and nodded.

"I believe the names came to David in *this* order for a reason. They were revealed to him en masse during his mystical vision for a specific purpose—to give him the names of the Lamed Vovniks so they could be saved. But I believe the *order* in which he was told these names contains another message. A message David has not yet accessed."

All eyes turned toward David. He felt the pressure on his shoulders grow heavier.

"How do I access it, Rabbi? Since time is so short, maybe you can give me a hint, put me in a trance, something."

"If only it were as easy as that." Cardoza sighed. "You're not a mathematician, neither am I. But mathematics is exactly what has led to the decoding of our sacred Torah—the Five Books of Moses: Genesis, Exodus, Leviticus, Numbers, and Deuteronomy. Here at the Gabrieli Kabbalah Center, we apply the same kinds of computer programs Israeli scientists use to search the Torah. Except here, we are using them to extract the names of the Lamed Vovniks written in code within Adam's Book of Names."

David nodded, remembering Rabbi ben Moshe's description of the book passed down from Adam through his sons, through countless generations, until it was lost. . . .

Rabbi Cardoza continued. "For even though Adam wrote the names of all creatures, the names of the Lamed Vovniks were buried within the text so their identities would be concealed—"

"But I've written only the names of the Lamed Vovniks. Are you saying there might be something else buried among them?" David's knuckles whitened on the arms of his chair.

"That's what we're going to find out." The rabbi scooped up the journal and went to the doorway. "Binyomin," he called softly to one of the skullcapped men, who rose at once to hurry over, his shiny bald forehead a gleaming contrast to his black yarmulke.

"Binyomin, make a copy of Professor Shepherd's journal and begin searching it. You'll notice that his names are written in a different order than we found on the papyri—try to unravel the reason. I know I don't need to remind you of the urgency."

The man took the book in his short pudgy fingers and sped off without comment.

"How does he search for a hidden message?" David was mystified. He couldn't imagine how the decoding program might work.

"It's a complicated process, but I'll try to explain in the quickest and simplest way I can." Cardoza returned to the table, adjusted the yarmulke on his head, shifting it forward. He cleared his throat and met David's gaze squarely.

"First off, you must understand that there is nothing ordinary about the Hebrew *alef-bet*. On the contrary, each letter is imbued with its own mystical powers."

"Like the gemstones." David leaned forward, suddenly wanting desperately to believe that all of these supposed powers would come together to make a difference. That his journal had another chapter, that the mystics in this city would help him find it.

"Exactly like the gemstones." Rabbi Cordoza's eyes bored into his. "Speaking of which, I'll take them from you now."

CHAPTER FORTY-THREE

SCOTTISH COUNTRYSIDE

"A spot more tea, my son?"

Bishop Ellsworth's veiny hand trembled as he poured Ceylon tea into Dillon McGrath's china cup. Dillon couldn't help but note how frail the old bishop had become as he lived out his retirement years.

"I regret so that I can't invite you to stay to supper, especially after you've come such a long way to see me, but unfortunately, my flight to London leaves in less than three hours. . . ."

The bishop shrugged apologetically, looking at Dillon with kindly gray eyes. "I truly detest having to rush you off. We have so much to catch up on."

"No apology necessary, your Excellency. *I* regret having come unannounced at such an inconvenient time." Dillon took a sip of the milk-laced tea, feeling regret for nothing whatsoever. He reached for a lemon tart on the plate the bishop's housekeeper had set on the low table between them before she'd bid the bishop a good holiday and gone home to her family.

There were just the two of them now in the quaint cottage. It looked small and humble, resting there in the long shadows of the crumbling stone castle that had once been a summer hunting lodge for the Crown.

Yet Dillon noticed that the china was Spode, that the tablecloth was the finest Irish linen money could buy, and that the bishop was dressed more for a night at the opera than an autumn holiday in the south of France. Even the curtains were of handmade lace and the octagonal clock ticking on the wall was solid gold, adorned with obsidian hands and numerals.

Still, with all the treasures embellishing the simple cottage, it was the ring upon Bishop Ellsworth's right index finger that commanded his attention, though he dared not let the old man see it.

The ruby shone like a drop of blood in its hammered gold setting. It was exactly as he remembered seeing it years ago at the conference in Rome when he had no inkling of the meaning of the inscription carved in its smooth face. Cabochon, just like the stone David had told him about. Like the eleven others described in the reference book.

Dillon swallowed the last crumbs of the tart and licked his lips. It was all he could do not to stare at the bishop's ring as the older man began clearing away the plates.

"Here, let me help you." Dillon rose and lifted the heavy silver tray. Following his host to the sink, he set the tea service down upon the counter, as the bishop murmured a thank you over his shoulder. But instead of turning back to retrieve the leftover tarts, Dillon seized the heavy, footed teapot and bashed the bishop across the back of the head. It connected with a sickening thwack.

The bony old cleric pitched forward, cracking his nose against the faucet before slumping to the floor.

Dillon felt only disdain as he knelt quickly beside the bishop, grabbing for his right hand. Mouth set, he tugged at the ring lodged on the old man's scrawny finger.

It stuck there, refusing to budge over the gnarled knuckle. Dillon leapt up to find the dish soap and squirted the liquid over the bishop's digit. With a single yank, the ring popped free like a cork exploding from a bottle of champagne.

Dillon spared one precious second to study the fabled gem before sliding the ruby cabochon onto his own finger. *Reuven.* He could read the Hebrew name clearly now.

"It appears you're going to miss your flight, your Excellency." He stepped over the inert body on the polished floor and scooped up the envelope the bishop had left propped atop his packed case. There was a Lufthansa insignia in the corner. Dillon flipped through it, smiled, and slipped the envelope inside his own breast pocket.

"I hope you remembered to buy travel insurance, your Excellency."

A moment later, he swung a leg over the borrowed moped and zoomed onto the tree-canopied country road that would lead him back to the abbey. His bags were already packed and waiting for him.

His own flight departed in less than three hours.

CHAPTER FORTY-FOUR

Rabbi Cardoza waited expectantly as David took his time digging out the stones from his pants pocket.

Now that the moment to relinquish them had come, David was reluctant, even though he knew this was where they belonged. Still, the agate had been in his possession for nearly two decades now. It felt odd to part with it.

He inhaled as he placed them in Cardoza's beefy palm.

The rabbi gazed down at the gems as if he'd been given the most precious gift in the world.

"Where will you put them?" David asked.

The rabbi looked up, gratitude and hope shining in his eyes. "Someplace very safe. They'll join the others we've recovered from the breastplate of the high priest. We must pray that, together again, their combined power can make a difference in this battle."

Cardoza slipped the gemstones into a small pouch he withdrew from the pocket of his long-sleeved white shirt. He replaced it, then straightened his skullcap once more, frowning as David's cell phone shrilled.

David snatched it from his pocket, his heart lurching.

"David . . . oh, David . . ."

It was Meredith. Speaking so tremulously he had to strain to hear her. As David listened, the tightness in his chest made him dizzy.

"What hospital are you in?" he managed when she fell silent. "Okay, try to calm down. I'll call you as soon as I know anything. I'll get her back, Meredith. I promise you, I'll get her back."

He closed the phone in a daze. *Hutch was dead. Meredith was badly injured. And Stacy . . .*

Slowly, he became aware that everyone in the room was staring at him.

"David?" Yael had gone pale.

"He had one blue eye, one brown." His voice was raw.

"Who, David?" Yael stood up, moved toward him. "Who are you talking about?"

He closed his eyes, seeing something no one else could—his Stacy in the hands of a monster.

"The murderer who took Stacy."

An hour later, Rabbi Cardoza regarded him with a mixture of compassion and urgency. "I know your thoughts are elsewhere, but we need to act while we still can. Are you ready to learn the power of letters and numbers?"

There doesn't seem to be much else I can do at the moment, David thought, still numb. *All flights throughout the Middle East are still grounded so I can't get to London, can't track down Crispin Mueller, can't tear him apart with my bare hands.*

"I'm listening."

"Good." The rabbi leaned forward in his chair, motioning David to take the seat beside him. "We use letters and numbers here to solve mysteries every day. Do you remember your Hebrew alef-bet?

Twenty-two letters—five of which are written differently when they end a word," he added.

David nodded. "That much has stuck with me from my bar mitzvah classes. Though not much more I'm afraid."

"What you probably didn't learn," the rabbi said, "is that every Hebrew letter has its own mystical power, a unique energy or vibration. Each letter also has a corresponding numerical value."

Handing David a chart of the Hebrew alphabet, he began scrawling its initial letters on a sheet of blank computer paper—*alef, bet, gimmel, daled, hey*—numbering them in sequence as he wrote.

"Hebrew numerology is called *gematria*. Here, the first ten letters line up with the numbers one through ten. So, *alef* equals one, *bet* equals two, and so on."

"And after ten?" David peered at the chart.

It was Yael who answered. "You count by tens. Later, by hundreds. Julius Caesar used a similar technique while he was building the Roman Empire in Gaul. He used substitution codes to send secret messages."

David raked his hand through his hair. "I hope there's not going to be a test."

"No test. We haven't the time to teach you more than the most rudimentary examples," Cardoza assured him.

Suddenly, David seized the chart of the alef-bet, studying it more closely.

"The letter *lamed* equals the number thirty," he said slowly. "And *vov* is six." He glanced up, as a flame of understanding sparked within him. "*Lamed Vov*. Thirty-six. The righteous ones—that's why they're called the Lamed Vovniks."

"Exactly." Yael came around the table to peer over his shoulder. "That's precisely how the mystics apply gematria. Kabbalists also believe that there is a mystical interconnection between words in the Torah which contain the same numerical value. And that studying these connected words can reveal hidden meanings not apparent on the surface."

"Hidden meanings?"

"Deeper meanings," she clarified, pushing a strand of hair behind her ears. "There are layers of knowledge in the Torah, some on the surface, and others so deeply hidden that centuries of mystics still haven't uncovered them."

"Jews aren't the only ones who employ gematria," Yosef told him. "The Arabs do as well. And the Sufis—they use it to explore depths of meaning in the Koran."

"Some say even your Founding Fathers used gematria in writing your nation's slogan, *e pluribus unum*—one out of many—" the rabbi said. "*Echad*, the Hebrew word for 'one,' has a numerical value of thirteen. The United States—*one* country, uniting the *thirteen* original colonies."

"That's amazing," David gave his head a shake. "My father was a U.S. senator. He would have loved to know that."

A soft knock at the door interrupted them.

"Yes, Rafi, come in," the rabbi called to the tall, gaunt man hesitating in the doorway.

"An e-mail just came through from Avi Raz. The only Percy Gaspard we've found died in a suspicious fire six months ago."

David and Yael glanced at each other. Another Lamed Vovnik murdered. Rabbi Cardoza cleared his throat, looking grave.

"Thank you, Rafi."

As the man returned to his work, Cardoza checked his watch. "We must move on," he said heavily. "Let's get to the Torah codes."

As David refocused his attention, the rabbi plunged ahead.

"Torah codes are nothing new. Theories about such hidden messages have circulated for thousands of years. As early as 1291, Rabbeinu Bechaye wrote about them in his commentary on the Book of Genesis. And in the sixteenth century, the mystic R. Moshe Cordovero bolstered the theory, claiming that every single letter of the Torah is filled with divine meanings."

"Even Sir Isaac Newton believed there were hidden messages in the Bible," Yael interrupted to tell David. "But as brilliant as he was, he was never able to prove it."

"Because he was born too soon," Yosef chuckled dryly. "He needed a computer to find his proof."

Cardoza twisted the cap off a bottle of water and took a deep swig. "It's true, David. And here's why no one found the hidden messages until the twentieth century—the codes are too subtle to be manually detected."

"Enter ELS," Yosef said.

David frowned. *ELS?*. "And that is? . . ."

"Equidistant letter sequences—or skips." The rabbi leaned back in his chair. "It's how the computer detects secret words and phrases concealed in the Torah and other texts. They pop out of the manuscript because the letters forming the hidden words fall at equidistant intervals from one another."

David's brows furrowed. "Run that by me a little slower."

"Let's say you pick a starting point anywhere in the Torah." Rabbi Cardoza was a patient teacher, David granted him that.

"From that letter you program the computer to skip ahead or backwards 'x' number of letters—for argument's sake, let's say ten. So the computer skips to the tenth letter, the twentieth, thirtieth, and so on, producing a printout comprised of every tenth letter."

To David's relief, he was beginning to see the pattern. "Once you have the printout, you comb through the results looking for words or phrases amidst the gibberish?"

"Right." Yosef's deep-set eyes reflected a glint of approval. "With the aid of a computer, you can run an ELS skip every possible way—forward, backward, diagonally, horizontally, and vertically. You can change both the length of the skip and the direction of the search from any starting point you choose. I'm sure you can see that such a search is nearly impossible using pen and paper, even if you work at it for years."

"But a computer can do it in a flash," David said, nodding. "So when you searched the papyri fragments from Adam's Book of Names, what skip did you use to find the Lamed Vovniks?"

A gleam showed in the rabbi's eyes. Yosef smiled, but it was Yael who answered him, her voice rich and throaty in the silence of the library.

"Thirty-six. The ELS skip that revealed the names of the Lamed Vovniks was thirty-six letters."

For a moment David didn't speak. He allowed the sheer simplicity of what he'd just learned to settle over him. Suddenly he felt very small as the concept of infinite knowledge—the vastness of God's brilliance and design in all things, throughout all of time—struck him like a firebolt. Although Adam named all of God's creatures and recorded them in a book written by his own hand, God yet concealed a secret within its text. The names of all the truly righteous souls.

David's head was aching from trying to puzzle it out.

"God knows everything," the rabbi said softly. "So He always knew—even from the beginning, even while Adam was writing his book—the identities of the Lamed Vovniks in every generation."

David pushed himself from his chair and began to pace around the room, the others falling silent watching him.

"We have free will—like Adam did," Cardoza continued. "God didn't force his hand as he wrote, and yet it's all there in Adam's book."

"The names of every Lamed Vovnik from the beginning of time . . ." David exhaled. "Concealed within Adam's list of every living creature." He'd been facing the glass doors, staring off in the direction of the men working at the tables, but abruptly spun around.

"If God knew the names of the Lamed Vovniks, He also knew the names of the Gnoseos and the other enemies of God."

"*Amelek.*" Yael's eyes widened. "In every generation, they rise up against the Jewish people, and against God."

"Amelek?" David shook his head. He'd never heard the term.

"The tribe that followed the Israelites as they wandered through the desert afer escaping from Egypt," Rabbi Cardoza explained. "They attacked the Israelites from the rear, killing thousands. The book of Exodus recounts the battle, relating how when Moses lifted his arms to God the Israelites beat back Amelek, but when he tired and his arms fell, Amelek gained. Then Aaron and Xur rushed to Moses' aid. One on either side of him, they held his arms up, and the Israelites defeated Amelek."

Yosef let out a weary sigh. "Although Israel ultimately decimated Amelek, our rabbis insist we always remember them. You see, David, Amelek rises again in every generation to destroy the Jews. It has done so, many times. Haman, Herod, Hitler, and even now—"

In every generation. The words had stopped David cold.

"What's the gematria of Amelek?" he blurted out.

"Two hundred forty," Rabbi Cardoza answered. "Why?"

David rushed to the doorway and scanned the library. "Where's Binyomin? I need my journal back."

The rabbi stared at him in surprise, then without a word, lumbered past him in search of the Kabbalist. Yael turned to David. "Why do you need it back? What are you thinking?"

"Have you searched the parchments of Adam's Book with a 240 skip for the names of the Gnoseos?"

"Not that I know of—" Yael broke off. "Let's try it. You could be right."

When Rabbi Cardoza and Binyomin returned with his journal, David quickly explained his theory.

"I think we should search both the parchments and my journal with an ELS skip of 240. Maybe we can uncover the identities of the Gnoseos and attack *them* from the rear before they can carry out their plan."

Rabbi Cardoza's eyes glittered with hope.

"Binyomin, quickly. Distribute copies of David's journal to the entire search team. Have them run a 240 ELS skip on both the journal and the parchment fragments concurrently."

He sank back in his chair and rubbed a hand over his eyes. "While we're waiting, I'd like you both to tell me everything you learned from Rabbi ben Moshe, *alav ha'shalom* — of blessed memory."

David dug out the rabbi's leather satchel from deep within his duffel and placed it on the table between them.

"My journal is only part of this mystery, Rabbi. Yael and I have been trying to figure out the connection between ben Moshe, this tarot card," he placed the tower card on the table, "and a Jewish printer in Krakow who was recently murdered for the printing plates."

David reached into the duffel again. "And this card we took from a Dark Angel who tried to kill us in New York," he said grimly. "It's identical to the rabbi's except they have different numbers written on the back."

David spread all of the items on the table and tried not to think about where Stacy was right now — and what Crispin Mueller might do to her.

Chapter Forty-five

It was no problem for Geoffrey Bales or either of the two other Dark Angels to obtain security clearance. Their credentials were impeccable. Lord Hallister had vouched for them and secured the proper documents, and why wouldn't he? Aiding a Dark Angel in eliminating one of the final Hidden Ones was an honor that would serve Lord Hallister well once the Gnoseos ascended from the Ark. He would be one of the heroes—along with us—Bales thought as he donned the dark green porter's uniform in the privacy of his rented flat.

The pants hung a bit long, but they'd have to do. There was no time for tailoring. Tonight, Lionell would hide the last of the weapons inside the wall of the men's loo at the pier. No one would suspect that an arsenal had been stored in a tidy hole behind the large metal paper towel dispenser. No one would suspect that three of the porters on duty as the *Queen Mary 2* sailed into safe harbor would be vying for the privilege of taking out a singular passenger as he disembarked.

Bales had a good feeling about this final assignment. He sauntered to the mirror where he'd taped Cherle's glossy color photograph to the dusty glass. He took his time, memorizing every crease and wrinkle on the man's smiling face.

He smirked back, knowing, somehow, that he'd be the one to put a bullet in Cherle's throat long before the old man ever got his land legs back.

The Ark

Crispin sniffed, waiting across from the cot where Stacy had begun to stir. The small underground chamber smelled stale and vaguely medicinal. He didn't like the odor, it reminded him too much of his years entombed in blackness—of the hospital where he'd spent the lost years of his youth. In a way it was fitting that this child who was so dear to David Shepherd was the one now lying semi-conscious on that cot.

What goes around comes around. And now it was coming back to Shepherd.

Ironic, Crispin thought, that David Shepherd's precious "daughter" looked to be about the same age as that Abby creature was back then. Her coloring was different, but both had that budding ripeness of a girl teetering on womanhood. The same wavy shoulder-length hair, full innocent mouth, and a gawky sort of promise.

An idea sprang into his mind and his pulse quickened. *Perhaps the ultimate punishment I could mete out to David Shepherd wouldn't be her death, but the knowledge that I'm bringing her with me to the new world—another vessel to be used, along with the other chosen females. . . .*

Crispin started. What was he thinking? She wasn't Abby. She was one of the Hidden Ones. She *had* to die, in order that the Gnoseos would live—and rise up to find the ultimate Source.

So be it. Shepherd the Noble would be tortured enough by his helplessness to save her—and the world.

Faint cries leaked through the walls. The women again. The unwilling vessels. It amused him that they thought someone might pay them any heed. They'd be taken from their pen soon enough. And he, as the Serpent, would get first choice as to which vessel would be his conduit for repopulating the world. He laughed aloud, a guttural sound rolling from deep within his chest.

The girl's eyes flew open.

Stacy winced at the pain in her head. It felt like her brains were receiving jolts of electricity, delivered out of sync with the rhythm of her heart. Everything looked gray for a moment, until she blinked several times and finally focused on a low rough ceiling overhead.

Move. Try. Sit up.

She managed to raise her head from the pillow, but fell back onto the cot as waves of nausea assaulted her.

Laughter. Laughter reached her ears. The same laughter she'd heard in her dream. Painfully, fighting the spinning room, she turned her head toward the source of the sound.

The man staring at her reminded her of a lion she'd seen at the Wild Animal Park in San Diego. Long tawny hair tumbled over his eyes and his smile was ferocious. She scrunched closer to the wall, wanting to get as far away from him as possible, only to hear him laugh again.

He rose from the chair and advanced toward her.

"What's so special about you? I've read that the Hidden Ones are not afflicted with the normal human shell around their souls. Nothing separates them from the Divine."

Stacy jammed her back into the wall, recoiling from the eyes boring into hers. "What . . . are you . . . talking about?"

He straightened, his mouth tight. "That's right. You don't know, do you? None of you do. Why am I wasting my time?"

He turned away from her. Went to the door. Soon it wouldn't matter.

"Your stepfather is coming for you, Stacy," he said from the door. "Yes, good news, isn't it? But for me, not you. Because I'm going to kill him once I take back what he stole from me."

Crispin raised his hands palms out, reassuringly. "Don't worry. I won't kill him right away. First I'm going to let him watch while I kill you."

CHAPTER FORTY-SIX

David awoke to the sound of his cell phone ringing, bolting upright in the armchair. *When had he dozed off?* As his eyes focused, he realized he'd been wakened by the whir of a printer spitting out the latest run of an ELS skip on his journal. His cell phone sat silent as a rock, charging on the table in front of him.

Why hadn't Crispin called back?

This waiting was impossible. Maddening. David felt superfluous. He had nothing more to give, no matter what any of them believed was still locked inside him. No more names had come to him, he was spent. Cardoza and the others had toiled through the night trying to decode his journal. But he knew nothing of computer printouts and nothing of meditation or sacred prayers. There was nothing more for him to do here. And Stacy needed him.

London was the last place he'd seen Crispin Mueller. It was the only place he could think of to start.

The Iranians had finally backed off, the security alert lifted, and the airport reopened some time around 4 A.M. His flight left at two this afternoon.

Stretching his tense muscles, David wove his way to the door and peered out at those working painstakingly in the next room. He saw Yael peering over her father's shoulder, her hair caught loosely in a clip atop her head. The long night's toll was etched in the drawn contours of her face, yet she still exuded the same tough grace he'd picked up on the moment she strode into Rabbi ben Moshe's office.

She lifted her head at that moment, as if sensing his glance, and offered him a wan smile.

"You look like you could use some fresh air," she told David.

"Take David to see what may be his only sunrise in Safed," Yosef said grimly. "It is truly spectacular and might be the last for all of us."

David walked silently beside her as they descended the stairs. A small buffet of fruit, cheese, olives, and juices had been set up in the staff lounge. While David poured coffee in insulated cups, Yael scooped up an orange and a paring knife. Glancing out at the waning cloak of night, they took their meager picnic outside, Yosef's words clamoring somberly in their ears.

"Can you carry both cups while we walk?" Yael asked. "There's some place I'd like to take you."

They walked the cobbled streets in silence as the grayness slowly gave way to pale opal light and the city of Safed quivered with the breath of a new day.

"Who knows how much time is left," she murmured as they turned a corner and headed down a narrow lane. "Days, hours. And yet . . ."

"I know. We can't just give up, can we?"

"My husband didn't." She fed David a section of peeled orange. "Yoni had a dream before he was sent into Lebanon. He dreamed of peace. A peace that would come long after he died."

She stopped at the entrance to a cemetery lined with graves, some flush with the grass, others raised and arranged in neat rows between paths studded with fig trees. David saw that each of the raised plots was framed by an attractive border of brick and cement and planted with abundant greenery.

"He's buried here in the military cemetery. He was only twenty-eight when he died." She turned to David, her eyes brimming with exhaustion and loss.

"I'm sorry," David said quietly.

Yael slipped the paring knife into the pocket of her khakis and stooped to gather up several pebbles, dropping them in her empty coffee cup.

Without thinking, David reached for her hand. Her fingers felt warm and strong, as full of life as she was. "I'm sorry about your husband—and about losing my temper yesterday. You didn't deserve that."

"*Lo davar*—forget it. I'm a Sabra, remember? We native Israelis are like the cactus we're named after—tough and prickly on the outside, mushy soft within. Don't tell anyone."

"Mushy soft. Is that so?" David asked, with a wry smile, surprised that she could forgive so easily. Another time, another place he might have kissed her. Instead he released her hand, and followed as she made her way down the narrow paths of the graveyard.

They walked on for a little ways until Yael stopped at the head-stone inscribed *Yonaton HarPaz*. "His soul is still here, you know," she said, her gaze fixed on the grassy outline of the grave. "The Kabbalists believe that the *nefesh*, the lowest of the three dimensions that make up the soul, remains to hover over the grave when someone is buried. Rabbi Cardoza told me the nefesh stays behind to protect the living in times of difficulty, while the two higher dimensions of the soul—the *ruach* and the *neshamah*—move on to higher realms."

"This definitely qualifies as a time of difficulty," David acknowledged. "How are they able to help?"

"The rabbi has told me that when the living come to the cemetery and ask the departed for their help, the nefesh flits up to the realm of the ruach and informs the ruach of the trouble below. The ruach in turn hurries up to the realm of the neshamah—closest to God—and the neshamah intervenes, asking God to have mercy on the world."

"That's why we're here, isn't it? To ask Yoni's nefesh to remind God we're in trouble. To ask for help." David stared down at the graceful ferns upon Yoni's grave, trying to take in the concept of both a hierarchy and a unity in one's soul. He'd always been taught that every person had a direct line to God, that no intermediaries were necessary. One could attend synagogue services and recite the ancient prayers, or one could go anywhere and compose personal prayers from the heart. All would be acceptable to God.

That was the teaching of traditional Judaism. These mystical beliefs of the Kabbalists were still foreign to him. Yet, remembering his own near-death experience and everything he'd learned in these pressure-packed few days, the idea that Yael could ask her husband's soul to intercede in the heavenly realm made as much sense as did the spirits of the Lamed Vovniks begging him to intercede on their behalf in the physical realm.

He watched her stoop to place the pebbles on Yoni's grave, adding them to others already there. David knew the reason, he'd done it himself when he'd visited his parents' graves. Yael was leaving behind a token of her visit.

He touched her shoulder and moved off, deciding to give her some privacy. He meandered off until he found himself at a concrete staircase leading downhill. He followed it down and came upon another cemetery nestled below. It was older, less orderly, but equally peaceful, with visitors praying at various tombs painted sky blue and piled with rocks.

It was only as he began reading some of the names carved on the tombstones that he realized this was the ancient burial place of famous Kabbalists.

A powerful sense of history enveloped him as he wandered through the sunlit cemetery and out again. He wandered the nearby lanes, walking uphill again. Before he realized it, he found himself in an alleyway where a blue sign with white letters pointed toward the Abuhav Synagogue.

David crossed the little outer courtyard of umber stones shaded by trees, and ducked inside the ancient *shul*.

Its interior was vast and empty. He craned his neck to peer, four stories up, at the vaulted domed ceiling rimmed with square windows. They spilled daylight onto the stone floor, studded with mosaics. The sunlight hurt his eyes and he winced, aware that his head was beginning to throb.

He shifted his gaze to the walls, painted a soothing celestial blue. Above them, myriad chandeliers dangled, and graceful archways bordered with lacelike painted ferns stretched toward the frescos that adorned the dome.

"Splendid, isn't it?"

He didn't startle at Yael's voice behind him.

"Very. And impressive," he replied without turning.

"You don't know it by half." She came forward and stood beside him, taking in the peaceful beauty of the place.

"This synagogue is bursting with Kabbalistic symbolism. The dome is not only architecturally stunning, it symbolizes Judaism's belief in one God. And those four pillars," she turned and gestured to the supporting columns, "represent the four elements of creation—air, water, fire, and earth—as well as the four worlds of Kabbalah—physical, emotional, intellectual, and spiritual."

David circled the interior, touching a hand to one of the columns and to the blue-painted railings wrapped around the *bimah*—the raised platform from which the Torah scrolls are read after they've been brought out of the ark.

"Did you notice the six steps up to the bimah?" she asked, watching him move toward the blue-framed platform. "They symbolize the six days of the week, while the bimah—higher than the steps—signifies the seventh day, the holiest day, the Sabbath."

David's headache was getting worse. In silence, he walked over to examine the painting of Jerusalem's Western Wall. It was nestled among three arks—the tall wooden cabinets containing the Torah scrolls. To his surprise, no matter where he stopped before the painting it appeared that the street at its bottom pointed straight toward him, as if he stood directly on its path.

"There's more." Yael smiled and gestured toward each of the arks in turn. "There are three by design—one for each of the patriarchs, Abraham, Isaac, and Jacob. And the arches—" Her arm moved in a graceful sweep above her head. "Nine of them, one for each month of pregnancy."

David felt surrounded by meaning, by an ancient symbolism that filled him with wonder. Every aspect of this majestic house of prayer had been imbued with mystical design. He'd always considered himself an educated man, but he was educated in the structure of governments, political processes, institutions, and behavior. He could talk knowledgeably about political theory, comparative government, and international relations. But Rabbi ben Moshe, Yael, and the Kabbalists in Safed had opened up a world he had never fathomed.

His great-grandfather, according to what his mother had told him, had been attuned to that world. For David, this was new terrain. *But perhaps,* he thought, letting the spiritual symbology flow over him, *there was more of his great-grandfather in him than he'd ever suspected.*

Standing in the synagogue, thinking of Stacy, of the Dark Angels and Crispin Mueller, and the dwindling presence of Lamed Vovniks in the world, David prayed this was true.

His head was now pounding. He closed his eyes to block the pain and tried to summon the names in his journal. *The Kabbalists had found thirty-four Lamed Vovniks from this generation among the thousands of names listed in his journal. But they were still missing two. Had he already written them? Or were they still inside him, hidden?*

Did the Gnoseos know those names? Why couldn't he—

Lightning-hot pain blinded him. He sank to his knees with a groan, pressing the heels of his hands into his eyes.

"David! Are you all right?"

Yael's voice came to him from far away, as if she was outside the synagogue, in the alley. He was alone beneath the domed ceiling with its frescos of harps and palm trees and biblical scenes. Alone in this holy place as pain eviscerated his skull.

He tried to stand. He had to get back to the Center, find some pain pills. He had a flight to catch soon. But another burst of pain knocked his legs out from under him.

He went down, sprawled on the stone slabs of the synagogue floor, writhing. Nothing existed but the pain.

And the faces . . . The voices . . . They were back—screaming, begging, demanding.

David tried to listen to them, but the agony crescendoed as if to shatter his skull. They were trying to reach him, he had to hear—

"David! Can you hear me?"

Yael was bent over him, but he didn't see her. He was staring at the ceiling, unblinking, his face contorted in anguish.

Perspiration poured down his temples and neck, rimming his shirt collar.

Frightened, Yael touched a cool hand to his brow, her own heart thudding. She was torn between running for help and staying with him. His skin was so clammy. Suddenly, in his unfocused eyes, she saw something change. An expression of peace replaced the torment and the muscles in his face relaxed. As she unfastened the top button of his shirt his body went slack.

David closed his eyes in exhaustion. "Jack Cherle," he muttered, his voice thick as wool. "Guillermo Torres." Yael caught her breath.

David's voice trailed off at the name haunting him most. "Stacy Lachman . . ."

He struggled to a sitting position, feeling empty and dazed. His headache was gone, as if it never existed. His mind was suddenly clear.

There were no more names in his head.

"We need to . . . get back. I have to tell them . . . the names."

She helped him to his feet. Unsteady, he leaned heavily on her and she slipped an arm around his waist.

"Are you sure you don't want to wait a moment? You're still aw-fully pale."

"Have to . . . hurry," David rasped, lurching toward the door.

He had the names. The final names. But he couldn't shake the feeling that there was something more. Something he was still missing.

Maybe when I get back, and speak to the mystics, he thought, blinking as he tried to get his legs to move toward the doorway, *they might know how to jog—*

Yael's head whipped sideways as they stumbled outside into the brightness of the courtyard. She heard the scruff of feet against stone as David sagged against her. She had to get him over to the bench.

"We need help here—" she started to call out.

And then she saw them enter from the alley.

Two of them. A man and a woman. *Tourists,* she thought with re-lief, glimpsing their polo shirts and walking shorts. "Please, can you help me get him over to that bench—"

They sprinted toward her but her relief died as she saw that the tall, sinewy man carried a length of raised pipe, and the woman, built like a Bulgarian discus thrower, gripped a knotted rope taut between two bricklike fists.

Yael glanced desperately toward the empty synagogue. *Too far, they'd never get the door bolted in time.*

"David, they've found us!"

David tottered as she released him and spun to face the Dark An-gels. He swayed forward, still weak, bracing himself against the sun-baked stone wall. With frantic determination, he willed his body to regroup, to obey the commands of his brain.

Adrenaline pumped through his blood, screaming at him to fight, but his muscles felt like wax. He saw Yael spring at the woman, who outweighed her by at least fifty pounds. Before he could take a step, the male was on him, swinging the pipe at his knees.

Pain ricocheted down his shins. He slammed to the ground with a scream. Through a fog of pain he saw Yael to his right, landing a kick to the woman's stomach, knocking her off-balance.

The hatchet-faced Dark Angel raised his ropey arm again. He swung the pipe at David's rib cage, but David managed to roll sideways along the pavers as the blow connected. Fire shot through his hip.

He heard a woman scream. *Yael!*

Panic gave him strength and, as the Dark Angel grabbed him by the collar to yank him upright, David jammed his fist into the hollow beneath the man's sternum. Hatchet-face exhaled all the fetid air in his lungs, bathing David in a stench like boiled liver. Before his enemy could suck new breath, David socked him again, driving his fist as high up under the man's rib cage as he could manage.

David saw Yael on the ground, one arm twisted beneath her body. The huge woman straddled her, pressing down on the rope stretched taut across Yael's throat. Her face was gray and fear catapulted David toward them.

But before he could get that far, he felt a three-hundred-pound weight slam into his back. He went down like a sandbag, Hatchet-face on top of him, both of them swinging and punching like crazed hockey players. Fists slammed against bone, elbows jabbed into nerve endings, and spit and blood flew across the courtyard.

Through the agony that seemed to envelop his entire body, David suddenly realized that though his torso was being pummelled without mercy, the goon was sparing his face and head.

Neither one of them has pulled a gun, David thought suddenly, deflecting a blow to his chest. Then he understood why.

They want me alive, they want the names. . . .

He didn't see the fist until it plowed into his stomach. Before he could roll, before he could breathe again, the pipe connected with his elbow. Endless pain sparked crimson lights behind his eyes. Gritting his teeth, struggling for air, he braced against the agonizing spasms and lurched sideways for better position as his enemy hurtled to his feet.

Hatchet-face was coming at him again, the pipe clenched to strike, but in one desperate motion David jacknifed his knees toward his chest and then kicked out with everything he had.

He connected with the Dark Angel's Solar Plexus. The man doubled over, dropping the pipe with a clatter as his hands dove reflexively to his ribs.

Instantly, David sprang toward the weapon, throwing himself over it even as he watched Yael's face turn purple. Her eyes bulged, she was using her knees, desperate to fight off the Herculean female strangling her.

Before he could move, he saw Yael wrench her twisted arm free. The sun flashed silver off her bracelet as she drove her clenched fist toward her attacker. Only at the last instant did he see it wasn't her bracelet glinting after all, it was the paring knife she'd been struggling to pull out from under her. As David watched, frozen, Yael thrust it with all of her strength into the side of the woman's neck.

Blood spurted out like sewage from a burst pipe. As the woman gurgled out a scream, Yael plunged the blade in again, piercing the hollow of her throat.

David seized the pipe. He fought to ignore the pain consuming him as he pushed himself to his feet. Sweat dripping in his eyes, he wheeled to confront the sinewy Dark Angel who was panting like an animal, preparing to come at him again.

"Yael, run! Get out of here," he shouted, but she didn't. Instead, she darted several feet to the side, brandishing the knife, her face set. With blood spattered across her cheeks and clothes, she looked feral.

The Dark Angel's gaze shifted quickly, back and forth, between the two of them—the lithe woman with the bloody knife and the man who waited to turn his own weapon against him.

With a roar he charged Yael, and David's stomach dropped. *He's going to use her as a shield.*

As the Dark Angel barreled toward her and David dove forward, Yael seemed frozen.

I won't get there in time, David realized in despair, but then he saw the steel in Yael's eyes.

She waited until the last possible instant, then dropped to a crouch and drove the knife straight into the Dark Angel's crotch.

His screams echoed in the courtyard until David ended them, slamming the pipe against his skull.

CHAPTER FORTY-SEVEN

The air in the Gabrieli Kabbalah Center had changed. It was infused with urgency—a frantic electricity that hummed through the entire second floor as Rabbi Cardoza and his staff searched the world from their computer banks, searching for Jack Cherle and Guillermo Torres.

No one knew where Stacy was, but in just a few hours David was going to do his damnedest to find out.

The Mossad was searching full out for the three Lamed Vovniks as well, thanks to a single phone call from Avi Raz. Rabbi Cardoza's quick update to Avi an hour ago was all it had taken. Within fifteen minutes, Avi had slashed through weeks of red tape and paperwork to launch the largest manhunt in the Israeli intelligence agency's history.

David winced as he bent over yet another computer printout of a 240 ELS skip analysis of his journal. So far, nothing of the Gnoseos was concealed in the text. Only gibberish.

Bruised and bloodied, David had refused all but the most rudimentary first aid. There was no time to bother with scrapes after he and Yael had limped back to the Center to summon the police. He'd merely slapped a bandage on the worst of the cuts and grappled with what he needed to do next.

David grimaced as he caught sight of Yael peering into the monitor across the table. A long welt burned angry across her neck where the rope had dug, bruising her larynx so badly it was painful for her to talk.

She'd very nearly died. They both had.

And Jack Cherle, Guillermo Torres, and Stacy would die, too, unless . . .

Unless Mossad found them. Or Interpol, or the CIA—or any of the other international agencies Mossad was contacting for help.

This ELS business is leading nowhere, David thought in frustration. He checked his watch, impatience mounting inside his chest, almost as painful as his battered ribcage and swollen fingers. Less than an hour before a car arrived to take him to Tel Aviv. Before he could get on his way to tracking Stacy.

He was finished here. He'd done what he'd come to do. Yael and Yosef had been right—Safed *had* released the final names trapped inside his head. But now there was nothing left for him to accomplish in this mystical city. And staying here might bring more danger, more Dark Angels, right to the door of the Kabbalists.

Yet something still nagged at him. He couldn't dismiss the feeling of something missed or forgotten. But what? Maybe there *was* something more he had to do here. Something Rabbi Cardoza put his finger on. The names in his journal. Why had they come to him in that specific order? Was it random, or was there a pattern he couldn't yet see?

If it was a hidden message, the gematria of the word "Amelek" had failed to reveal it. *What if I need to apply a different ELS to the journal . . . a different word . . . like "Gnoseos?"*

Standing up quickly, he sought out Binyomin and asked him the gematria of the word Gnoseos. "Try a skip based on that," David urged him.

As the computer pages were spit out, his discouragement deepened. Nothing new was materializing within these lines of text, only the same kind of gobbledygook "Amelek" had produced.

David groaned as he lifted his duffel—lighter now, because the rabbi's satchel and its contents were gone. Everything, including the gemstones.

At the thought of the agate he'd brought to Rabbi ben Moshe, he hesitated.

Crispin's taunt replayed itself in his mind.

You have something of mine. And I have something of yours.

Crispin wanted him to believe he'd trade the gemstone for Stacy. David knew it was a trick, but without the agate in hand, how could he call Crispin's bluff?

He saw Yael glance up from her monitor. Her gaze rested on him a moment, then she came around the table. To say good-bye, he thought.

"Is it time to leave already?" Her usually rich voice was painfully raspy and strange.

"The car should be here any minute. I've exhausted my usefulness here."

The searching look she sent him gave him pause.

"Don't be so sure. I want to run an idea by you—about the tarot cards. Remember the notebook Rabbi ben Moshe gave us?" She touched her throat as she spoke, as if to lessen the pain. "He wrote about the Gnoseos' insistence on secret passwords and talismans. They went to enough trouble to kill the printer for the plates. The cards must be extremely secret—and extremely important."

David set his duffel on the chair beside him. "All the Gnoseos we've come across have them," he agreed. "Hold on—maybe it's a Gnoseos identification card. Sort of like a driver's license—"

"Or." Yael bit her lower lip. "A passport," she said slowly.

A *passport.*

"A passport to where? For what? They want to destroy this world," David countered, "not travel it."

"True." Her green eyes squinted in thought. "But what if they're all gathering someplace to celebrate the end of the world . . . all the Gnoseos together? . . ."

David's pulse quickened. "And how better to prove they belong there—that they're invited to the victory party—than to produce a secret passport?"

"Exactly." Yael's eyes flashed. "Passport, invitation. Whatever. They'd need tangible proof. A ticket in."

"Handy then that I have Gillis's."

She raised her chin and held his gaze. "I'll need one, too. I'm going with you."

"*No, Yael.*"

"My flight is booked. My seat is right behind yours. I'm not letting you search for Stacy alone." She lowered her voice. The softness accentuated its strained quality. He could barely catch the words. "Wait here. I'll get Rabbi ben Moshe's tarot card. I saw where Rabbi Cardoza put it."

David touched her arm as she turned toward the doorway.

"I need the gemstone, too, Yael. I need the agate."

For a long moment she looked at him and he could read the uncertainty, the conflict, in her face. Without saying a word, she hurried from the library.

Yael was going with him to London. David found himself surprisingly heartened. And if they were right about the purpose of the tarot cards, they'd have two passports to Gnoseosville—wherever that might be. Maybe the cards would get them to Stacy. Or to someone who knew where Crispin had her.

He pulled the mysterious card from his wallet and studied it again, trying to decipher its symbolism. People jumping from the shattered turret of the tower.

Suicide? No. Destruction, death, chaos, the tarot reader had said.

And rebirth. His gaze narrowed on the lightning slashing through the sky behind the tower—there'd been plenty of electrical wrath from Mother Nature lately.

And the drawbridge, the one that reminded him of the Tower Bridge in London.

London. Where he'd just crossed paths with Crispin . . . where he was headed to find Stacy. . . .

Yael crossed the room toward him, her leather tote swinging at her hip. "I brought them both," she murmured without flicking an eyelash. "They were exactly where I remembered."

Suddenly David felt a needlelike tingle run up his spine. His ears buzzed as if the conversation in the library was magnified.

It was exactly where I remembered. Remembered . . .

"Zakhor." He grabbed Yael's wrist. "Remember."

She tilted her head, regarding him quizzically. "What else do I need to remember?" she asked, clearly puzzled.

"Not you. Me. They told *me* to remember. They kept shouting at me to remember . . . zakhor. Maybe that's what I'm supposed to re-member now. The word zakhor."

Yael's eyes went wide. She rushed to the nearest table and scrib-bled numbers on a slip of paper. "Here's the gematria of zakhor—"

233. David yanked out his journal and opened it to the first page, the first name.

"D," he told Yael. With his finger he counted off a skip of 233 let-ters. "The next one is I," he told her.

Counting furiously, he proceeded to give her a U, then an A, his mind and fingers flying at breakneck speed. Could this really be it? The key to the puzzle in his journal?

Yael scribbled the letters as he rattled them off: S, T, E, F, A, N, O, E, D, U, A, R, D, O . . .

Yael gasped. "Oh, my God, David . . . it spells DiStefano Eduardo—Eduardo DiStefano. The prime minister of Italy!"

"Rabbi Cardoza!" David shouted across the library. The rabbi wheeled toward him, startled by the excitement in David's voice. He hurried over, his leathery face worried.

"Run an ELS skip of zakhor through my entire journal, Rabbi. I think we'll find the names of the Gnoseos. Yael and I just pulled out the first one encoded there. There have to be more."

"What name, David?"

His voice shook. "Eduardo DiStefano, the prime minister of Italy."

Cardoza's jaw dropped. He was stunned, but only for an instant. "Binyomin, quickly!" he called over his shoulder.

When David phoned the Center from the car, as he and Yael sped to Tel Aviv's Ben Gurion airport, Rabbi Cardoza read him the list the computer was spitting out.

When David heard him say "Mueller, Crispin" he felt as if someone had just thrown an electric switch while his finger was in the socket. *This was it. The Gnoseos. A list of their names, written as a subtext within his journal.*

Not only had he been given the names of the Lamed Vovniks, but also the names of their enemies. Through the phone he heard Rabbi Cardoza read off another name. "Wanamaker . . ."

A buzzing filled his ears. *Judd?* That's how the Dark Angels found us at the tarot reader's shop—Judd called them the minute we left the restaurant . . .

"David, did you hear me? I said I've just called Avi." Rabbi Cardoza's voice intruded on the clamor in his brain. "He's put all the agencies on alert. Interpol says DiStefano arrived in London yesterday."

"Get MI6 involved," David told him. "My hunch is that they'll find all of the Gnoseos descending on London."

David's cell rang again as he and Yael stood in Ben Gurion Airport waiting for a shuttle to ferry them across the tarmac to their plane.

"The little girl isn't sleeping well, I'm afraid. She keeps crying out for you to come save her."

"You son-of-a-bitch." Red rage swirled before David's eyes. He didn't care that several heads had turned toward him. "Where is she?"

"She's with me, of course. Not far from where we last set eyes on each other."

"London." David met Yael's eyes.

"You get an A, Professor." Crispin's voice mocked him.

"And you get an F for effort. Your two Dark Angels are flat on a slab in the coroner's office."

Crispin laughed. "You flatter me, my friend. You think I sent them? No, it's others who give the Dark Angels their orders. This matter is between you and —"

"Let me talk to her, Mueller. Prove she's still alive."

"Don't you trust me?" the other man taunted, his glee so transparent David was overwhelmed with the desire to throttle him.

"I want to hear her voice."

"And so you shall. After you follow one more instruction. Then you can hear the sweet tones of your precious Stacy. And if you manage to follow directions correctly, and return what is mine — who knows? I just might spare her."

"Where do I find you?" David bit out.

"Let's not get ahead of ourselves," Mueller chided. "There is another matter that interests me. I hear you've written a book."

"Several."

"You know the one I mean. I hope for your daughter's sake you have it with you. I'd like to read it."

David's words stung like ice. "Where . . . do . . . I . . . find . . . you?"

"Get yourself to Trinity Square Memorial Gardens. Then give the little girl a ring."

Click.

David's gut burned so fiercely he could barely breathe.

He waited until they'd been cleared to board before he quietly briefed Yael.

"I'm supposed to call him from Trinity Square Memorial Gardens. Ever been there?"

She looked back at him as they made their way toward the plane. "A long time ago. It's near the Tower of London. A memorial to Britain's merchant seamen and navy who served in both World Wars—the ones who have no grave but the sea."

She waited until the flight attendant had squeezed past them to assist an elderly passenger before continuing. "I walked through it on my very first trip to London. There's a sunken garden and . . ." She broke off.

"What, Yael? What else?"

"Crispin Mueller has a sense of irony. There's a wall, David. A wall full of names."

Chapter Forty-eight

The Ark

Crispin's muscles were locked in fury as DiStefano ripped into him. His father stood near the door of the computer alcove, looking as if he wouldn't lift a finger if DiStefano were to charge at his only son with a machete.

"Your business here is to do one thing and only one thing, my dear Serpent." DiStefano's words dripped like acid. "You're to find the last Hidden One, not waste precious minutes slithering around the one who's here. We could have already dispensed with her had you focused on finding the last name. Jack Cherle will be dead this afternoon once his pleasure ship docks at Southampton. We are so damned close," he spat, "and yet you dawdle."

Crispin opened his mouth to retort, but DiStefano cut him off before he could utter a syllable.

"Sit back down at that computer and find the last damned name."

Crispin flushed the color of new wine. As his hand clenched

tighter around his cane he imagined how it would feel to thwack it across DiStefano's face. More than once.

"You heard the Head of the Circle." His father's voice was tight and wooden. Erik Mueller jerked the door open, his eyes shuttered as he looked back at his son. "Take your seat and finish the job you were assigned."

The door slammed behind him.

"The Lamed Vovniks *are* my damned assignment," Crispin bit out, limping in fury toward DiStefano. "After all I've done I have more right than anyone to see what's so special about these so-called righteous ones."

"Dealings with the Hidden Ones are the exclusive duties of the Dark Angels." The gray hair at DiStefano's temples was darkened with sweat. "If you can't find the final name, we'll have to pry it from David Shepherd's journal. Is that how you want to be remembered? As the Serpent who choked in the final moments? Who failed to deliver at the brink of victory? Or as the one man who single-handedly uncloaked each of the thirty-six hidden ones?"

Crispin slammed his cane against the floor. "Get out so I can work."

DiStefano's eyes held his for an endless moment.

"Don't think to leave this room until you have the name."

A vein in Crispin's neck throbbed as DiStefano left him alone.

Who in bloody hell does he think he is, confining me to this room like a child? It's my work that has taken us this far in a single generation. When has anyone else ever identified even half as many Hidden Ones? The world is disintegrating because of what I've achieved. And because of my contribution, the end is inevitable.

Leaning his cane against the file drawers, Crispin called up his calculation log. It didn't matter that he wouldn't be going to the surface anymore. He didn't need to. His plan was already in place. He could accomplish everything he yearned for down here in the Ark.

When Shepherd reached Trinity Square Memorial Gardens and dialed up his precious little girl's phone, it would be Raoul who scrutinized the caller ID. Raoul who would be lying in wait with Enrique at the seafarers' memorial—mere steps away, hidden behind the curved garden wall.

They didn't know their orders had come from him and not DiStefano. It had taken no more than a few knowing keystrokes to hack in to DiStefano's secure server and send the Dark Angels the text-mail instructions. Momentarily, Raoul and Enrique would bring Shepherd, his journal, and the gemstone down into the Ark.

Soon it would be time for a much anticipated—and very private—reunion.

Once Shepherd gets here, the game is mine. He'll be trapped. Helpless to save his daughter. Helpless to save the world. Or himself. Then I'll publicly reveal the final name, and the Circle—everyone in the Ark—will cheer me for bringing about our triumph.

He gazed at the calculation log where the final name was highlighted in red.

If his father and DiStefano had treated him with the deference he deserved, he would have handed them the name on the spot. Now they could squirm and worry. And they'd welcome David Shepherd when the Dark Angels delivered him, thinking they still needed him.

But it was Crispin who needed Shepherd—who needed the satisfaction of closure, final closure. Before the Ascension, he needed to see Shepherd suffer. As he had suffered, locked in the darkness all those years.

With a few keystrokes, he once more logged into DiStefano's server and typed an official order that would set the end in motion.

The thirty-sixth name—and the command to find him.

Guillermo Torres.

CHAPTER FORTY-NINE

Dillon stared at his reflection in the mirror above the sinks in the congested restroom. He looked like hell, and without doubt that was where he was going. And there was a good chance he'd be there sooner rather than later.

He was very conscious of the snug fit of the gemstone ring as he washed his hands. Was it his imagination, or was it really as heavy as it felt?

There was no time now for guilt or second thoughts, he told himself as he checked his watch. He had a connection to make within the hour.

But as he started toward the door, a man barreled through it, obviously frantic to answer the call of nature. He crashed into Dillon, his briefcase and umbrella sent flying as his suitcase slammed against Dillon's hip.

Wincing, Dillon stooped to retrieve the man's umbrella as the sweating, broad-shouldered stranger began to scoop up the scattered contents of his briefcase from the tile floor.

Dillon froze as he spotted a Tower card seconds before the man shoved it back into his briefcase along with a passport wallet and grooming kit.

"Here you go, my friend," Dillon said with a smile, handing over the umbrella.

"My fault, sorry, eh? In a bit of a hurry." The man with the thick German accent was already striding urgently toward the urinals.

Dillon leaned against the wall outside the restroom. When the German bustled out a minute later, he fell into step with him.

"It seems we have something in common." He flashed the colorful tarot card he pulled from his breast pocket, identical to the one in the German's briefcase.

The other man's deep-set eyes lit with recognition. His jowly cheeks relaxed into a smile. "Exciting times we're living in, eh?"

"To say the least." Dillon shortened his stride to keep even with his new acquaintance.

"Since we're both going to the same place, why don't we share a cab?" Dillon offered. He pushed open the door and stepped out into the faint gray drizzle misting the London streets.

"I was thinking exactly the same thing."

A porter lifted a hand to summon them a waiting cab from the queue, then thumped the German's bulky green suitcase into the boot. Dillon's new friend leaned forward and told the driver their destination as Dillon slammed the cab door.

"Tower Hill. Drop us at The Monument."

He couldn't stop thinking about her as he wandered the lower tunnels. *Elizabeth.*

Perhaps it was the dankness down here, the smell of the earth and bedrock, the endless trickle of water dripping grooves into the rock wall behind the rear staircase.

Or was it the faint cries of the women he could hear as he skirted their holding area?

He thought of Anne Boleyn, locked in the Tower of London, which rose so famously on the surface high above the Ark. She had been a prisoner, too.

As he neared the rear staircase, he suddenly turned, drawn toward the chasm hidden deep within the shadows. He picked his way down a darkened tunnel to the underground well. Running his hand along the moisture-slicked guardrail rimming it, he felt an odd thrill. Even he had no idea how deep it dropped.

No matter, he reminded himself. He wasn't going down. He and the others were going up. To a new world high above, finally unfettered and reunited with their spiritual Source.

It was what he'd wanted and worked for as far back as he remembered. What his ancestors had striven for without success.

He ought to be overjoyed that this miracle was happening during his lifetime. He thought of his wife, meticulously storing their scant belongings in the room they'd been assigned on the upper level. And felt nothing.

Perhaps if Elizabeth were down here with him . . .

Never once had he questioned his faith. The search for inner knowing, for ascension, was something he'd been raised with, something he'd yearned for since his youth.

But now that it was imminent and he was about to leave the physical world, he found himself strangely reluctant to leave everything he knew. And he knew he loved Elizabeth.

She was more real to him than this subterranean Ark, more real than all the plans and plots and murders it had taken to reach this day. Gazing into the blackness of the chasm, he could see once more the uncertainty Elizabeth had tried to mask when he told her he was going away.

It was too late to change things. Reaching into his pocket, he palmed the small silver charm Elizabeth had taken from her bracelet one morning at dawn. A champagne-glass charm her older sister had given her on her twenty-first birthday. Elizabeth had said she wanted him to have it because he'd taught her how to drink in life. He'd kept it with the loose change in his pocket, the jingling sound a constant reminder of their love.

Opening his hand, he stared at the miniature champagne glass. It was of this world, the evil physical realm, he reminded himself. There would be no place for champagne in the next world. And there would be no place for Elizabeth.

With a sharp snap of his wrist, he hurled the charm into the gaping blackness and listened for it to be swallowed up. He never heard it touch bottom.

CHAPTER FIFTY

MEXICO CITY

Guillermo Torres paced up and down the surgical wing of the maternity floor, his breath coming faster as each moment passed.

He'd been waiting for this day for nine long months, praying for a healthy baby. Now his prayers were about to be answered, and his heart was overflowing with anticipation and joy.

Rosa had miscarried twice before, but thanks to the Virgin Mother the bleeding this time had stopped during the second month and their baby was now full term. Today he would hold his child in his arms.

He paused for a moment and sent up a fervent prayer for the doctors performing the C-section, for his wife's swift healing, and above all, for a healthy child to finally bless their home.

Tears pricked his eyes and he wiped them away with the back of his sleeve. He was only twenty-two, the baby of the family, and his brothers had always teased him for being sentimental. He laughed at them instead of being insulted. He was glad he felt so deeply about everything and couldn't understand why more people didn't feel touched by life the way he did.

Guillermo peered up at the clock above the nurse's station. *When?* It had been thirty-five minutes since he'd kissed Rosa good-bye as they wheeled her into the operating room. When would they come get him to put on his gown, allow him to stand beside his wife as the miracle happened?

When would his mother get here to see her new grandchild? Half the family was on their way from Toluca.

Downstairs, two doctors carrying clipboards strolled through the emergency room of Nuevo Hospital Juarez and stepped into the elevator.

They didn't exchange any words as the car lifted them toward the third floor. They didn't need to. Stepping off the elevator, they walked through the maze of polished, antiseptic hallways with the ease of men who belonged there.

But neither of them had ever sworn an oath to save lives.

5,900 MILES AWAY
BARCELONA, SPAIN

Guillermo Torres owned the stage. As he crooned "What A Wonderful World," he could feel the warmth of the audience caress him like a generous lover. They were with him, this tapas bar crowd, and they applauded long and hard as he finished the first set.

He glanced over at Armando, the owner of the bar, who kept promising him a nightime gig. If today didn't convince his boss that he could keep an audience riveted to their seats, drinking and applauding all night long, nothing could.

Guillermo loved singing almost as much as he loved teaching. Music was his passion. The language of his soul. And it gave him almost as much pleasure to impart its complex lushness to his students, as it did to bring an appreciative audience to its feet.

As the applause at last faded, he slid onto a barstool. As usual, a shot of Pernod and a small plate of vinegary *boquerones*, a chunk of *Cabrales* cheese, and a glass filled with olives were waiting for him. Claudia knew his tastes.

But as he tossed an olive in his mouth, it was a slim mustachioed bartender who came from the kitchen balancing serving plates of garlic mushrooms, fried cheese, and cumin chicken.

Guillermo had never seen him before in his life. "Where's Claudia? She was here earlier."

"Sick." The man shrugged his slim shoulders. "Female problems." He nodded toward Guillermo's empty shot glass.

"Another?"

Why not? Guillermo thought, pushing the glass across the bar.

A woman from the audience sauntered over just then, sliding a hand along his arm, standing a little too close as she told him in a breathy voice how much she enjoyed his singing. He never saw the bartender refill his glass, nor did he see him flick a droplet of liquid from a tiny silver flask that was swiftly repocketed.

He only knew that the tapas were good, the Pernod was excellent and the woman smiling so invitingly into his eyes wore a low-cut red dress and an intoxicating perfume.

Guillermo drank deeply. Life was good.

ATLANTA, GEORGIA
4,600 MILES AWAY

Guillermo Torres lived for baseball. He'd come up from the farm clubs in Puerto Rico, slugged his way out of the bush leagues and into the majors, and now was closing in on 3,000 hits.

But he was not at his best today. He was still sore from sliding into home yesterday and slamming his hip hard against the plate. Good thing this was only a charity exhibition game against local policemen, raising money for victims of domestic abuse.

Guillermo sat on the boards of a half dozen national charities, but this cause meant the most to him because he'd spent his childhood helplessly watching his own mother being beaten by his stepfather. Now his mother was perched proudly just behind the dugout with his wife and two children as the police officers ran out onto the field.

He didn't notice the overweight fan in the Braves jersey who ambled in with his cardboard tray of beer and pizza and squeezed into an empty seat four rows behind his family. Guillermo waved to the cheering crowd as he ran out onto the field.

When the fatal shot rang out near the end of the first inning, everyone thought it was the crack of Guillermo's bat.

LONDON

David stared through the rain at the man exiting the cab in front of the Tower Monument. It looked like . . . it couldn't be . . .

Dillon.

"Driver, stop. Let us out here," he ordered, hurriedly fishing euros from his pocket.

"Trinity Square is over there, what are you doing?" Yael asked.

But David was already lunging onto the wet pavement, his gaze locked on the two men approaching the Tower Monument.

Yael had jumped out beside him. As the cab whisked away, she touched his sleeve.

"Do you know them?"

"One of them." His jaw was tight. "My best friend, Dillon McGrath. The priest who sent me to Rabbi ben Moshe."

The friend who couldn't find my passport. Who couldn't find Eva either. The same night I sent him to my house, she turned up dead. The police are looking for me—but he never explained why he had to leave the country.

"What the hell is Dillon doing in London?" he muttered.

"Who's the other man—do you know him?"

"Not yet." David started across the street. Dillon and his companion were already walking briskly down King William Street toward London Bridge. The shorter man popped a black umbrella against the misting rain. Dillon pulled his collar higher, hunching his shoulders as he kept pace with his hefty companion.

David was oblivious to the rain collecting on his eyelashes, streaming down his cheeks. Yael's steps matched his, and he sensed her rising tension as all around them, preoccupied Londoners hurried through the rain.

"I take it there's a reason you haven't called out to him," she said.

"I'm not sure . . . if I can trust him." David's lips faltered on the words. He'd never imagined saying something like that about Dillon. The implications hung in the damp air, bleak as the sky overhead.

"You think he had something to do with Eva's murder?"

David had pushed away his suspicions before, but he couldn't any longer. Seeing Dillon in London, knowing that Crispin was here . . . and Stacy . . .

"I'm even wondering if he had something to do with ben Moshe's murder. It kills me to say it, but he knew I was going to be with ben Moshe that afternoon."

"They're turning onto Arthur Street," Yael interrupted breathlessly. "We'd better drop back a few paces."

Foot traffic was thinner here in the industrial area nearer the docks and David didn't want to risk Dillon spotting him. The Thames gleamed a dull pewter in the distance as he slowed his pace. They were getting farther from Trinity Square with every step.

As if sharing his thoughts, Yael glanced at him, biting her lip. "What about the phone call to Crispin?"

Torn, David held his panic at bay. "First I need to see where he's going. Then we'll double back."

And hope to hell, he thought desperately, *that Mueller hasn't grown tired of waiting.*

Tension throbbed through him in painful waves as he watched Dillon and the other man hurrying along the street, continuing as it merged into Swan Lane. *Am I putting Stacy at risk over nothing?* Dillon was the truest man he'd ever known. Maybe he was getting paranoid. The Gnoseos had turned his life so upside down he was doubting his closest friend. A man who had devoted his life to the service of God—not to evil.

Dillon could be of help right now. All I have to do is call out. . . .

But he couldn't bring himself to do it—the words stuck behind his teeth like lumps of clay.

Then he saw the next street Dillon and his companion were turning into. His brain screamed in alarm.

Angel's Passage.

Dark Angels?

Yael gripped his wrist. "They're going into that warehouse, David."

"And so am I. You with me?"

She quickened her pace, but kept her tone low and even. "Haven't you noticed? Every last step."

CHAPTER FIFTY-ONE

THE ARK

Where were those sounds coming from?

Stacy pressed her ear to each of the four walls, listening as intently as she could. The sobs were so faint, so indistinct, she couldn't be certain. But she knew she wasn't imagining them.

Someone was in pain or afraid. If she could only get out of here, she could try to help them.

What a joke. She couldn't even help herself. She tried the door for the hundredth time, jiggling the knob in every direction, only increasing her frustration. She had no idea how long she'd been here, or what was going to happen to her next—she only knew that in the end the lion-man was planning to kill her.

David's coming. She clung to that knowledge, holding on to every shred of hope. She wanted to feel happy about David coming for her, but instead she was terrified. She knew the man was telling the truth when he said he'd kill her and then kill David. Just like she knew the man who'd kidnapped her had already killed Mom and Hutch.

The tears streamed down her face faster than she could swipe them away. *Mom.* She couldn't erase the image of her mother sprawled in the gravel, blood trickling from her head. *Where was Mom now?* she thought, rocking back and forth with sobs. *Still lying there? Did Len know? Did David?*

She tried to stop the tears, telling herself to search the room. *There must be something here I can use to trip that man when he comes back. If I can just get past him while the door's open, I can run. I'm fast. My reflexes are excellent and I have good instincts. That's what Coach Wilson always says. I'll dodge around him—his limp will slow him down. I can run, get away. . . .*

She froze in the center of the room as, suddenly, the key clicked into the lock. *No, not yet!*

Frantically, she stared around the barren room. There was nothing to trip him with. . . .

The door opened with a rush of air. Stacy shrunk back, fear lodged in her throat.

A man she'd never seen before strode into the room.

CHAPTER FIFTY-TWO

As soon as Dillon and his companion disappeared through the warehouse door at 8 Angel Passage, the building became indistinguishable from every shuttered two-story warehouse around it.

David quickened his pace as the drizzle hardened into a steady tap of rain, causing Yael to shiver as she hurried along beside him.

"I think we should wait, David—listen first before we go in there," she said, blinking away raindrops. "Unless you're ready to barge right in and confront him."

"Not yet. Let's check out the delivery door." David sidestepped puddles as they made their way to the rear of the building.

He stopped so abruptly, Yael stumbled into him. They both flattened themselves against the side of the building as they spotted the flurry of activity around the loading ramp. David scrutinized the white truck backed up against the dock. An assembly line of workers were unloading suitcases and boxes, methodically handing them off to men who hustled them inside.

"Look at their badges," Yael whispered.

David nodded, his stomach twisting with disbelief. The badges clipped to the workers' belts were chillingly familiar. Even from this distance, he could make out the shape of the tower, of the lightning slash in the sky.

The tarot card.

"We've found them, David. We have to get inside."

He hunched his shoulders against the rain. "Then we follow Dillon."

"What about Stacy?"

"If this is some kind of Gnoseos headquarters, Crispin might be right here—with her. We may have just saved ourselves a telephone call."

"And gained the element of surprise." Even as she said the words, David tugged out Gillis's Tower card. She did the same with the rabbi's.

"We walk through the front door like we belong," he said tersely, wheeling toward the main entrance to the building. *And pray this is leading us to Stacy.*

"You sure you want in on this, Yael? You could go back to scope out Trinity Square—"

"I said every step of the way, remember?" She hurried past him to the front and tried to push open the steel door.

Locked.

"Open sesame," David muttered. He rapped on the door. Then, noticing the peep hole, he raised the Tower card and plastered it in front of the convex lens.

The door opened almost immediately. A man roughly the same size and build as Gillis stood there, doing his best impression of a Brink's truck. A Brinks truck packing a machine gun.

Unsmiling, he held out his free hand for the Tower cards. David fought off the sensation of being in a surreal dream as the man scrutinized their cards. This was no dream. It was a nightmare. Dillon was a Gnoseos. A traitor.

Dillon.

He swallowed down the bile in his throat, trying to assume non-chalance as the guard handed back their cards and stepped aside for them to enter.

"Down the hall to your right." He gestured with the machine gun. "Baggage?"

"All taken care of." David brushed passed him as if he had all the time in the world, a hand at Yael's waist.

The warehouse interior was nearly empty save for half a dozen other armed men, who looked both alert and single-minded. *Dark Angels.* Farther back in the shadows were boxes, suitcases, and floor-to-ceiling cases of bottled water. *Provisions.*

He could hear Yael's shallow breaths as they reached the end of the hallway and were confronted by a plain wood door. Leading, one would suppose, to the warehouse manager's office.

But it wasn't an office. As David pushed the door wide, they realized they were in a subway station entrance. A flight of cement stairs rimmed by a round metal banister led steeply down. Tiny orbs of light glowed like ghosts' eyes from the sides of the steps, dwindling away to pale pinpoints of light. He heard Yael draw in her breath beside him.

It was a damned good thing he'd conquered his fear of heights or he'd never have mustered the courage to descend those steps, much less in quasi-darkness. He could glimpse nothing of the bottom—the stairs just curved away far below, giving no indication where—or if—they ended.

An eerie desperation thumped in David's chest as he launched himself down the staircase, Yael right behind him. He was certain that Dillon had come this way just minutes before. The dank air was still layered with the scent of his friend's Aramis cologne.

He heard Yael's footsteps clacking behind him. She hadn't shown a single flicker of fear, which was more than he could say for himself. His trepidation accelerated as their descent steepened.

There was no sign of an end to these stairs.

"Coming back up is going to be a bitch," Yael whispered behind him.

David could only hope they wouldn't have to race up pursued by a flock of Dark Angels. He kept that thought to himself.

The light grew still murkier, the air even colder.

Yael's sandaled feet felt like blocks of ice. She'd spent many of her adult years sifting through underground excavations, but never had she encountered anything as strange and foreboding as this seemingly infinite set of stairs.

Just when she decided they were doomed to trudge downward forever, a cement landing came into view. She breathed a sigh of relief and hurried toward it.

But when they halted, there was only a closed metal door to their right and yet another staircase continuing downward. This one twisted in a harsh spiral of steel and copper, plunging down a hole bored through the bedrock surrounding the landing.

"My God," Yael breathed.

David had never seen anything like this. He felt as if he were descending into the underworld, and wouldn't have been at all surprised to find himself standing at the banks of the River Styx.

"Your choice . . . the door or the stairs." Yael cast him a questioning glance as she rubbed her aching calves.

David chose the door. Futilely, he tugged at it.

"It'll make too much commotion if we try to break in—let's take our chances with the stairs."

"I wonder how many years it took them to tunnel this far down." She hated the raspiness of her voice, but at least she still had one. She braced herself against the rock wall, stretching to work on the kinks. All of her bruises seemed on fire and the burn at her throat was throbbing.

She wondered if it had occurred to David that they'd come down here without a single weapon.

"Is it too late to point out that we're going in unarmed against the enemies of God?"

"We have good on our side, right?" David was only half joking. He wished he'd thought to buy a pocketknife after they'd left the airport. But the point was moot.

The air smelled even mustier as they started down the next set of steps. "Watch out," David cautioned as his head disappeared down the hole. "These steps are slippery."

"Condensation." Yael concentrated on maintaining her footing, fixing her gaze on the rungs one by one, avoiding the danger of staring down the dizzying spiral.

Suddenly from far above, they heard footsteps and low voices. Others were coming down behind them.

They probably know where they're headed, she thought.

David and Yael trudged on, picking their way down the slick metal steps. David had never been this far below ground. He wondered if either one of them would ever see daylight again.

He shook the thought away, concentrating instead on the Lamed Vovniks, reminding himself that as long as any of the thirty-six still drew breath, there was hope.

From below he could now distinguish a hum of voices and the sound of rushing water.

"I think we're coming late to the party," Yael murmured.

"Just hope no one figures out we're crashers."

Moments later, they emerged from the vertical cylinder of rock as the staircase plunged into a large, dimly lit cavern.

Taking the last of the steps, David stared across the open space at the two giant bronze sculptures near the far wall. Cast in the shape of a double ouroboros, they towered outside a double doorway, yet appeared almost miniscule in comparison with the craggy rock wall soaring beyond them.

But it was the freestanding column of jagged rock to his right that drew his scrutiny as they reached bottom. Rearing upward like a tower, it was crowned by a jutting protuberance—a balcony hewn from the rock. It looked like a primitive observation post. *Or like the Pope's balcony*, David thought, half-expecting to see the Gnoseos' leader come out to wave to his minions.

His gaze narrowed on the gleam of glass doors beyond the balcony. *There's a room behind it. That's where the door on the landing must lead.* He thought he caught movement beyond the glass—someone was up there.

Then his attention shifted to the reception desk ten feet ahead. A cigarette-thin woman with shiny dark hair glowered at them. The large crystal ouroboros brooch pinned to the jacket of her red wool suit glittered like ice.

But he was more concerned with the Dark Angel posted behind her, a shrewd-looking black man with legs planted apart, his eyes glinting as steely a gray as the pistol at his hip.

No way are we in Kansas anymore.

The woman pursed lips painted the same shade as her suit, waving them forward with impatience.

"This way. You're the last to check in. We need to verify your passports."

CHAPTER FIFTY-THREE

Storming down the hall, Crispin was blind to the people giving him a wide berth. He veered toward the rear staircase leading to the lower level, and charged recklessly down it, one leg at a time, the tip of his cane rapping harshly against the winding metal steps.

A black rage enveloped him. Where the hell was Shepherd? *He's playing with me*, Crispin fumed. Raoul had just reported that Shepherd and the Israeli woman had arrived at Heathrow over two hours ago. *Why hadn't they reached Trinity Square and made the damned phone call?* Raoul and Enrique had scoured the park and the memorial garden—no sign of them. *No phone call.*

Maybe hearing the little girl scream would get Shepherd's attention. His teeth ground together as he envisioned snapping her arm like a pretzel as Shepherd listened to her cries.

He yanked the key from his pocket and plunged it into the lock, but to his surprise, the door swung inward before he even turned the key.

What was this?

An empty room, that's what it was. Incredulous, Crispin stared at the bare cot, the vacant chair, the barren corners.

He let out an incoherent roar of rage.

He punched the buttons on his phone. "She's gone!" he shouted, reaching the Dark Angels' command center on the floor above. "The room is empty! Who do you *think* I mean? The last Hidden One—*find her!*"

By the time he'd spun around, bells were beginning to clang the alert. Rage still burning like hot coals in his chest, Crispin hobbled through the corridor and up the rear stairs, his face mottled with fury as a dozen Dark Angels poured past him down the steps.

As he reached the landing, he came face to face with DiStefano.

"A word, Serpent." DiStefano's expression was remarkably calm.

"We have to find the girl," Crispin snarled.

"Oh, we will. There's no place for her to hide, is there?" DiStefano tilted his head, a slight smile curling his mouth.

"I don't know what games you're playing or why you didn't come straight to me with Guillermo Torres's name," he said. "And I won't ask who sent the assassination order from my server, Serpent. I'll just tell you, it's done. Three men named Guillermo Torres were eliminated today." His eyes gleamed with satisfaction. "And Jack Cherle's ship is docking as we speak—another Hidden One to be dispatched momentarily. That leaves us only the girl."

"I want her brought to me when she's found."

Ice glinted in DiStefano's eyes. "She will be *killed* when she's found," he countered smoothly. "This is no longer about you, Serpent. Your role is over, successfully completed, I might add. Our time has arrived. There is no longer any reason to keep Stacy Lachman alive. David Shepherd has failed to stop us and once her life is snuffed out, we win. Your only concern now is to prepare yourself for the end—and our beginning."

On the words, a rumble shuddered through the tunnel's ceiling of rock. Both men looked up.

"Cherle." DiStefano consulted his watch and smiled. "He's dead, or will be very soon. Only one to go."

Crispin's mind was racing. *Not yet.* He wasn't ready.

Once, this was exactly the way he'd planned it. But now it was all wrong—something was missing. Discovering Shepherd's connection to Stacy Lachman had changed everything. Now he wanted it all—the gemstone that had been stolen from him, retribution for the years he'd lost in that coma, the satisfaction of vengeance. *Then the Ascension. Not a moment before.*

He turned from DiStefano without a word. *If the leader of the Circle thinks he can stop me, he's dead wrong. If I get my hands on the girl first, she's mine. And I'll decide when it's time for her to die.*

SOUTHAMPTON

Three long-range rifles thundered within milliseconds.

Jack Cherle crumpled to the pavement as his family screamed and people dove for cover.

"Clean kill, mates. See you in London." Geoffrey Bales's voice crackled through the other two Dark Angels' earpieces, even as their vehicles pulled away from the docks.

Bales tugged out his BlackBerry and began to type with one hand as he drove.

"It's done."

Chapter Fifty-four

David and Yael placed their tarot cards on the reception desk. David held his breath as the woman in the power suit picked each one up and scrutinized it—front, then back. *She's checking out the numbers,* he realized.

Rapid-fire, she typed into the computer before her, then leaned forward to frown at the screen. Her head flew up and she stared hard at Yael.

She's not buying it, David thought, his heart hammering as he pretended to be absorbed by the mammoth Lichtenstein on the wall to his right. *Any minute now that Dark Angel's going to raise his gun and pick us off.*

Beside him, he sensed Yael's tension. Sweat dripped from his armpits. *I should spring now, catch him off balance. . . .*

But before his limbs could react, the woman barked at Yael. "Your name. What is it?"

At that the Dark Angel advanced, his broad fingers tightening on the gun. "Is there a problem?"

"There is no problem." Yael spoke coolly. "You have my name right there. And you have my card."

"That's the problem," the woman countered. "This card was issued to a man."

"That's impossible," David said.

"Clearly, you've made a mistake." Yael's tone was frigid. If David didn't know better, he'd have thought she was truly affronted. "I want to speak to Prime Minister DiStefano. Or Crispin Mueller. *Now.*"

For the first time, the woman appeared unsure. She glanced over her shoulder at the Dark Angel, as if seeking guidance.

Glaring at the Dark Angel, David pressed her. "Tell him to put that weapon down," he ordered. "She has her card. Obviously, the numbers are mixed up. If we're the last to arrive, then it's apparent no one else is coming."

He leaned closer, inches from her face. "And do you think anyone on the outside would have access to these cards? Use your head," he finished in a scornful tone.

The woman was visibly struggling, torn between adherence to the Gnoseos code of secrecy and the obvious discrepancy before her.

"But it says Paul Wright—"

"*Paula* Wright." Yael turned to David, her teeth clenched. "Who'd expect incompetency at a moment like this?" she hissed. "Typos on this crucial day? Unacceptable."

He pointed at the Dark Angel. "You. Get DiStefano at once. He can settle this matter without wasting any more time."

"That won't be necessary." Hastily, the woman opened a drawer and produced two small key rings, each dangling a single gold key. David heard Yael let out a tiny breath, and the clamor of his own heart slowed infinitesimally.

"James Gillis, you're in Room Seventeen in the D corridor on the main floor. Paula Wright, Room Forty-two in the C corridor." She jerked her thumb to the right. "Lower level, near the back stairs."

Yael snatched up her key ring and stomped down the corridor, the picture of unmollified outrage.

"Let's go, James, since we're now so *late*."

David had to force himself not to glance back. "That was close," he muttered under his breath as he caught up to her. "You were impressive back there."

"I took a gamble. Can you believe this place?" she whispered, as they merged into the flow of people in the wide corridor.

The tunnel was so congested they might have been back in New York. But this was no Big Apple. It was stark, eerie, and dimly lit with a combination of bare bulbs and fat candles perched on high ledges. The architecture was a startling blend of metal and natural rock, and the air reeked with a fusty odor from the seepage puddled along the edges of the walls. Yet the atmosphere crackled with expectancy and excitement.

David had never imagined anything like this. The bunker was a weird cross between a cave and a fallout shelter. It was far larger than he'd expected, even for the two thousand people who'd been issued the secret tarot cards.

Where in this godforsaken maze is Stacy? he thought as he scanned the jubilant faces coming at him. Every person he passed looked ordinary, but they were all enemies. His enemies and the world's.

Stacy might be the sole hope he had of defeating them, but he hadn't a clue where to start looking for her.

Walking quickly, they passed a large auditorium flanked by the ouroboros sculptures, then a dining hall, a kitchen.

There's slim chance of finding her in a public area, David thought as they hurried past.

To his relief, other than an occasional nod or a smile, no one in the tunnel paid much attention to them as they made their way toward the rear stairs.

Suddenly, a low rumble shuddered through the rock. Candles wobbled on their perches, and David and Yael glanced up in alarm.

"What was that? The soles of my feet are still vibrating," Yael muttered.

"I don't know, but I don't like it. All we need is for this place to catch on fire." David scowled. "We have to find Stacy and get out of here."

All around them, a low murmur of excitement thrummed through the passersby. Then came a shrill clang of bells, one after the other, echoing through the hallway.

"It must be time," a man shouted excitedly.

"To the auditorium!" a woman's voice sang out.

More shouts went up. "To the auditorium! To victory!"

As everyone around them charged in the direction from which David and Yael had just come, the two of them pressed on, running now toward the rear of the tunnel.

David's heart pounded more from fear than exertion. Time was evaporating and he had no clue where to look for Stacy in this vast godforsaken hellhole. But with everyone now congregating in the auditorium, maybe he and Yael could search the more remote parts of the bunker with less chance of detection.

The thought had no more flickered through his mind before he saw four Dark Angels, guns drawn, running at them from both directions.

He and Yael froze. But to their astonishment, the Dark Angels charged right past them. Except for one.

"Have you seen a teenage girl with blond hair and a gray sweatshirt?" he demanded.

Stacy. David shook his head, his mouth too dry to speak, even if he'd wanted to.

The Dark Angel pointed down the hall. "Head to the auditorium—we need the corridors clear to search. If you spot her, grab her and bring her to the reception desk. She's the last Hidden One."

"Oh, my. Of course, we will." Yael gazed at him open-mouthed, the picture of compliance.

"How'd she get away?" David forced out the words.

"That's what we'd like to know." The Dark Angel scowled at him, suddenly stepping closer. "Where were you two heading?"

David held up his room key. "I forgot something in my room."

"Leave it," the man ordered. "We need these halls cleared."

Screw you, David thought, but he and Yael turned obediently and pretended to go back the way they'd come. But the instant the Dark Angel disappeared behind them, he grabbed Yael's hand.

"Come on, we're going below." They bolted headlong for the rear staircase, praying no one else would try to stop them.

As the corridor ended, they skidded to a halt, staring in dismay at the six narrow passageways confronting them, labeled A through F.

"The assigned rooms are down there—they're probably just sleeping quarters," Yael panted.

David's heart sank. This place was bigger than he'd thought. Each corridor appeared endless, and seemed to hold dozens of doors. *What if Stacy was hidden behind one of them?*

Desperately, he tried to think. His instinct told him to go down. "Let's check below first and work our way up." He was already sprinting toward the rear staircase.

The clanging of the bells had stopped, he realized, as he took the spiraling stairs two at a time.

There were few people left on the lower level, save for several Dark Angels they spotted searching room to room in the alphabetically marked passageways that mirrored those above.

"Here," Yael said, darting toward a floorplan painted on the rock wall behind the stairs. "This might save us some time."

Frantically, David scanned the diagram. "Look—that balcony we saw—it leads to a Situation Room."

"Like a war room," Yael murmured. "Far above the arena, and probably impenetrable."

She glanced nervously behind her, where Dark Angels were still moving methodically away from them, searching along the D corridor.

"The brass are probably gathered up there," David said. "That might be where Crispin had Stacy."

A perfect venue for an execution, he thought, but quickly blocked the image from his mind.

"She could still be down here somewhere," Yael argued. "There's a trash containment center down this hall, and a fan room, and . . . what's this?" She pointed to a circular area just behind the rear staircase marked OFF LIMITS. "Off Limits? Do you think—"

David's mouth tightened. "One way to find out."

They took off, heading for the area behind the staircase. When they reached the area marked OFF LIMITS, they found only an underground well surrounded by a safety railing.

"Well, that's a dead end." David stared into the plummeting chasm, then raked a hand through his hair. His ribs were killing him. But he refused to acknowledge the pain.

"There's the containment center." Yael pointed to the squat metal tank in the shadows of the hall.

"I'll check it out," David said grimly.

The door was locked, as he expected. Grabbing hold of the built-in ladder, he began climbing toward the top as Yael glanced warily around. No one else was back here. *At the moment.*

"Hurry," she urged, then fell silent as he neared the top.

She understood his need to search everywhere. But the longer they lingered here, the greater the chance they'd be caught. She held her breath as he wrestled open the trap door at the top—and didn't exhale until his feet were thudding against the rungs of the ladder in descent.

"Nothing inside but garbage. Where could she be hiding?"

They both startled at a creaking noise nearby. Yael whirled and saw a large rat skittering from an alcove she hadn't noticed earlier. It was nearly invisible, a small opening tucked beneath a natural jut in the rock wall.

"There's something back there. Where there's a rat, there's usually food."

David hurried toward the recess and she followed, her hands clenched at the thought of his stepdaughter alone down here in this horrible place.

They both spotted the door at the same time. It was unmarked and might have easily gone unnoticed in this remote area of the bunker.

The perfect place to keep a hostage, Yael thought.

The door was ajar. She pushed it wide and noticed a faint medicinal odor. "Oh my God."

The closetlike space appeared empty. David groped along the walls for a light switch, and a pale fluorescent glow lightened the room. They saw a chair, a bureau, and an unmade cot. Remnants of what looked like a cheese sandwich remained on a tray at the foot of the bed.

"She was here. We probably missed her by minutes." David felt as if the world was swallowing him up.

"Look at this!" Yael had dropped to her knees beside the cot and scooped up a rubber message bracelet from the slate floor. The words "Aim High" were stamped into the stretchy yellow rubber.

"It's hers." David's voice was thick. "I bought it for her when she visited me last summer."

He stared at the narrow band for a moment, then forced it over his swollen hand. Though it gripped his wrist tightly, uncomfortably, it made him feel closer to Stacy. "She was right here. That bastard—"

"Why aren't you upstairs? What are you doing in here?"

David and Yael wheeled as a deep voice filled the tiny room.

David did a double take. He didn't recognize the Dark Angel leveling a gun at them, but he immediately recognized the short, broad-shouldered man blocking the doorway.

Alberto Ortega, former secretary-general of the UN.

David had met him once, back when his father was still alive, at a White House reception he'd attended with his parents and the Wanamakers and several other senators' families.

Wanamaker. I wonder how far back that connection goes. Who drafted whom?

"David Shepherd." Ortega's eyebrows shot up. He took a step into the room. "How did you get down here? Never mind. It doesn't matter."

He unclipped a beeper from his belt. "In twenty seconds, this hall will be teeming with Dark Angels," he remarked conversationally, his finger poised at the keypad. "Not that my friend Domino here can't handle the two of you."

The Dark Angel with lank reddish hair and a matching soul patch drew back his lips in a charming smile. "And with double the pleasure I took killing your housekeeper."

David went still as the air, his mind contorted with confusion and fury. *Then Dillon didn't kill Eva?*

"I trust you've brought your book of names." Ortega advanced a step.

"Got it right here." On the words, David swung his duffel like a baseball bat, knocking the beeper from Ortega's fingers. The impact sent it clattering into the corner as David charged Ortega, jamming his right fist into that smug face. He pistoned his arm again and rearranged the swarthy features into a bloody mask of split flesh and broken teeth. Ortega toppled backwards into Domino, and in the instant they tottered off balance, David lunged for the Dark Angel's gun.

A shot exploded and he heard Yael curse behind him. His fingers closed on the red-hot barrel. Sweat poured down his face as he ignored the searing pain and wrestled for the gun. Domino outweighed him by a good thirty pounds, and David fought to keep his death hold on the weapon.

As Ortega staggered out of the way, Domino twisted the gun, forcing David's wrist backwards on itself. Pain ripped up his arm, his knees buckled for an instant. The groan that whistled through his teeth brought a smile to his opponent's face.

"Kill them!" Ortega gasped, struggling to his knees, blood spraying from what was left of his mouth. Yael flew at him like a 120-pound rocket, slamming him onto his back and into a thin pool of his own blood.

Straddling him, she stabbed her room key into his left eye. He tried to protect his face, blood seeping through his fingers, but she rammed the key again, this time into the hollow of his throat as his screams reverberated in her ears.

David heard them from a distance, from someplace deep inside his agony, as he and Domino exchanged vicious body blows. His ribs crackled as if he'd been rammed by a bull.

The gun. I can't let go of the gun, he thought through a haze of desperation as Domino landed another savage punch.

Crashing his free fist into Domino's Adam's apple, he felt the man's tendons give way, watched the killer's eyes momentarily roll back in pain. And then Domino was smiling at him, even as he drove his fist down like an anvil onto David's skull.

Lights danced before David's eyes as he sank to his knees. His hand clasped empty air. He saw the gun swiveling toward his head. Willing his body, he tried to jacknife forward, to go for the gun or at least keep himself a moving target.

But before his muscles could uncoil, another man appeared behind the Dark Angel. Using both hands, the newcomer crashed a rock the size of a melon against the back of Domino's head.

David blinked hard. Wondered if his vision was jarred by the blow he'd taken to the head. He focused his eyes.

Incredulity filled him. The man standing over Domino was Dillon McGrath.

CHAPTER FIFTY-FIVE

It was dark, so dark that Stacy couldn't see her own hands in front of her as she crawled along the sheet metal tunnel. The man had warned her to be as quiet as possible, to move slowly but steadily forward. But with every inch she wriggled along the narrow passageway, her weight creaked on the metal, and she tensed with fear that the sound could be heard below.

"The ventilation shaft is tight, probably quite dusty," the man had told her, talking fast and looking all around as he hoisted her up through a trapdoor. They'd run to a side tunnel a short distance from where the lion-man had kept her.

"You'll have to go a ways before another corridor opens to your right. When it does, take it. Keep going—it's a long way. I'll meet you where it ends. No matter what you hear, don't stop, get to the end and wait for me there. Do you understand?"

Stacy didn't understand anything anymore. Now, squeezing her way down the tiny tunnel, the hairs on her neck suddenly stood on end as she heard the clang of alarm bells.

The lion-man knows I'm gone. Her heart was hammering so hard it hurt. She tried not to think about him looking for her. Or about how cold she was, how lonely, how scared. She hoped she could trust the man who'd let her out, hoped she'd get to see her mom and David again. She just wanted things to be normal again.

Shivering, she forced herself to continue on. When she felt the side wall to her right disappear, she tried to manuever herself around the tight bend. It took several minutes of squirming and holding her breath as she twisted herself into the passage.

Her mouth was dry from the dust, her hands so cold they were numb. She wanted to get out of this cold metal prison so badly she could scream. But she couldn't scream. The lion-man would come. And the man with the different-colored eyes. She had to stay quiet.

She hadn't inched very far along the second tunnel when she thought she heard voices. *They're coming for me!* She stopped and listened, fear eating through her stomach.

Voices. She was right. She listened harder, straining to catch words.

It was women, arguing, angry. *The women who were crying?* They weren't crying now.

"Let them come for us. We'll fight them with our nails and our teeth."

"We have the knives we snuck from our dinner trays. They've been sharpened on the rocks."

"We can kill some of them, at least, before they kill us."

But behind the determined voices, she heard other sounds. Some of the women were weeping. Pleading.

"If you fight them, they'll kill all of us."

"Oh God, I don't want to die."

Stacy froze. Who were they? Prisoners? Like she was? What was going to happen to them?

She heard the man's voice again in her head. *Keep going, don't stop no matter what. Get to the other end.*

I can't do it. She heard a sob from her own throat. *I can't just leave those women.*

There was no room to turn around. Slowly, painfully, she began inching herself backwards the way she'd come.

Toward the voices.

CHAPTER FIFTY-SIX

David launched himself at Dillon and slammed him against the doorframe.

"What the hell are you doing here?" he snarled.

"Saving your life, for God's sake." Dillon's blue eyes flashed into his. "Some way to thank me, by the way."

"Thank you for what? Trying to end the world? Is *that* what all your metaphysics study is really about—*Father*? Did you confiscate my passport when you let this monster into my house to kill Eva?"

"Eva? She's dead? God in heaven!" The shock on Dillon's face appeared genuine. He shook his head, as if trying to clear it, then shoved David away.

"Well, your friend here might not be." He sounded shaken. "So unless you're up for another go-round, I suggest we discuss this above ground—while we can still get out of here."

Yael stood beside David, aiming Domino's gun at Dillon. "David, he did just save your life," she said warily.

David's head was spinning with confusion as he tried to reconcile

Dillon bashing Domino in the head, Eva's murder, the missing passport, and his very presence in the bunker.

"Look out!" Dillon snapped as Domino snaked an arm toward David's pant leg.

David wheeled and kicked the Dark Angel in the jaw. After Domino's head lolled to the side, his body slumping into unconsciousness, they all three sprinted toward the back staircase. "What *are* you doing here, then?" David demanded.

"It's a long story. After you told me about the Hebrew lettering on your agate, it triggered a memory. I'd seen something similar before. I checked a volume on Jewish magic to see if it had anything on gemstones," Dillon said breathlessly as they reached the stairs. "Found an entire section on the magical gemstones of the high priest's breastplate."

"Go on," David panted.

"Years ago I met a bishop in Rome. He's since been exposed for abusing young boys. Same poor kids he invited to his weekly Bible breakfasts. But it was his ring I remembered. Unusual—a smooth-faced ruby with Hebrew lettering."

"The ruby from Aaron's breastplate?" Yael gasped, her cheeks flushed with the exertion of running up the stairs.

"I tracked him to the Scottish countryside. Took it from him. To return to the Israelis. But then I discovered this strange tarot card among his travel papers."

Dillon was extremely fit, yet his breath was coming hard. "He kept talking about having to catch a flight to London. So that's where I headed. Ran into a German at Heathrow. He carried the same card. I attached myself to him, ended up here. Now you tell *me* what the hell is going on."

They were halfway to the landing. David stopped short, ignoring the sharp pain wracking every inch of his body.

Beside him, Yael and Dillon pressed themselves against the railing, gasping for breath.

"Stacy's here," David said raggedly. "These maniacs are trying to end the world. Those voices . . . those names I heard . . . they belong to the people these monsters have been methodically killing. Stacy's one of them—maybe the last one. We have to find her and get her out!"

"God help us." Dillon went pale beneath his ruddiness. "Where is she?"

"I don't know. You might want to have a few words with God and help us find out," David said between clenched teeth. "Before they catch us and kill us too."

CHAPTER FIFTY-SEVEN

The voices grew louder.

I'm going in the right direction, Stacy thought. *But how will I get down to where they are?*

She scurried faster, feeling her lungs closing up from the stirred dust. Her fingers had skimmed along room ducts as she'd crawled. Slatted ones, like the ones in houses. The voices had to be coming from a duct nearby.

Suddenly, as she reached the bend once more, the women sounded like they were right below her. She ran her hands along both walls, trying to find a duct—or another trapdoor. There had to be more than one.

She twisted her way back through the bend. It was even harder going backwards, and at first she got stuck. But she wedged through and then she found it—a trapdoor, like the one the man had told her to replace when he'd hoisted her into the shaft.

Cautiously, holding her breath, she gripped it by the sides and slowly began pushing it away. It was heavy, like the other one, but when she managed to move it several inches, she was able to peer into the tunnel below. She heard the women—they were close now.

"You may want to fight and die, Irina, but I want to stay alive," one of them sobbed.

A girl with a throaty voice answered her. "Be a coward if you want, Louisa, but I want to get back to my Mario. And I will die trying."

Stacy shoved the panel the last few inches. The opening was the same size as the one she'd come up through. But the floor looked so far away.

Taking a deep breath, she slid her legs through the opening, bracing her elbows against the sides of the shaft until her feet dangled as low as they could go.

Pretend you're Michael Jordan, dropping from a rim shot, she told herself as she slid her hands to grip the lip of the opening.

She hesitated, and then let herself go.

She landed hard and felt something pull in her ankle. *There's no time for the disabled bench,* she thought, sucking in her breath. She was in a tunnel much like the one where she'd been held. It was deserted. But the women were close by, she could still hear them arguing.

Stacy pushed herself to her feet, and limped along the tunnel toward their voices. She passed several paintings, all of them creepy—dark colors, with snakes and weird symbols. She hurried on, freezing as she caught sight of the wrought-iron gate down the passageway. Her heart lurched. It looked like a prison gate.

She half-ran toward it—and then she saw them. Several dozen young women locked in an enormous room. It was arranged with beds, like a dormitory. The women looked worn and pale, like they hadn't seen sunlight in years. They were younger than her mom, Stacy noticed, and a few didn't look much older than she was. But their shoulders were hunched like old women's, and their hair hung long and unkempt.

What were they doing here?

One of the women gasped as she saw Stacy limping toward the

gate. Suddenly they were all lined up there, staring at her with in-credulous, hollow eyes.

"Who are you?"

It was the one with the throaty voice. She was pretty, with dark hair and large eyes fringed by long lashes.

"I'm Stacy. Who . . . who are you? Why are you all in here?"

"Irina. My name is Irina." The young woman gripped the bars tightly. "Thank you, merciful God," she whispered with a glance upward. She peered at Stacy again, her face taut with hope. "We are prisoners. Help us! There's a key."

"Where is it?" Stacy scanned the walls, seeing no shelves or hooks.

"Down the tunnel. Behind one of the paintings. Quick!"

"Which one?" She was already hurrying back toward the pic-tures, her ankle throbbing more with each step.

"We don't know," another voice called down the tunnel. "We just see them take it from behind one of them. Hurry, please hurry."

Stacy lifted one painting after another off the wall. *Where was the key?* Any second she thought to hear someone coming. She would end up locked behind the gate with them.

Thinking of those worn desperate faces, she struggled with the largest painting, nearly toppling backwards as it popped from its hook. And then she saw it. A large black key, shaped like an F, hung on a nail behind the painting.

Fingers shaking, she grabbed it and forced herself to run despite the pain in her bad ankle. Her hands were trembling so violently it was difficult to fit the key in the lock, but she managed it at last, and as the gate sprang open she was nearly trampled.

The women rushed wildly past her, fleeing down the tunnel. Only Irina stopped. Kissed Stacy on the cheek, sobbing softly. Then grabbed her hand.

"Come with us, little angel—run!"

CHAPTER FIFTY-EIGHT

"I assume you have a game plan." Dillon peered cautiously up the stairs.

"I'm pretty open to suggestions." David swiped at the sweat on his brow. "What was yours?"

"To get whatever gemstones they might have."

"Have you seen any?" Yael's head whipped toward him.

"Two—inside a lighted glass case. They're up in that war room behind the balcony. Where the bigwigs meet."

"You were up there?" David's eyebrows shot up.

Dillon's mouth twisted into a grimace. "Briefly. Tagging along with my new best friend. As we were coming down the stairs, one of his colleagues popped out of that glass door wanting to speak to him inside. I didn't get further than the doorway, but there was no mistaking what was in that case."

"Are the stones accessible?" David asked.

"If we can break the case. But getting in there . . ." Dillon shook his head grimly. "I went down below hunting for a weapons cache. An axe, a metal pipe, anything. Instead, all I found were friends."

Yael smiled faintly at him, extending a hand streaked with blood. "Yael HarPaz."

"Sorry, can't imagine what happened to my manners," David muttered, then his gaze met Dillon's. He was filled with a regret he couldn't even begin to express. "I should have trusted you," he said thickly. "Forgive me."

"Pick up the tab on our next three breakfast excursions, and we'll call it even."

Suddenly from below came the rush of pounding footsteps.

"Let's get out of here," David said in alarm. They surged toward the main level, but as they reached it and started toward the auditorium, they were stopped by the sight of a half dozen Dark Angels bounding toward them.

"What have we here?" A woman's voice spoke from behind.

David recognized it immediately. Rocked by disbelief, he wheeled and stared into the imperious eyes of Katharine Wanamaker.

Katharine Wanamaker. The woman who'd consoled his mother for months after his father's fatal heart attack. The woman who'd always prepared Waldorf salad at holiday dinners, even though David was the only one who ate it.

"Why don't you get Judd," he told her between clenched teeth. "We'll have a family reunion."

Her laughter trilled mockingly. "For all Judd knows, I'm in Georgetown locking up a major bequest to the symphony."

He doesn't know, David thought. "Judd called you after we left the restaurant in New York, didn't he? He didn't give us up—*you* did."

He lunged for her, dragged her against him, and spun around to face the Dark Angels. Yael darted forward, pressing the barrel of Domino's gun into Katharine's neck as Dillon braced himself for the onrush of attackers.

"Stop right there, or she's dead!" David shouted.

He could hear the stampede rushing toward them up the stairwell. Panic kicked adrenaline through his bloodstream.

In seconds they'd be swamped from both directions by Dark Angels.

Where was Stacy?

As Katharine struggled to break free, he tightened his grip.

"Move again and I'll shoot," Yael warned her.

The Dark Angels rushing down the tunnel hadn't slowed.

"Where's my daughter?" David's voice sliced into Katharine's ear, even as he dug his fingers deeper into her flesh.

"Even if I knew, I wouldn't tell you. Give up, David." She twisted her head toward him, her eyes malevolent. "You can't win."

"Where's Mueller—"

She never had a chance to answer. The Dark Angels skidded to a halt, their attention suddenly diverted by the horde of women swarming at them from the stairs.

"What in the world?" Dillon gaped at the bedraggled figures racing as if all hell pursued them.

"Get them back down there!" Katharine ordered the Dark Angels.

David roared at her. "All I want to hear from you is where Crispin Mueller is hiding himself! And where he has Stacy!"

Through the pandemonium now raging in the tunnel, Yael clicked off the gun's safety.

"Stacy!" David shouted at Katharine. "*Where's Stacy?*"

Caught up in the chaotic stampede of women on the stairs, Stacy heard something through the thunder engulfing her. It was faint, far off, but she heard it—David's voice. He was shouting her name.

"David!" The cry tore from her throat, and she stumbled on the steel steps. Irina's hand steadied her. She recovered quickly, her breath bunching in her throat.

If she fell now, she'd be trampled. The women were running like maddened cattle in an old western movie. She ran faster, gasping for air, praying for it to be true, for David to be here. . . .

As she crested the staircase she found herself in a tunnel just like the one below—this one filled with people.

Her eyes frantically scanned the faces—David!

She screamed his name and he turned his head toward her, amazement on his face. It seemed to be happening in slow motion. Then she saw the joy in his eyes and she broke free of Irina and darted toward him.

But someone grabbed her around the waist, yanking her off her feet. She writhed and screamed, and saw David shove the woman he was holding away to leap toward her.

"Let me go!" she screamed, twisting her head up at her captor, and then she screamed again. Terror bubbled through her.

The man holding her was the one with the different-colored eyes. The man who'd killed Hutch. Who'd hurt her mother.

"David, help me—" she shrieked, but then she saw another man tackle him and heard the deafening blast of a gun.

David collided with the ground, his jaw slamming into the floor. Black circles shimmied before his eyes and he heard a gunshot. Opening his eyes, he tried to lift his head, but two Dark Angels were pinning him down. He saw Yael a few feet away, her arm twisted behind her back, a Dark Angel now brandishing Domino's gun. He heard Dillon grunt and the thwack of blows. Despair overtook the pain.

"Take the Hidden One up to the Situation Room," Katharine urged.

The man holding Stacy shouted orders. "You—hold Shepherd and the other two in the reception area while I find out what the Leader plans to do with them." He glared at the other Dark Angels. "Why are the rest of you standing there like baboons?" He was already dragging Stacy away. "Round up those women. Go!"

All David knew was that Stacy was crying. The sounds were tearing his heart, fading away down the hall as he struggled uselessly against the men pinning him.

He wanted to kill the monster who'd grabbed Stacy almost as much as he wanted to kill Crispin Mueller. *What good was my vision, what was the point of my hearing their pleas? I've failed everyone*, he thought as he was yanked roughly to his feet, as the three of them were hauled along the tunnel toward the reception desk.

He winced when he saw the size of the welt swelling along Yael's cheek. Blood dribbled from Dillon's nose. And some of the fleeing women, whoever they were, had already been recaptured.

It's over.

A black-haired man emerged from the auditorium and strode briskly toward them. He was tall, suave, and self-assured. *A honcho*, David thought, his eyes eviscerating the man. He could feel the Dark Angels straighten as the man approached.

"Prime Minister DiStefano, we've found Shepherd. What would you like us to do with him?"

DiStefano.

Before DiStefano could open his mouth, a figure burst from beneath the reception desk with a howl of fury.

A woman.

Streaking toward DiStefano and wielding a blur of long, glinting metal. She fell on him, plunging her weapon into his heart, burrowing it deep with a strength that defied her slight stature.

His mouth agape in shock, DiStefano emitted only a low gurgle and then toppled backwards.

Stunned, the Dark Angels froze an instant before releasing their grip on the prisoners. Shouting for help, two of them rushed toward the fallen man, while the other three dove for the attacker.

Crazed, she slashed the bloodied knife through the air with frenzied determination, holding them at bay. Then with a shriek, she whirled and bolted for the staircase.

Yael was running too. Panting hard, she reached the nearest of the ouroboros sculptures. Desperately, she wedged herself between it and the rock face.

This has to work. You have to do it.

Bracing her back against the jagged wall, she summoned her strength and shoved at the ouroboros. Grunting, she ignored the rock biting into her spine, struggling to budge the sculpture even as Dillon fought with the crew-cut Dark Angel who'd released her.

Dillon's fist shot out. His right hook sent Crew-cut down on his back, the ruby leaving a blood-red imprint emblazed on his cheek.

Yael focused with single-minded intensity on the heavy bronze sculpture, so cold and immovable against her sweating palms.

In a move seared into his brain from a Steven Seagal movie, Dillon took a flying leap and landed squarely on his opponent's chest with both feet, shattering his ribs. An agonizing screech pierced the air as the man writhed.

Dillon ignored the revulsion screaming in his soul and grabbed the man's gun.

He spun around.

David was sprinting up the staircase like a madman. Suddenly five more thugs came thundering down the stairs, blocking his path in a wall of guns and muscle. David jumped the banister, his hands clutching the steel as he swung himself beneath the steps and dropped to the ground. His knees buckled, and pain was etched across his face. But he seemed beyond caring as he bolted for the protected rear of the jagged rock tower supporting the balcony, pursued by Dark Angels scrambling down the stairs.

With sweat beading along his upper lip, Dillon leveled Crew-cut's gun and fired, peeling off one shot after the next.

The thug in the lead reeled backwards, grabbing his shoulder, but the others surged, unfazed, streaking across the reception area after David. Suddenly Dillon heard a deafening scream from Yael. As he watched in horrified fascination, she shoved the sculpture forward with all her might.

It wobbled back and forth—then, for an interminable instant, it hung in the air, balanced at an impossible angle. As Yael's face contorted with effort, it toppled over. Crashing with a roar that resounded through the bunker like an explosion, the burnished metal crushed the men pursuing David.

For a moment Dillon's emotions whirled. Remorse for the grisly loss of life, wild hope that they might yet make it out alive.

Then he felt something else. Blood, warm and sticky. Spurting from his chest. He stared down in disbelief. There was no pain, only a strange whirring in his ears. He staggered a step, dropped to the ground. And then heard only silence.

Yael fought to block out the carnage she'd created as she pried a dead Dark Angel's fingers from his gun and started for the stairs.

CHAPTER FIFTY-NINE

What in the world is going on down there?

Crispin Mueller slammed his cane against the floor of the Situation Room and surged from his chair. Ignoring the flash of fear in Stacy Lachman's eyes, he limped swiftly onto the balcony. He leaned on the railing hewn from rock and peered incredulously at the pandemonium below.

An ouroboros sculpture lay angled across the twisted bodies of several Dark Angels. He could see another prone form a few feet away, a man centered in a pool of his own blood.

It was a scene of chaos. People shouting, streaming pell-mell from the auditorium, confused and panicked.

Squinting, he scanned the throng milling in the reception area. Only moments ago, he had observed DiStefano striding toward Shepherd, imprisoned by the Dark Angels. He'd been waiting for them to drag Shepherd up here so the fun could begin.

Now, incredibly, DiStefano lay in a heap, his shirt purpled with blood.

Where was Shepherd? How had he broken from his captors? How had one man wrought this much chaos?

Not for long, he vowed, the rage popping like pistons in his skull. He flew back to the doorway, his cane thumping, his jaw taut.

"DiStefano's dead. And I don't see Shepherd anywhere."

"How can that be?" Odiambo Mofulatsi, the South African diamond broker who ranked third in command, came out to the balcony, scowling. "Where's Ortega? And your father? Why aren't they up here?"

Crispin ignored him. "Raoul, bring the Hidden One out here. It's time."

The frightened girl shrank back in the chair Raoul had pushed her into, her eyes glistening with a mixture of fear and dread as the Dark Angel loomed over her. When his hand clamped around her wrist and his strong fingers dug into her skin, she stopped breathing, her heart frozen with terror. Though she tried to twist away, he easily dragged her across the room and onto the open curved balcony.

Mueller leaned his cane against the stone. He balanced his weight on his good leg. At his nod, Raoul shoved the girl toward him and Crispin scooped her up and hoisted her onto the ledge. Whimpering, she tried to squirm herself back onto the balcony, but his sinewy arms held her firm.

"Hold still or I'll let go." His breath burned hot in her ears.

Crispin smiled at the girl's choked cry, at the absolute terror in her eyes. A surge of power ran through him.

"What are you waiting for?" Raoul demanded. His eyes bored into Mueller's. "She's all that stands in the way of the Ascent. *Do it!*"

Crispin ignored him. There was no way he was going to end this without exacting what he wanted from Shepherd. The agate. And the supreme satisfaction of forcing David Shepherd to watch *this* girl fall.

The crowd below stilled at the sight of the girl he held on the ledge.

"The last Hidden One!" someone cried.

"The Serpent himself has her," another excited voice crowed.

The Serpent. His name washed over the crowd, a chant, a prayer. Crispin's face shone with pleasure. *They* did *know what he'd done.* It buoyed him. He grinned, flooded with total confidence.

Mofulatsi bustled forward to address the crowd. "Back into the auditorium—everyone. Now. Prepare yourselves as you were told. Our Ascent is imminent."

Katharine Wanamaker and a few others began to hurry toward the auditorium, but most lingered below, fascinated by the scenario on the balcony.

"Now!" the towering African shouted, pointing his long arm.

Crispin snapped over his shoulder at Raoul. "Go find Shepherd and bring him here. Quickly!"

"We don't need Shepherd any longer," Mofulatsi barked. "Raoul, I want you to locate Alberto Ortega and Erik Mueller. They must be here with us at the moment we destroy God's rotten world."

White rage eclipsed Crispin Mueller's vision as Raoul rushed out to fulfill Mofulatsi's orders. He resisted the overpowering urge to fling the girl off the balcony, to prove he didn't need anyone's permission to achieve what he'd worked harder for than any of them.

Instead, the rage bellowed from his throat, thundering off the walls of the Ark, echoing through the cavern below.

"David Shepherd! Show yourself! A life is hanging in the balance. A precious life. The last of your Hidden Ones. Come save her, if you dare."

Furiously, he scanned the reception area—but there was no sign of Shepherd. The only movement was from the remaining Gnoseos faithful filing back to the auditorium.

"Are you afraid, Shepherd? Too cowardly to save her? Come up here and stop me—I dare you!"

His rage mounted as seconds ticked past without the coward showing himself. He bared his teeth, consumed by hatred, and for an instant, loosened his grip around the girl's waist. It was just long enough for her to slide forward on the balcony's rim, her legs flailing wildly to push herself back towards safety. Her scream echoed, even after he'd locked her once more in his grip.

"I dare you, Shepherd. I dare you!"

Sweat poured down David's face, streamed from his armpits. His fingers were shredded, his palms torn bloody by the rock. His breath wheezed in shallow pants as he cautiously picked his way up the back of the godforsaken tower of rock soaring toward the balcony.

He had no pick axe, no rope, no purchase on the jagged, nearly vertical column. All he had were his fingers. His knees. His feet groping for a toehold as he scaled the rock, serpentining to wherever he could find purchase.

Hutch's guidance played across his memory. *One foot at a time. Don't look down. Keep your eye on the summit.* He refused to wonder about Yael. About Dillon. Were they alive? Hurt? Or still fighting?

He couldn't afford to distract himself from the climb. Crispin was shouting for him. Roaring insanely. He blocked the words from his mind and shook the sweat from his eyes.

The mountain is like a woman, Hutch had told him on his first advanced climb, when he was old enough to appreciate the metaphor. *Mold yourself against her. Become one with her.*

His body embraced the wall. His hands groped for the next fissure. He was a rock. He was one with the tower.

A scream pierced the air. Stacy's scream—from directly above him. His hand faltered, grasped at empty air, and his foot skidded out from under him.

CHAPTER SIXTY

Crispin tensed as he caught the timbre of his father's voice filling the Situation Room. *It's about damned time.* But his filial irritation vanished when he heard a female voice, speaking in an Israeli accent.

"What is this place? What are you doing?"

She sounded desperate. Frightened. Crispin smiled.

"Look who I found skulking on the stairs," his father announced, dragging Yael HarPaz onto the balcony.

"Well, then." Crispin's smile deepened as he regarded the terrified girl balanced precariously on the balcony. "Your hero can't be far away."

"It's time to end this," Mofulatsi told Crispin impatiently. "What in this evil world is keeping Ortega?" He consulted his watch, but his head jerked up as Raoul burst onto the balcony.

"Ortega's dead. Domino, too." His mismatched eyes latched onto Stacy Lachman's stark white face. "There's no reason to wait. Kill her."

Mofulatsi stepped forward with an air of decisive authority. "I am the highest in command now. Serpent, bring her to me. The honor of the final death is mine."

"No!" Crispin sneered, his gaze scouring the hall below with limitless wrath. "We end this when *I* say. *Shepherd! Where are you, Shepherd?*"

"Right here." David flung himself over the rear lip of the wall and onto the balcony. The Gnoseos and Yael spun in shock as he stalked toward Crispin.

David ignored them. All of his attention was concentrated on Crispin.

"I thought you wanted to make a trade."

CHAPTER SIXTY-ONE

David extended his raw and bloody palm. The agate glinted upon it, nearly as bright as the lust in Crispin's eyes. "Come and get it— if you dare," David taunted softly.

He held his breath, not daring to glance at Stacy's terrified face, to absorb her quiet sobs. His gaze was locked with Mueller's, and everything rested upon this moment.

"Bring her to me," David said, "and you can have the agate."

"I'll have the agate anyway." Mueller smirked at him. "After you watch her fall."

"I guessed you wouldn't be man enough to take it out of my hand." David tossed the agate up in the air, then caught it. "Even as a kid, you were nothing but a bully. Look at you now. Hiding behind a child. Who's the coward, Mueller?"

"This is nonsense," Mofulatsi exploded. "Serpent, *bring me that girl*. Raoul, kill them!"

David's gaze flicked to the olive-skinned man as Raoul jerked up a gun. *His eyes!* Shock, then rage, surged through David. *One blue eye, one brown. It was him.*

He was face to face with the animal who'd killed Hutch. Who'd kidnapped Stacy. Who was about to put a bullet through him and Yael.

David had nothing to lose. All eyes were on him and the gun was leveled at his head. "Sure you don't want it back?"

His heart slamming against his bruised ribs, he edged a step closer to Crispin, then another, waggling the agate just out of the other man's reach.

"I want my years back!" Crispin screamed. "You went forward to the light, while I was dragged back into darkness. You were *given* the names I had to spend every day and night searching for."

"Poor Crispin." David's lip curled. "You want the agate, Mueller? Here!"

Crispin gasped as he flung it in a soaring arc. A gunshot thundered. In the split second that Mueller's startled gaze followed the agate's flight over the lip of the balcony, David leaped forward, hurling himself at Stacy and looping an arm around her waist. He yanked her toward him, but Crispin still had her locked in an iron grip.

"David!" Stacy clawed at his shoulders.

He held on desperately, straining every muscle to the point of torture trying to snatch her to safety. Suddenly, he saw Erik Mueller grab up his son's cane from where it leaned against the balcony. David braced himself to absorb the blow.

Instead he watched with shock as Mueller slammed the cane against his son's shoulders. Crispin yelped in surprise and pain, his knees buckling and his grip on Stacy slipping. It was all David needed. He swept her free, up and over the balcony.

He wheeled with her in his arms in time to see Mofulatsi lunge at Yael, trying to wrestle the gun away before she could fire again. She'd taken down Raoul, who was moaning, his thigh twisted and bloody, his face a mask of pain as he writhed on the floor.

Before David's brain could process all the chaos engulfing him, he felt a tractor mow into his legs. He crashed to his knees, Stacy toppling with him. With a shriek, she scooted aside as Crispin threw himself onto David and began to pummel him.

Stacy froze, tears streaking her cheeks, her face etched with terror. But she was only frozen for a moment. When she saw Crispin pounding his fists into David's face, she flew at him like a tornado, sinking her teeth into his arm, grabbing handfuls of his long hair. She yanked with all her might, ripping strands from his scalp before he sent her flying with a backwards buck of his torso.

David drove his fist into Crispin's midsection, dazing him just long enough to reverse their positions, David now pinning Crispin to the floor, his hands closing like a vise around the Gnoseos' throat.

Yael kicked out at Mofulatsi, scraping the heel of her sandal down hard along his shin. Then she brought her knee up hard, ramming it into his groin.

The big man doubled over with a scream of agony, finally relinquishing his hold on the gun. Before he could recover, she jerked the firearm free. At the same moment, Erik Mueller leaped toward him and brought the cane down hard against Mofulatsi's skull.

"Traitor!" Crispin croaked. He was gasping for air, futilely clawing at David's fingers to pry them from his throat. "Damn you . . . father . . . help me!"

Erik swung the cane again at Mofulatsi without even turning his head in Crispin's direction.

Yael gulped for breath. Her wrist was raw, burning from the imprint of Mofulatsi's thick fingers. But she had the gun. With the metallic tang of her own blood hot against her tongue, she spun toward Raoul—he was still down, blood pooling crimson around him as he struggled for breath.

She swallowed down nausea and whirled, rushing inside to the glass display case.

Two gemstones emblazoned with Hebrew lettering glistened up at her—the amethyst and the emerald. *Gad* and *Zebulon*.

Gritting her teeth, she smashed the barrel of the gun into the glass.

It held. Cursing, she tried again, hitting it with all of her strength. Sweat poured down her face. The glass hadn't even cracked. Yael closed her eyes, pictured the glass shattering, and slammed the barrel down again. There was an explosion of glass like crystal rain and triumph swept through her.

A jagged shard sliced her arm as she reached past it for the stones. She ignored the fiery sting, clenching the amethyst and emerald in her palm.

Was it her imagination or were the stones really glowing?

There was no time to study them. She plunged them inside her sweat-soaked bra and a shiver washed over her, tingling down to her toes.

Then Erik Mueller pushed Stacy into the room, away from the carnage on the balcony.

"Yael," David was shouting to her, his voice hoarse. "Get Stacy out of here! More Dark Angels could be on their way."

"No—I won't go without you," Stacy cried, trembling uncontrollably.

Erik dragged her toward the glass door and the staircase beyond. "You have to go, child—the world depends on you!"

"No!" She broke free of him, trying to run back onto the balcony, but Erik seized her arm.

"You don't understand. It's too dangerous for you here—there are plenty of others who want to kill you—we have to get you out!"

"Take your hands off her." Yael had the gun trained at his chest. "Right now."

Stacy blinked at her in dismay. "Don't hurt him. He let me out of that terrible room. He showed me the secret way out!"

Yael bit her lip, her brain whirling with indecision, her body throbbing with pain. She tried to wrap her mind around what Stacy was saying, weighing it with what she'd seen herself.

Mueller had found her on the stairs outside, trying to break into the Situation Room. He'd convinced her that he wanted to help save Stacy, that he'd had a change of heart. That all of his life he'd been blind, unquestioning—and wrong about the world of God. There *was* goodness in this world, he'd decided. He told her that he'd found it in a woman named Elizabeth. A woman he loved. And his sect had inadvertently proved it to him. Their systematic murders of the Lamed Vovniks had stolen goodness from the world, unleashing only destruction.

Yael had been skeptical, but Erik Mueller had claimed he no longer wanted the world to end. He had a plan. They'd enter the Situation Room together, she pretending to be his hostage while maintaining possession of her gun. He'd struck his own son, then attacked Mofulatsi. He was intent on saving Stacy now, even as David choked the life from his flesh and blood.

"Take her, Yael!" David shouted frantically. "Stace, it's all right. I'll be right behind you."

Yael sprang toward the girl. "Come on, Stacy. You heard him, he'll catch up to us."

She grabbed Stacy's arm and tugged her through the glass door to the landing. Erik watched them start up the stairs, turmoil roiling through him. He started to follow them, wondering if he'd saved his Elizabeth. Then he turned back, hesitating.

Shouldn't he now save his son?

Before he had the chance to decide, Raoul staggered in from the balcony, his swarthy face now white as milk, his lower body bathed in blood.

"Traitor!" the Dark Angel roared. He raised a gun and blasted a shot through Erik's forehead. Erik Mueller dropped where he stood.

Swaying, Raoul tottered back onto the balcony, ignoring the fire screaming from his thigh with every step. He was woozy. He was dying. He'd lost too much blood.

David Shepherd was busy throttling the Serpent. He wouldn't even see what was coming. With a sickly smile, Raoul aimed the gun straight at Shepherd's head. He'd enjoy this last kill. More than any other since he'd put an end to his grandfather.

With a gruesome smile, he pulled the trigger—and heard nothing but a hollow click.

David started at the sound, turning his head toward it—and away from the man beneath him. He caught a dark blur at the corner of his vision and ducked just as the butt of a gun whizzed past his ear. Suddenly, one hundred and eighty pounds of blood-soaked venom flew at him. He rolled aside, wincing as the gun butt connected with his spine.

The cane. Somehow David managed to snag it as he scrambled gracelessly to his feet. He was stunned that he could still stand. His lungs burning with every breath, his broken ribs searing, he faced the killer.

With sour breath and a power honed by years of training, Raoul leaped at him. David rammed the tip of Crispin's cane into the Dark Angel's bullet-torn thigh. An agonizing scream sang from his throat as he hurtled backwards, cracking his skull against the jagged rock wall.

David drew a shaky breath, repulsed by the gore. At least Raoul wouldn't be killing anyone ever again.

And Crispin . . .

David turned, his eyes narrowing. Crispin had managed to crawl to the front lip of the balcony and to drag himself to his feet. He leaned over, bellowing into the cavern below.

"Come out, you fools! The Hidden One is escaping! Up the . . ."

David slammed into him, raising the cane, but he'd underestimated the power in Crispin's upper body. With one arm, Mueller grabbed the cane from him, knocking David off balance and nearly over the balcony. Teeth bared, Crispin shoved again, and David's torso dipped over the ledge.

He jerked himself back, and suddenly felt a strange sensation in his hip—the amber in his pocket seemed to tingle. A shot of adrenaline zipped through him like an electrical jolt.

"You wanted the agate, Mueller? Then why don't you go get it?" He punched Mueller in the gut, then grabbed him by his belt and heaved him over the balcony.

Mueller hit the ground before a scream could gurgle from his throat.

Then David was running, barreling down the stairs, sprinting for the reception area. *He had to find the agate.*

His gaze skimmed the toppled ouroboros, the bodies . . .

His heart stopped.

Dillon.

David rushed to him, sank to his knees. He groped for a pulse even knowing he wouldn't find one. Dillon was already cold.

Grief swamped him. And so did shame. How had he doubted his truest friend? How could he leave him here now?

He glanced toward the auditorium. The door was creaking open. Nearly two thousand Gnoseos—restless for their deliverance.

Find the agate.

Frantic, he pushed himself to his feet. That was when he noticed the bishop's ring. The ring Dillon had risked his life to retrieve.

Quickly, David bent to tug it from his friend's finger. As he did, he saw the agate. An inch from Dillon's sleeve, glowing like seaglass. As he snatched it up, both stones from the breastplate of Aaron seemed to shimmer in his palm, more brightly with each passing second.

He was beyond wondering how the agate had come to land so near the ruby. He was beyond wondering anything except how to get out of here alive.

There was a murmur of voices, people were beginning to trickle from the auditorium. Clutching the stones in his bloodied fist, he sprinted for the stairs.

And then he was running, running for the surface, running for his life.

He heard a shout. Footsteps pounding. They were coming after him.

How far ahead were Yael and Stacy? he wondered dizzily, his chest heaving with every step. He wouldn't make it. His vision was wavering and he was dripping a crimson trail of blood. Weakness numbed his legs.

But he couldn't stop.

Trembling, he pushed on, slipping once on the condensation slicking the steps. Then he reached the second landing. He climbed more, heard scuffling feet and female voices above him. *Yael and Stacy.*

Angry shouts and sounds of pursuit drove him on.

By the time he stumbled into the warehouse, he could barely stand. Avi Raz caught him, dragged him through the room filled with boxes, more boxes than had been there before, and now swarming with dark-suited men carrying walkie-talkies and guns.

"Thanks . . . for bringing . . . the cavalry," David gasped.

Avi was soaked with sweat. "You got up here just in time."

All around them, other men were bustling about, positioning cables and wires and explosives with deliberate urgency. Some were hustling the women who'd escaped toward ambulances.

Then David was sucking in fresh air, squinting into the daylight. Staggering with Avi to the loading platform behind the building where Stacy and Yael waited in the back of an idling delivery truck.

They were miles from the warehouse at 8 Angel Passage when the explosion roared through the secret bunker far below the city of London, collapsing the lair deep within the earth. Miles from the tunnels where the Gnoseos swarmed like wasps in a hive, buzzing with their anticipation of victory, even as the fiery blast annihilated them from the face of the earth.

With a single blast that shook London like an earthquake, the sect that had plotted for centuries to overthrow the world God created was reduced to a whirling underground maelstrom of cinders, smoke, and ashes. The Tower of London stood firm, as it had for centuries, and the china in Buckingham Palace barely rattled on the royal shelves.

CHAPTER SIXTY-TWO

WARSAW, 904 MILES AWAY

While the ground shook beneath London, thirteen-year-old Stanislaw Nowicki climbed the stairs to the bimah in his small synagogue. As he prepared to don his *tallit* for the first time, he recited the special *bracha* for putting on the prayer shawl and took a deep breath. Then the rabbi pointed to the line in the Torah where Stanislaw would begin to read his bar mitzvah portion.

And as he chanted the ancient Hebrew in a clear young voice, the waters of the River Thames quieted once more.

COPENHAGEN, 412 MILES AWAY

Lise Kolinka bent toward her thirteenth birthday cake, lips pursed, her face bathed with the glow of candlelight. As she closed her eyes to make a birthday wish, rain began to pound from the skies over Arizona. By the time she had blown out all of her candles, there was a downpour in the American Southwest, extinguishing the virulent wildfires, washing the mountains clean, renewing the scorched earth.

CHICAGO, 4,261 MILES AWAY

Keisha Jones spent every Saturday working alongside her Aunt Doris at the Stony Island food pantry on Chicago's South Side. Today, on her way to help sort donated canned goods, the thirteen-year-old girl jingled the spare change she'd found in the street. When she handed it to Mrs. Wallace and learned it was enough to buy one family eggs and bread for the entire week, a shiver of happiness radiated through her. She decided that next week she'd donate half of her babysitting money, too.

And off the coast of Japan, a tsunami that was roiling deep beneath the sea eased itself back down across the ocean floor, settling like boiled water taken off the burner.

SHANGHAI, 7,073 MILES AWAY

Chen Ho sat beside his beloved grandfather, patiently reading him the daily newspaper. He had to repeat things often because his grandfather was hard of hearing as well as blind. But Chen didn't mind. His homework would wait—his mother's father had few pleasures left to him besides keeping up with the outside world and drinking his nightly glass of beer.

As Chen turned the page, he saw that his grandfather had fallen asleep. A smile settled over his heart. He folded the paper, knowing exactly where to pick up later.

At the same time in Turkey, a cry of joy went up as rescuers unearthed a dozen children miraculously found alive beneath the rubble of a schoolhouse.

In Mathiaka, Sierra Leone—in Luvena, Russia—in Tokaji, Hungary—and in twenty-eight more villages and cities around the world, a new generation of Lamed Vovniks reached the stage of spiritual maturity, one by one.

Pure of heart, their souls filled with goodness and compassion, not one of them realized—not one of them would ever know—the awesome power of their very existence.

CHAPTER SIXTY-THREE

Tiberias' waterfront promenade was brilliant with swaying palm trees, packed food stalls, and strolling tourists as David scanned the throng for Yael. When he spotted her at the opposite end of the *tayyelet*, he felt a small shock at the sight of her in lemon-yellow capri pants and a black silk t-shirt. Somehow the image he carried in his mind always had her in that green silk jacket and black skirt she'd been wearing the morning she strode into Rabbi ben Moshe's study and demanded he give her the agate.

The agate was back in Jerusalem now. Along with the amber, and the other stones from Aaron's breastplate they'd recovered from the Gnoseos.

His journal was in his hand. This would be its final journey.

As he wove his way through the crowd toward Yael, the events of the past month whirled by in a blur. He'd spent a week in Santa

Monica with Stacy as a guest of Meredith and her husband. It hadn't felt as strange as he'd imagined, being in Len Lachman's house. Stacy had wanted him close. So close he had been.

He was still on a leave of absence from Georgetown. Still reeling from the deaths of Dillon, Hutch, and Eva.

Still hurting from the bruises and broken ribs. But those injuries would heal and fade. He only hoped Stacy's memories would as well.

The strange thing was, she hadn't wanted to know much of what had precipitated her ordeal. David had been planning to tell her that he'd explain when she was older. But there'd been no need. Instinctively, it seemed, Stacy had asked few questions, appearing comfortable to let go of what she'd been through. Lamed Vovniks, he remembered, had no idea who they really were.

Meredith had taken her for a few sessions with a therapist, who'd pronounced Stacy untraumatized by her ordeal. David was content to wait until she wanted to know more.

As he skirted a family hurrying toward a falafel stand, he caught the glint of silver earrings swinging from behind Yael's dark coppery hair. She was close enough now that he could see her smile. See the strands of multicolored glass beads at her throat. See the smooth swing of her hips.

She slowed as she neared him, the smile blooming in her eyes. She rose up on tiptoe and brushed her lips against his for a feather of a second.

"I've rented the fishing boat. We have it for the entire afternoon."

"Should we take along a picnic?"

She smiled.

An hour later, they were far from the noisy shoreline, alone on the blue wooden boat, heading for deeper water. The sea was calm, glistening in the sunlight like a jewel beneath the city of Tiberias, which—like Safed—was one of Israel's four holiest cities.

The Israelis called this lake the Kinneret, the Christians knew it as the Sea of Galilee, where Jesus recruited his apostles from among the fishermen who toiled there.

David waited until they were surrounded by nothing but sky and water, the people on hillsides a distant blur.

Then he set down his oars. As Yael watched in silence, he lifted his journal from the seat beside him and dropped it over the side of the boat. It floated for a minute, the pages going soft as the cool water washed against their ink. And then the red leather book slowly disappeared beneath the glassy surface, sinking to the bottom of the lake, taking its holy secrets to the deep.

Yael glanced at the sack of food beside her, then carefully maneuvered her way across the boat to sit beside David.

"Before our picnic, there's something I'd like to ask you."

"Ask away."

"I've received an invitation to be a visiting professor at Georgetown for the next term. Did you by any chance have something to do with that?"

David struggled to keep a poker face, but he could smell her perfume, and that made it difficult for him to resist a smile.

"What if I did? Would you consider it?"

She pursed her lips and stretched her long legs before her as if studying the salmon-colored polish gleaming on her sandaled toes.

"I suppose it would depend. Is there much of a social life for the faculty?"

"Well, you've already missed the Labor Day picnic. But Dean Myer fries a mean turkey for his New Year's Day bash. I don't have a date."

"Fried turkey . . ." Slowly, she turned toward him. "That might just be the best offer I've had today."

She wrapped her arms around his neck, her hair falling back as she tilted her face up to his. "I do have a few qualms about your East Coast winters."

"Not to worry. I think we can manage to keep warm." David kissed her then, as the boat drifted. He lost himself in the softness of her lips, the lull of the sea, and the peace of knowing that the secret names of the Lamed Vovniks were concealed once more.